VICTORIA JENKINS

THE
ACCUSATION

Published by Bookouture in 2020

An imprint of Storyfire Ltd.
Carmelite House
50 Victoria Embankment
London EC4Y 0DZ

www.bookouture.com

ISBN: 978-1-83888-759-9
eBook ISBN: 978-1-83888-758-2

THE
ACCUSATION

BOOKS BY VICTORIA JENKINS

The Divorce
The Argument

THE DETECTIVES KING AND LANE SERIES
The Girls in the Water
The First one to Die
Nobody's Child
A Promise to the Dead

PROLOGUE

'Tell us what happened.'

I sat up against the flat hospital pillow and tried not to focus on the throbbing inside my head. This was the worst kind of headache – one that stayed after sleep – and I feared that something far more sinister had been done to me than they were letting on, some damage the doctors had yet to realise the full severity of. I couldn't allow myself to be injured. I was needed too much.

Two pairs of eyes watched me expectantly, waiting for me to fill in the missing details of the previous evening's events. I wanted more than anything to give them what they asked, but I just couldn't.

'Where's…' I began, but the question was strangled on my tongue, lost to a single tear that slipped from my left eye and slid onto my cold cheek.

'She's fine,' the female reassured me.

When I closed my eyes, I saw the tree the car had collided with; I heard the screech of brakes and the crunch of metal as the bonnet crumpled against the trunk of the oak, folding in on itself like an accordion. A rush of darkness flooded me, greens and browns muted by the night, and I remembered the last thought that crept from my mind as my eyes fell shut and consciousness escaped me: that just a split second could change everything, and that nothing was ever going to be the same again.

'Tell us what happened,' the man said again.

But I couldn't.

'I'm sorry,' I said, making eye contact now. 'I don't remember.'

ONE

It was just past 10.30 when I slipped my jacket from the back of my chair and swallowed the remaining contents of my wine glass, a too-sweet mouthful that quickly added to the dizzying effects of those it followed. I'd only had a couple of glasses since getting to the restaurant a few hours earlier, but it had been so long since I'd last drunk alcohol that it felt as though I'd finished the bottle alone. Amy shook her blonde head, a mock frown stamped on her youthful face, a face that even at thirty-nine (though not until quarter to midnight, as she kept reminding us; even in utero she had timed her arrivals ready to party) could allow her to pass as someone still in her twenties.

'Quitting already? Such a lightweight.'

I smiled. 'I've made a promise,' I reminded them, having already told them about Lily's job interview the following day. She had failed her driving test – it was all over as soon as they hit the interchange on the way in to Cardiff, she told me; a motorbike overtaking her to the right and two lanes that filtered into one throwing her confidence – and so my role as Mum's taxi service continued, while I reminded myself almost daily that it wouldn't last much longer and that I might, possibly, miss my position once the post was made redundant. Besides, I wanted to know where Lily was. While she was with me, there was no chance of her meeting up with a certain someone else.

'Circuits tomorrow?'

I rolled my eyes at Laura's reminder, regretting the day, months earlier, when I'd agreed to sign up to the classes with her. Laura had always been more athletic than I was and had been back to her pre-baby weight while I was still sitting on the sofa eating biscuits. I had agreed to go to circuits as I'd needed something to motivate me, but even that one weekly session already felt like a burden, something I pursued through a sense of duty to Laura more than anything else. That and the fact that I didn't want to look like a quitter.

'Can't wait,' I said, smiling at her cynical raised eyebrow. I sidled around the far end of the table to give Amy a hug. 'Happy birthday. Enjoy the weekend.'

'Oh,' she said with a wink, 'I most definitely will.'

Amy's twenty-eight-year-old boyfriend of all of three months had booked them into a spa hotel somewhere in Somerset as a birthday surprise, a no-expense-spared, champagne-on-arrival overnight break that was basically an elaborately decorated dirty weekend. Amy's existence was as far removed from Laura's and mine as it could be. Like me, Laura was married with two children. She worked for a local estate agent and her weekends were mostly booked up with soft-play parties, toddler gym classes and whatever sport her eight-year-old son had decided he was into that week. Amy was enjoying the kind of lifestyle neither Laura nor I had ever really had, even in our twenties, staying out late during the week and dating men she had no intention of pursuing any kind of relationship with. Her job as a freelance fashion journalist meant she travelled extensively and was rarely home for periods of more than a few weeks, and I didn't mind admitting that I sometimes lived a separate life through her stories, wondering what might have been had things been different. Though it all seemed exciting and glamorous, I doubted I'd have had the energy to keep up.

'Text me when you get in,' Laura told me, ever the concerned mother.

'Will do.'

I left the restaurant and zipped my jacket to my chin as I headed down the main road that led to the town centre, wishing I'd opted for a pair of tights instead of going out with bare legs. It was mid October but already felt much later, the air gripped by a winter that was promising continual rain and grey skies for the next few weeks. Smokers stood beneath the wooden shelter erected to the side of one of the town centre's pubs, smoke circling the air in acrid plumes. I passed drawn-down shop shutters and dimly lit windows, only the pubs and the takeaways still open. This place had become my home, or maybe I had grown into it, though I had often wondered why someone like Amy chose to stay here. When I'd asked her why she'd never made a permanent move away, her answer was a simple one: that it was purely a base and would always be home to her. I had envied her the attachment she felt.

My path snaked left, taking me past the castle that dominated the centre of the town, a feat of medieval architecture mostly taken for granted by those of us who lived within a two-mile radius of it. When I'd first arrived here, over a decade ago – having spent some years in Cardiff before making the move north – I'd made a point of finding out what I could about the history of the place, but as with everything else, the novelty soon wore off and the building and its grounds became as everyday as the shops that stood opposite it. I still sometimes found myself enthralled by the sounds of these streets: the busy traffic and the dull thud of distant music; the familiar rise and lull of noise.

For a moment, I was distracted by thoughts of my previous life. I felt my surroundings melt into nothing around me, replaced by a dark void that left me isolated. I was standing at the front door of the old flat, my back pressed to the wall, the roar of blood in my ears pouring over me like a tsunami. The silence of the place was suffocating, reminding me that I was alone; I could still smell the damp that clung in places to the wallpaper. The memory was as vivid as if I had been there just the day before.

I crossed the main road and headed towards the park, leaving my thoughts with the geese that stood silently at the edge of the castle's moat. I could have stayed on the lit main roads, but the difference was a good ten minutes, and my legs were pimpled with goose bumps. I couldn't wait to take off the shoes I had chosen to wear. They would never have been my usual choice, and I knew that had I been meeting up with just Laura, I would have opted for something far more comfortable. There was something about Amy, some effect she had that I'm sure she didn't consciously intend, that made me feel the need to make more of an effort, to make more of myself. Perhaps it was a good thing. Perhaps not. Either way, the feeling of having her friendship warmed me, and I wrapped myself in it as I entered the darkened park.

I was just within the boundary of the main gate when I heard the woman's voice.

'Help me!'

It took a moment for my eyes to adjust to the darkness. The street lights were behind me, their glow illuminating yellow puddles in the lane I'd just left. To the left of me was the children's play area, the swings and slides of various sizes partitioned off from the rest of the park. To the right stretched the football fields, lined with tall hedgerows that cut off the housing estate behind them. Towards the end of the fields, just in front of the block of public toilets, I could make out two figures, their bodies morphing into one confused mass as they grappled with one another.

'Help me!'

Without thinking, I ran towards them. If it hadn't been for the alcohol that warmed my chest, I might not have been so brave, but I acted without thinking, knowing that responding to the woman's pleas was the right thing to do. As I ran, I stumbled in my heels and twisted my ankle, cursing beneath my breath as I steadied myself. When I looked up, a man was running away, disappearing between the trees. He was carrying a bag in his left hand. The woman was on the ground, her voice having fallen silent. I grappled for my mobile phone in my bag, hobbling quickly towards her.

'Are you okay?' I called, realising the stupidity of the question.

It was only when I neared her, when I crouched to the ground beside her, that I saw the blood. It stained the top she was wearing: a high-necked white blouse with intricate lace detail, worn beneath a long dark cardigan.

'Help me,' she said again, but her voice was smaller, almost strangled. Her accent wasn't Welsh; it was southern and lilting, as though it might have faded over time. When she turned her head away from me, I saw the stab wound in her neck, a two-inch incision that was draining her blood into the hard ground on which she'd fallen.

'Oh shit.'

I unlocked my phone in my shaking hand and began to dial 999. 'Ambulance,' I spluttered. 'Stay with me,' I urged her, not knowing what else to say; sounding like every television soap I had ever watched. 'Yes,' I said, when a female voice spoke at the other end of the line. 'Um, I'm in Lewis Evans Park in Caerphilly, the one just off Castle Street. I'm with a woman who's been stabbed.'

'Is she breathing?' the operator asked me.

'Yes, she's breathing, she's conscious, she's just spoken to me.'

'Okay. Where has she been stabbed?'

'In the neck.'

'Don't try to move her, all right?' the woman instructed me. 'I want you to stay with her and keep talking to her until the ambulance arrives. They're on their way now. What's your name?'

'Jenna.'

'Okay, Jenna. Do you know the woman's name?'

'No, I…'

I was still crouched on the ground, my body looming over hers in a way that I realised was probably intimidating. I sat down on the concrete beside her, not caring whether her blood ended up on me, and with my free hand found hers, gently rubbing her cold knuckles with my thumb.

'What's your name?' I asked her.

'Charlotte.'

'Her name's Charlotte.'

'Okay,' the operator said again, her reassuring tone doing little to calm my increasing panic. I realised I had no idea where the man I'd seen running away might have gone. For all I knew, he could still be in the park somewhere, watching us, waiting to make a return. 'Do you have something you could use to apply pressure to the wound?'

Stupidly, I looked around me, as though a bandage or a towel might magically appear on the ground beside us. 'My jacket. I could use my jacket. What do I do?' I propped the phone between my right shoulder and my ear as I slipped my left arm from the jacket, the chill of the night air biting at my bare skin. I should have had more of an idea of what to do, but panic overruled common sense, and all memories I had of any previous training were lost.

'I want you to put the jacket over the wound and apply pressure, okay? Hold it in place until the ambulance arrives.'

'How long are they going to be?' I asked, shivering with shock as I straightened one of my jacket sleeves, folded it in half and then pressed it against the wound in Charlotte's neck. She winced in pain at the contact and I apologised hurriedly, praying that the paramedics would get there soon.

I had done plenty of first-aid courses in the past, but nothing could have prepared me for the reality of being faced with a stabbing victim. I wondered why I had chosen to take the shortcut home;

why it was me who'd been the one to find this woman. We all live so innocently, shielded in the bubbles we create for ourselves, watching the news with a sigh or a tut at the state of the world, comfortable with our cups of tea and plates of biscuits while we witness the unfolding of other people's tragedies. None of us really believes that any of these terrible things we see on our screens could happen to us. If we did, no one would ever leave the house.

'They're on their way,' the operator repeated, which I knew could mean two or twenty minutes.

'You're not from around here, are you?' I asked Charlotte, in an effort to keep her talking as instructed. 'You have a pretty accent.'

'Thank you,' she said, her words still small and strangled.

I wanted to ask her what happened, what she was doing here on her own, why she had taken such a risk at this time of night, and then I realised the naivety of my question. I had done the same: walked alone through a quiet, darkened park, inviting any trouble that happened to be lurking, all the while oblivious to the fact that I might be doing so. And then reality kicked me in the stomach, making the carbonara and tiramisu churn in my guts. If I had left the restaurant just minutes earlier – if Charlotte hadn't happened to be here too – I might have been the one lying on the ground with a stab wound in my neck.

'Do you live around here?'

As soon as the question left my lips, I realised how ridiculous I sounded. I was trying to stop the woman's blood seeping from her neck – blood I could feel damp against my fingertips, warm and sticky – yet at the same time I was trying to spark a casual conversation as though we were two people who had happened to meet by chance, one of whom found it difficult to cope with awkward silences.

'Not far,' she managed, though her breath was short and raspy.

'Her eyes are beginning to close.' I spoke into the phone, too loudly, panic escaping me in a hurried burst of sound.

'Keep applying pressure to that wound, Jenna. Talk about anything – it doesn't matter what it is, just try to keep her awake.'

'I live over there,' I said abruptly, pointing as though Charlotte might pay attention to the gesture. 'It's all right, this town, isn't it? I mean, there are worse places to live, I suppose. I run a coffee shop. The irony is, I don't even like coffee. I don't generally tell people that – wouldn't really do much to help business, would it?' I could hear myself rambling, but I couldn't bring myself to stop. The sound of my voice was drowning out the other noises that filled my head, the ones of fear and sickness and panic that would prevent me from helping her if I allowed them to overwhelm me.

Charlotte shook her head slightly, the effort it took to do so draining her of the last of her energy. Her face fell to one side, and I repositioned myself, clambering across her while trying to keep pressure on the wound.

'Try not to move. Just stay with me, okay? Don't close your eyes. Charlotte?' I put my phone on the ground and clicked the fingers of my free hand in front of her face. 'Charlotte! Shit!' I grabbed the phone. 'I'm losing her! For God's sake, please, where are they?'

As the operator began to answer me, trying to calm me with her measured tones, I heard the ambulance in the distance, its siren steadying my heart rate. 'They're coming,' I told her. 'I think they're coming.'

Within less than half a minute, the far end of the park was lit with headlights, and I was frantically waving my phone in the air, its torch turned on, desperate to be spotted in the darkness. 'Over here! Quickly!'

The engine was cut, and I waited for the sound of boots on concrete, still pressing the jacket to Charlotte's neck, still praying she'd stay with me until the arrival of someone who knew what they were doing. I felt a hand on my shoulder, heavy yet reassuring.

'Okay, let's take a look at her. What's your name, love?'

When she didn't answer, the paramedic looked at me.

'Charlotte,' I told him. 'Her name's Charlotte.'

'All right, Charlotte love, I want you to try to stay awake, okay? Stay with us.'

He gestured to his female colleague, who reached for the large box she had carried with her from the ambulance. I stood and stepped back, almost losing my balance. I had been crouching so long, my legs felt numb, and now the blood rushed back to them. Charlotte's eyes had fallen shut.

'Is she going to be okay?' I asked, my words barely audible, the voice that escaped me not sounding like mine.

'Wait with us until the police arrive,' the female paramedic said, not looking up at me. 'They'll want to speak to you.'

I nodded, the most I seemed able to manage. I couldn't tear my eyes from the sight of them hovering over her, looming and retreating as they produced more and more equipment, and the feeling of uselessness that not long ago had consumed me was replaced by the sensation of being absent, as though I was not really there and this wasn't really happening. I was standing apart from my body, watching myself watching.

There was a surge in noise as further sirens approached. The paramedics were talking, to Charlotte and to each other, their words increasingly rapid. There was engine noise, there were lights and a sudden rush of people, and while my eyes were still focused on what few glimpses of Charlotte I was able to snatch, a hand on my arm ushered me away, moving me towards the pool of light around the police car.

'Are you okay?' the officer asked me. I realised I had barely acknowledged him; I couldn't have said what he looked like or how old he might have been. I nodded and felt something being put around me, then remembered that my jacket was still with Charlotte, soaked in the blood that had seeped from her wound.

'You called the ambulance?' the officer asked me.

I nodded, apparently unable to form words, exhausted by the ordeal and by the not-knowing what would happen to the woman now. What if she died? If I had got there two minutes earlier, could I have stopped what had happened? If I had acted more quickly – put pressure on the wound before being instructed to do so by the 999 operator – would she have had a better chance of surviving her injuries? What if something I had done had made her condition worse without my realising?

'Are you okay?' he asked again.

He said something more, to someone else, but I didn't hear his words. He caught me as I fell forward, and the next thing I knew, I was sobbing into his jacket, the weight of the trauma trying to drag me to earth.

TWO

There was blood on my dress, in my hair, on my hands. I turned my key in the door quietly, not wanting to disturb the silence of the house. The only sound was the faint murmur of the television from the living room. Damien had waited up for me; either that or he had fallen asleep on the sofa, the remote control probably still at hand.

I clicked the front door shut gently behind me and stood in the darkness of the hallway, the soft glow of lamplight escaping in cracks from the living room door to my right, quiet washing over me. There was usually something so reassuring about that late-night peace, a kind of comfort in knowing that the girls were upstairs, safely tucked in their beds. The house was secured and the night that stretched ahead of me, beautiful with its dark promise of a restful sleep, would roll into a new morning, always bringing with it a fresh start. That night, it didn't feel that way. That night, I felt as though the darkness was a threat and not a comfort, as though I had brought something into the house with me.

There was a mirror hanging on the wall to my right; an old-fashioned rectangular sheet of glass framed in gold that had belonged to Damien's late grandmother. There was a smear of something on its surface – make-up, perhaps. I imagined Lily standing there, peering close to her reflection, her fingertips lightly tracing the soft flesh beneath her lower lashes before they connected with the glass and left a smudge of foundation that would stay there until someone cleaned it away. She had started wearing more make-up than usual, her customary flick of mascara and smear of lip gloss replaced with a look that was too heavy, too old for her youthful skin. She was grown up, and yet she wasn't. She was a young woman, but still a little girl.

When I looked beyond the smear of make-up, I saw my own reflection, pale and almost not-there, ghost-like. There was blood on my face, two lines of badly painted brownish-red camouflage at my jawline, and my make-up had smudged around my eyes, casting dark shadows beneath them. I looked as though I was ready for a bad-taste Halloween fancy dress party; as though if I stared at my reflection for long enough, I might raise the corner of a sinister smile.

The living room door opened and Damien appeared.

'Where have you been? I was just about to call the—' One look at me and he stopped short. His gaze lingered on my chin and then moved down my dress, resting on my hands, my bloodstained fingers. 'What the hell's happened to you?'

I had no idea what the time was. The officers who had taken my statement in the park had insisted on driving me home, despite the house being just a few streets away, and yet they could have taken me anywhere, I wouldn't have noticed. I had lost all sense of place and time.

Damien moved towards me and wrapped his arms around me, and I found myself crying again, my tears soaking his T-shirt. It smelt familiar: the favourite aftershave he always wore.

'Are you hurt?' he asked, the words spoken into my hair.

I shook my head.

'Tell me what happened.'

He pulled away from me and studied my face for a moment before leading me down the hallway to the kitchen. I wished I was able to read his thoughts – to know what the look on his face meant – but I was too preoccupied with the memory of what had happened, still feeling the horror of the other woman's blood on my skin, so close I could almost taste it on my tongue.

In the kitchen, I propped myself shakily on a stool at the breakfast bar while Damien put the kettle on. When I asked him for paracetamol, he found a box and snapped two white tablets from their plastic strip, then brought me a glass of water.

'I've been calling you,' he said. 'I was worried.' I hadn't looked at my phone since the call with the 999 operator had ended. There is nothing more annoying than the sound of a mobile phone conversation in a restaurant, and so I made it a habit to always turn mine to silent whenever I was out. In the park, I hadn't had a chance to think about the fact that Damien might have been trying to get hold of me, and it occurred to me then that Laura would have been doing the same, holding me to my word when I'd told her I would text when I got home.

I glanced at the clock above the microwave. It was ten to two. Nowhere other than the dodgy club above the discount store would be open at that time, and no one over the age of twenty-five or under the influence of fewer than six drinks would ever go there.

'What's happened?' There was something strange in his voice, something that dreaded the answer before he had even given voice to the question.

'Someone was stabbed,' I said, the words sounding as though they were coming from someone else's body, the experience of it all still not quite belonging to me. 'A woman in the park. She… I helped her.'

'Jesus Christ.'

Damien came to stand beside me, and I allowed the weight of my body to rest against his. He waited for the words for come, for me to spill the story of what had happened during those past few hours in my own time, and when I was finished, he continued to hold me, not saying anything.

'So did you actually see it happen?'

I shook my head. 'I saw someone running away, but that was it. I wasn't near enough to get a decent look.' I pulled away from him, feeling awkward at our prolonged closeness. Things had been strained between us for a while, and we rarely embraced. 'I'm sorry I worried you. Are the girls okay?'

'They're fine. Amelia fell asleep watching *Mary Poppins*.'

'Poor you,' I said with a smile. Since taking her to the cinema to see the remake, she had become obsessed with the original, learning all the words to the songs and singing each in her best faux-posh Julie Andrews voice, with the occasional mockney Dick Van Dyke effort thrown in for good measure. 'Lily all right?'

Damien nodded. 'On that bloody phone till God knows what time again.' He rolled his eyes and I said nothing, a frisson of guilt curling in my stomach. I would talk to her about it when we were alone tomorrow, but at that moment I couldn't bring myself to linger on the subject.

'Is she going to be okay?'

It took me a moment to realise he was no longer referring to Lily. 'I don't know. She'd lost consciousness by the time the ambulance left.'

'Jesus.' He shook his head and went to the kettle. It had boiled a while earlier, but he hadn't yet got around to making the tea. I watched him as he took tea bags from a jar beneath the windowsill, sugar from the one next to it. 'Stabbed,' he muttered, more to himself than to me, and shook his head again.

While he finished making the tea, I went upstairs to wash and change before coming back down to join him. We took our drinks through to the living room and sat side by side on the sofa. I should have been exhausted, yet my body had somehow pushed through it, my brain too wired to find rest. I told him about the paramedics, the police, my statement, the short journey home in the back of the police car, filling the next hour with talk of nothing but what had happened.

'I need the loo.' Eventually I put a hand on Damien's knee and pushed myself up from the sofa. I didn't need the toilet; it was an excuse to leave the room. The more we had talked, the more my thoughts had drifted to Lily and her late-night phone call. They were becoming something of a habit.

I pulled the living room door closed behind me and went upstairs to my older daughter's bedroom. Her room was a mess – clothes abandoned on the carpet, a cosmetics bag emptied over the dressing table, dirty plates and glasses everywhere. Her duvet was crumpled and piled high, and if it weren't for the cascade of dark hair that escaped from the top of it, I might have thought at first glance that she wasn't there.

As always, her mobile phone was close to hand, precariously balanced on the edge of the bedside table. I reached for it and tapped in the code, having watched her in the car the previous day and memorised it. I didn't feel guilty; she had lied to me, and I was doing this for her own good.

Password incorrect, the phone informed me. I typed in the six-digit combination again, making sure I hit each number correctly. Wrong again. Putting the phone back on the bedside table, I stared at the mountain of duvet that was my daughter and wondered exactly when our relationship had changed. There had been a time not so long ago when she would have talked to me about anything, when I had considered myself – perhaps naively, maybe optimistically – her friend as much as her mother.

Whatever had altered between us, one thing was clear. Lily was one step ahead of me.

THREE

The following morning, Lily came downstairs wearing skin-tight jeans and a top that grazed her waist, giving the occasional flash of her belly button. Her body had changed so much recently, with the childlike narrowness of her hips giving way to curves that made her look older than her years. She was becoming beautiful. The problem was, she knew it. I didn't want her to become one of those girls – one of those duck-lipped, bushy-eyebrowed Instagram teens – who had become a stereotype for an entire generation, and I had always hoped that intelligence would be enough to deter her from following the herd.

'You were back late last night,' she said casually, passing a hand over my loose hair as she walked past me. 'All-night rave up at Spoons?'

I flashed her a sarcastic smile and shoved a box of cereal in her direction. 'We're out of bread,' I told her, trying to maintain a sense of normality, hoping my dark thoughts and the truth of last night wouldn't make themselves known in my pallid complexion. I had decided not to tell Lily about what had happened, knowing she might slip up and mention it in front of Amelia. My younger daughter was sensitive enough already, and I wanted the park to remain a safe place, not somewhere she would fear.

The thought that danger lay so close to our home was disturbing. As far as I knew, Lily had no plans to go anywhere other than her job interview that day, and if she did intend to go elsewhere, I was going to insist that either Damien or I gave her a lift, though I'd find out where she was going first before offering my husband's services; if she was going to visit *him*, I didn't want Damien to find out, not before I'd had a chance to speak to him about it.

Lily pulled a face at the cereal and went to the fridge instead, pulling out a tub of yoghurt and a carton of strawberries. On top of the microwave, where it was plugged into its charger, my phone beeped. It was a message from Ffion, who was in charge of the coffee shop that day.

Ellie has called in sick, but Kirstin said she'd cover. Just letting you know x

I texted back. *Thanks, that's great. I'll call you later.*

I trusted Ffion with the running of the coffee shop, though Saturdays were our busiest day. Time allowing, I resolved to pop in at some point that afternoon.

Amelia's voice seeped from the living room, intermingled with the grating tones of Dick Van Dyke. '*The more I laugh*,' she sang, '*the more I fill with glee…*'

'I can't cope with that much longer,' Lily said, shooting a glare at the closed door. 'Seriously… how many more times is she going to watch it?'

Though I agreed with the sentiment, I didn't care how many times Amelia watched the film; I was glad that at least one person in the house could find something to smile about.

'She's happy,' I said. 'Leave her be.'

I caught the face Lily pulled. 'You okay, Mother? Someone drink a bit too much last night?'

'Yeah, something like that.'

Thoughts of Charlotte kept me distracted from Lily's increasingly annoying attitude. She had recently developed a confidence that was far from attractive; if anything, it was making her look like a spoiled brat. I was going to tell her so, but not while we were in the house and there was a chance Amelia might overhear. I was also keen to keep the conversation away from Damien, so I saved it until we were alone in the car, where I approached the subject that had sat silently between us with a little more force than I should have.

'You're still seeing him, aren't you?'

The sigh was audible enough to be offensive, as though I was inconveniencing her by wanting to know the details of her private life. If this was any normal teenage relationship I wouldn't have been so insistent, but I had reason to be concerned. A few weeks earlier, Amy had told me she'd seen Lily in a restaurant with a man, a man who according to her was at least late twenties, maybe early thirties. When I confronted Lily about it, she at first tried to deny that she'd been where Amy claimed to have seen her. Then I showed her the photograph that Amy had taken: a distant shot, poorly lit, that had only captured the back of the man and a side profile of Lily but was more than enough to prove that it was indeed her and she'd been caught red-handed – or in this case, red-faced – guilty as charged. Her outrage at Amy's invasion of her privacy made itself known in a screaming tantrum that was followed by a series of slammed doors.

The following day, when she'd calmed down a fraction, I'd tried to talk to her about it. I asked her who he was and where they had met, but she was not exactly forthcoming with details, only repeating that he didn't treat her like a little kid, which was apparently all that Damien and I did. She tried to tell me that it had been dinner, nothing more, and that there was nothing serious going on between the two of them. I'd made her promise not to see him again, and in yet another example of my astounding naivety, I'd believed her when she'd told me she wouldn't.

I had made attempts to find out who this man could be, trawling through Lily's social media profiles and employing Amy's help to find out what we could about him, but my efforts at playing private investigator had led me nowhere. I still didn't know his name. Now I felt as though Lily – as though the two of them together – had been laughing at me, and the thought made me determined to find him and make sure he was never able to bother a teenage girl again.

'I can't believe you're still on about this.' Lily raised a leg and put her foot on the dashboard.

'Oh really? And why would that be?'

'I told you I wouldn't see him again, and I haven't. Have you sent your little spies out looking for evidence?'

I ignored the comment, but my lack of concentration on the road meant I almost ran a red light. From somewhere behind me came the blast of a horn. Lily reached dramatically for the door handle, as though she had narrowly missed a near-death collision.

'Who were you on the phone to for so long last night?'

The sigh became more infuriating each time it was expelled from between her pouting lips.

'Maisie.'

I glanced at her, checking for telltale signs of duplicity, but the problem was, I didn't know when she was lying and when she was telling the truth. She was a good liar, and the implications of that were frightening.

'So if I call Maisie later and ask if she spoke to you last night, she'll confirm that, will she?'

'Yes, Detective Morgan, she will.'

Her reply sent irritation pulsing through me. I loved my daughter, but there were times when I caught myself thinking that I didn't like her very much, immediately followed by guilt that the notion had even flitted through my brain. It was a phase, I realised that – she wouldn't be this sarcastic and disrespectful forever. At least, I hoped not.

I made a mental note to call Maisie's mother later. Lily liked to think herself smart, but she'd got her brains from me, so I could play her at her own game.

'Swear to it,' I said. 'On Amelia's life, swear that you're not seeing him any more.'

I don't know why I said that. I hate using people's lives to swear by, though I'm not superstitious in the slightest. It was something Damien did that I always chided him for, and yet there I was asking Lily to use her sister to prove to me she wasn't telling yet more lies.

She pouted. 'I swear on Amelia's life that I'm not seeing him any more. There. You happy now?'

But of course I wasn't happy. I didn't believe her.

'Where did you meet him?'

Another exaggerated exhalation. 'For God's sake, I've just told you I'm not seeing him, okay? What is wrong with you?'

'I don't want him preying on anyone else. How old is he?'

I'd never got this information from her; it remained a mystery, along with all the other details she was keeping hidden from me. I had hoped Amy had been wrong when she had estimated his age; that he looked older than he was, or that the lighting had been too poor for her to get a fair impression.

Lily didn't answer, instead turning her head from me and focusing her attention on the window as though something fascinating had just passed us by.

'You know it's not normal for men of his age to bother with teenage girls, don't you?'

Her silence was more frustrating than having her shout at me, but before I could tell her so, she decided to offer me a response.

'It's not like that.'

'So you are still seeing him?'

'For God's sake, no, I'm not, I'm just saying it wasn't like that. Not everything has to be about sex, does it? Just because you got knocked up young doesn't mean we're all headed the same way.'

I stopped the car. It was stupid and childish, I realised that – too late, of course, in the way that regret always floods upon us. Beneath my sweater I could feel my heart pumping painfully, too fast, and when Lily turned to look at me, her face was enough to tell me that she knew she'd pushed me too far this time.

'Get out.'

We were only a few streets from the offices where she was booked in for an interview – a call-centre job, weekends and one evening during the week. She had taken on multiple part-time jobs since she'd turned sixteen almost two years earlier, but her lack of staying power meant she'd already had more employers than I'd had in my entire adult life. She knew her way to the building from where we'd stopped, but still, I shouldn't have done it. A red mist descended, and at that moment I couldn't see through it. I thought of Charlotte, her blood seeping from her neck – the life draining from her – and it made my foolish, selfish daughter all the more infuriating.

'What?'

'Get out of the car.'

Realising I meant it, she grabbed her bag from the floor and opened the door, giving it a good slam behind her, then sauntered off down the pavement, refusing to look back. I waited there a while, watching her disappear around the corner at the end of the street.

It wasn't her I was cross with, not really. Yes, she was lippy and rude and all the obnoxious things teenagers seem best capable of being, but in truth it was me I was angriest with, for the lack of control I seemed to have over what my daughter was doing. I hated that she was lying to me, though I had no right to be angry about it – no right to be angry with her for anything – not when it was me who was carrying the biggest lie of all.

FOUR

After leaving Lily – and sending her a grovelling text to apologise for our argument and for making her get out of the car – I stopped at Sainsbury's to buy flowers. Before going in, I replied to the text Laura had sent me the night before, asking whether I was home safely and gently mocking me for being forgetful.

> *Sorry. What am I like! Lovely to see you both last night – we'll have to do it again soon. I'm not feeling too great, so going to have to give circuits later a miss. Sorry x*

I quickly dismissed the idea of calling her, not wanting to get into a conversation about what had happened. I had already been over the previous night's events too many times, having to relive the scene again and again, each time haunted by the sight of the blood that had seeped from the other woman's skin onto mine.

In the supermarket, I spent a disproportionate amount of time deliberating over what colour flowers to buy – reds too romantic, yellows too cheery – though my procrastination was nothing more than a means of delaying my visit to the hospital, of having to face whatever awaited me there. The long hours between the previous night and that afternoon had been riddled with varying degrees of guilt, each relating to a different aspect of what had happened in the park. I should have acted quicker. I should have been better prepared. I could have been kinder, couldn't I, more compassionate with my words? Instead, I'd panicked. Talked nonsense.

After paying for a bouquet of pale pinks and creams – perhaps too feminine, but they were the only choice after a carefully considered process of elimination – I returned to the car. I'd had a text back from Laura: *Okay, no worries. Hope you're feeling better soon x*

I had heard one of the paramedics say that Charlotte would be taken to the Royal Gwent Hospital in Newport; I had called that morning and been told which ward she had been moved to following emergency surgery during the night. It occurred to me as I carried the bouquet through the front doors of the hospital's main building that perhaps she wouldn't be allowed flowers on the ward. I had explained to the nurse I'd spoken to that morning that I was the person who had called the ambulance and stayed with Charlotte until it had arrived. I'd asked how she was – stable, I was told, and lucky – but the thought of enquiring whether she might be able to accept gifts hadn't come to mind; why would it when there were so many other things to think about?

I got lost in the labyrinthine mass of the hospital's corridors and had to stop to ask a passing caretaker to point me in the right direction. Once I reached the ward, there was no need to find a member of staff; there was a board near the nurses' station with the patients' names printed in marker pen. Charlotte Copeland. Room 6. It occurred to me that they didn't seem particularly concerned about patients' safety, nor their privacy, but the thought was fleeting, quickly replaced by the swell of a headache that had been growing in severity since that morning. My palm was sweating around the stems of the bouquet. I was wearing only a thin cardigan over my T-shirt, having left my bulky winter coat in the car, and yet it felt as though I was overdressed, a thin trickle of sweat running down from the top of my spine.

Charlotte's room was at the end of the corridor. She was lying beneath a thin hospital sheet. Her head was turned from the door to face the window, which framed a panoramic view of the city, with the transporter bridge visible in the distance, a smudge of grey cloud hanging above it. She might have been sleeping, but the tilt of her head – too far back for her to be comfortable – suggested that she wasn't.

I paused on the threshold, unsure of what to say. The longer the moment drew on, the more inappropriate it began to feel, so I cleared my throat and spoke her name. She pushed a hand to the mattress, using it to propel herself upright. When she turned, my eyes were drawn to the dressing that covered the left side of her throat, then to her face, which was the pallid grey of exhaustion and trauma.

'How are you feeling?' I asked stupidly.

The scream was ear-splitting, bursting through the door and echoing down the corridor. I looked at her with horror, realising that her expression was a mirror of mine. My mouth fell open as though I too might scream; instead, she repeated her own cry, this time somehow louder and even more insistent.

Within moments, a nurse came running down the corridor, her hurried footsteps frantically click-clicking on the tiled floor. 'What's going on?' she asked, her face red and flustered. She was overweight, and her uniform pulled around her waist, her stomach straining to be freed from its incarceration. I felt ashamed at the thought, uncharitable, but it helped in that moment to keep me distracted from the echoes of Charlotte's screams and her unexpected reaction to seeing me.

'It's her,' Charlotte said, her voice much stronger than it had been the previous evening. 'It's her!'

The nurse looked at me, her eyes narrowed. 'You can't bring those in here,' she said, gesturing impatiently to the flowers I carried.

I shook my head and mumbled an apology. The flowers were the least of my concerns, particularly when the screaming recommenced.

'Charlotte,' the nurse said, hurrying to her side. 'Stop this. Calm yourself down.' She turned in a panic, as though hoping another member of staff might be free to come to her rescue. 'Charlotte,' she said again, repeating her name over and over as the hysterical woman continued to scream. 'You need to take it easy – you'll burst your stitches.'

All the time she had been screaming, Charlotte had managed not to take her eyes from me, and though the nurse's panicked attempts to calm her should at times have blocked her view, she had found a way of keeping me in sight. I felt the weight of her stare rest upon my skin, settling there like something I would never be able to wash clean.

'You're not listening to me,' she shouted, trying to push the nurse aside. 'It's her!'

A second nurse brushed past me as she entered the room. 'What's going on?'

'I'm not sure,' the first said, as though neither Charlotte nor I was present. 'Could you show this woman to the relatives' room, please?' She looked at me, waiting for me to object. I could have left – I could easily have outrun them both and fled from the hospital – but I stayed because I had no reason not to.

I nodded. 'Fine,' I said, not really knowing what else to say. 'I'll…' I looked down at the flowers still dangling from my hand, the blooms that had appeared so beautiful just an hour earlier now seeming drained of life, defeated. 'I'll wait there.'

I followed the second nurse from the room, hearing the voice of the first as she continued to try to calm a hysterical Charlotte.

'There's water there, if you'd like some,' the second nurse told me as she pushed open the door of the relatives' waiting room. She gestured to a dispenser in the corner, though there were no cups in the plastic funnel designed to store them. There was a bookcase against the right-hand wall, stocked with an array of dog-eared paperbacks and children's books. I wondered how long people were expected to stay there, and just what they were waiting for. It seemed to me that no stories could detract from the misery that must so often have played out within those four walls.

I knew then, from the mock politeness in the nurse's words, that something was very wrong and that I had been sent here to wait for someone else, someone who would ask for some explanation. I hadn't got one. There wasn't one. What had happened in Room 6 played over and over in my head, and with each repeat I hoped I might spot something different, something previously unnoticed, yet there was nothing. No matter how many times I viewed the scene, it remained the same. Charlotte's reaction was inexplicable, and so I waited for the police to arrive so that I could tell them there had been some sort of mistake.

FIVE

For the second time in twenty-four hours, it felt as though I was living someone else's life. The wrong things were happening to me, things I had no control over and felt certain were meant for somebody else. I was sitting in a cell at the local police station, all personal items – car keys, purse, mobile phone – having been taken from me and bagged at the custody desk. I had been photographed and had my fingerprints taken, a DNA sample scraped from the inside of my cheek, but other than to ask for my name and other details, no one had really yet spoken to me. Apparently I would be allowed a phone call, though I hadn't had a chance to make it yet. The thought of calling Damien and telling him what had happened filled me with dread, though I knew that had everything been right between us, it wouldn't have.

I was surrounded by brick walls, with nothing but the bare toilet in the corner for company. I was determined not to be reduced to having to use it, even though my bladder was near fit to burst. The thought of how many people – what type of people – had sat here in this box over the years, their minds plagued with the same waking nightmares that filled my head, helped keep everything else at bay for a while. I wondered how many of those other people had been innocent.

No matter how I tried to distract myself, I was unable to shut off the sound of Charlotte Copeland's voice. It might as well have been in that cell with me, so loud were the echoes it had left. How had she managed to get things so wrong? I had only tried to help her, though I could never for a moment have anticipated where that decision would lead me.

A tiny window in the top of one wall was the only source of light in the cell, and though I scanned the room for the camera I was sure must be installed somewhere, I couldn't see it. Eventually, after what felt like an age, someone came to unlock the door. I was taken back to the custody sergeant, who passed me a phone and told me I could call my husband.

With shaking hands, I keyed in Damien's mobile number. It was one of few I had memorised.

Pick up, I thought, when it started to ring. Please, Damien… pick up.

It rang through to answerphone. 'Damien, it's me. I…' Even now, I'm not sure why I said what I did. 'I'm going to be back late… I'm sorry. Tell the girls I'll make it up to them tomorrow. We'll get a pizza in or something. I'll explain when I see you, but there's nothing to worry about. Love you.'

The custody sergeant, having listened for the duration of the message, pulled an expression that I decided to ignore. Once I'd returned the phone to him, the officer who had escorted me from my cell took me back there.

It was several more hours before I saw another human being. A middle-aged female officer, stern-faced and grey-haired, unlocked the door and passed me a tray of food that looked so unappealing it made aeroplane meals seem appetising. I took it from her and placed it on the bench beside me, with no intention of touching the contents.

'When will I be interviewed?' I asked.

'We're waiting for the duty solicitor.'

I could have cried, but I didn't want to show any signs of weakness. The thought of having to stay in that room any longer, my family once again not knowing where I was or what had happened to me, made me feel sick. I already regretted not telling Damien the truth, but I hadn't dreamed I would be there so long. I had lied to him, despite my recent fears that he had been lying to me for some time.

'How long can you keep me here?' I asked, but my question was met with only the closing of the cell door as the officer left.

I dropped back onto the bench, pulling my knees up to my chest and covering myself with the thin blanket. I tried not to think about where Damien was – what he was doing and who he might be with – but I couldn't distract myself enough. If the reason for his recent distance was another woman, my absence would do nothing but push him closer to her. I waited, my mind plagued with the darkest of thoughts, my back and shoulders stiff with tension. I refused an offer of food while I waited for the arrival of the duty solicitor, who was apparently in no hurry to come to my aid. Having based my expectations on television dramas and crime novels, I was expecting a middle-aged man in an ill-fitting suit, someone with cigarette breath and an air of disillusionment, so when, at nearly eight o'clock that evening, I was finally introduced to a smartly dressed woman younger than I was, it threw me into a further state of ill-prepared panic. I had no idea what would happen to me, or what I should do to help myself. All I knew was that the woman I had visited in hospital – the woman whose life I might have saved – was accusing me of being her attacker.

'Follow me,' was all the solicitor said. She led me through a set of double doors to a room marked as Interview Room 2, where she opened the door and gestured to the nearest seat at the table to the left of the room.

I sat on the metal chair and listened to the door close behind us. There was a tape recorder on the table, a clock on the far wall; a camera installed in one of the corners of the ceiling. Other than that, the room was empty. I had no idea what happened next. I had never been arrested before – I had never been within the walls of a police station before – and though I'd watched plenty of police dramas on television, I doubted they were sufficient to prepare me for whatever the next couple of hours might hold.

The solicitor smoothed the skirt of her fitted dress before sitting beside me. 'You've been accused of a violent assault,' she said, as though I might need reminding of the fact. 'At the moment, the accusation made by the victim is currently all that stands against you, so my advice is to tell the truth and stick to the facts.'

'What do you mean, "at the moment"?'

'In order to charge you, the police will need evidence beyond the accusation.'

'I didn't do it,' I told her, feeling certain already that this woman didn't believe me. She was supposed to be on my side, yet it occurred to me that she was unlikely to care what happened to me. I hadn't hired her; I wasn't paying her. The title 'duty solicitor' seemed apt; she was there through obligation, not because she wanted to help prove my innocence.

'Then they won't find any evidence.'

She spoke so simply, as though everything was as straightforward as her tone implied. But I knew it wasn't. I would be guilty until proven innocent, and how was I supposed to do that? I had been there with the victim. The police had seen me there. If Charlotte Copeland, for whatever reason, wanted to accuse me of causing the injuries that had led her to that hospital bed, they would believe her, wouldn't they? Why would she lie?

'Will I be charged?' I asked quietly, hearing the tremor in my voice.

'As I said, not without evidence.'

'And if I am? What happens then?'

'If that happens, you'll need a solicitor to make an application for bail.'

'You won't do that?'

'I'm here as duty solicitor. Who you employ after this is entirely up to you, but as I said, it may not come to that. Give your account of what happened as simply and honestly as you can. Try not to get too emotional – just stick with the facts. If there are any questions you're unsure about, wait for me to step in, okay?'

I nodded, but it was without conviction. Beneath my T-shirt, my heart was pounding, and a rush of blood to my brain had prompted a headache that was fierce and relentless.

A moment later, the door opened, and two plain-clothes officers came in. The man introduced himself as DC Cooper and his female colleague as DC Henderson. He clicked a button on the tape recorder and spoke their names again before giving the name of the duty solicitor, Louisa Jones.

'Interview with Jenna Morgan commencing,' he said with a glance at the clock, 'at eight seventeen pm. You understand the allegation that's been made against you, Mrs Morgan?'

I nodded.

'Please speak for the recording, Mrs Morgan.'

'Yes, I understand.' My voice didn't sound like mine. It was brittle and sharp, already defensive.

'Charlotte Copeland has identified you as the person responsible for her assault,' said DC Henderson. 'We'd like you to take us through your version of what happened the night before last.'

'My version?' I glanced at Louisa, remembering her words about being honest and sticking to the facts. 'I've already told you what happened. I told the officers at the park last night.'

'If you could tell us again, please.'

I started at the restaurant, explaining why I was there, and ended with the police arriving at the park. I recalled each moment in as much detail as possible, from feeling cold and wishing I'd worn a pair of tights, to panicking that I was doing something wrong and not following the 999 operator's instructions properly. I didn't want to say that I saved Charlotte's life – she might well have survived without my efforts – yet at the same time I wanted to make them realise that my being there could only have been a good thing. I had tried to help her. Now I was paying for it in the worst of ways.

'Last night, when you spoke with our colleagues, you didn't offer much in the way of a description of the man you say you saw fleeing the park?'

There was an inflection at the end of DC Cooper's sentence; it was a question, not a statement.

'It was dark. He was wearing dark clothes, and I was at least… I don't know… two hundred metres away.'

'Quite a distance, then. How can you be sure it was a man?'

'I can't. I mean… I'm pretty sure it was a man.'

The two officers sitting opposite me were offering little in the way of reassurance, but then why would they? As far as they were concerned, I was guilty, identified in person by the victim. I had no defence to help me, and yet surely anyone could see the implausibility of the accusation made against me. Why would I have stabbed her, then stayed with her and helped her until the paramedics and the police arrived?

'Mrs Morgan.' DC Cooper leaned forward and studied me across the table as though I hadn't already been in the room with them for the previous fifteen minutes. 'Had you had any contact with Charlotte Copeland before last night?'

I noticed that the tone of his voice had changed, the politeness abandoned. I shook my head. 'I've never seen her before.'

'So you have no idea why she might want to accuse you of the assault against her?'

'No,' I said, trying to keep my voice as steady and level as possible. 'I can only assume that she's confused. Of course she recognises me – I was there with her. She was in a bad way before the ambulance arrived. The loss of blood… it must all seem like a blur to her. Perhaps she thinks—'

I was stopped short by the touch of Louisa's hand on my knee beneath the table.

'It's not Mrs Morgan's job to explain the accusation made against her, Detective.'

'We're just establishing the facts,' DC Cooper stated, eyeing the solicitor with impatience.

'You're missing the crucial fact that you have no evidence with which to charge Mrs Morgan,' Louisa said, looking from one officer to the other. When neither spoke, she continued, 'Holding her here any longer is a waste of everyone's time.'

The two officers exchanged a glance that confirmed her statement as correct. I should have felt relief, but there was nothing but the terrifying sickness that had lodged in my chest and was threatening to steal the breath from my body.

DC Cooper sat forward. 'Interview paused at eight forty-two pm.' He stood, and DC Henderson followed.

After they'd left the room, I found myself unable to speak, though there was plenty I wanted to say. The solicitor and I sat in silence, as though both unsure what we were waiting for. A short time later, DC Cooper returned alone.

'Follow me,' he said.

Louisa scraped back her chair as though everything was done and dusted, but I knew even then that it was far from finished. 'What happens now?'

'I'll show you back to your room,' DC Cooper said, as though he was a hotel employee and I was a paying guest; as though his parting phrase was sufficient to answer the flurry of questions that had settled in my head like a snowdrift, blocking any escape I might have had from my thoughts. When I looked at Louisa, she offered little more in terms of reassurance.

'I thought I'd be released?'

'They can hold you for up to twenty-four hours,' she replied. 'If no further evidence comes to light, they'll release you. Find yourself a solicitor. Just in case.'

I followed them both from the interview room and along the main corridor, back to the cell where a sleepless night awaited me.

SIX

I was released without charge under further investigation on Sunday morning. I had never heard the phrase 'under further investigation' before, though it was obvious that the police had no intention of dropping their suspicion of me. I wondered why they had kept me overnight just to release me without charge, but when I asked the desk sergeant who returned my belongings to me, his response was vague, a non-committal, 'we'll be in touch' apparently considered sufficient to clear up my confusion.

It was nearly eleven o'clock by the time I arrived home on Sunday morning. The first sound I heard upon stepping into the house was that of my younger daughter's tears, and it pierced my heart more sharply than any knife could have done. It didn't take me long to realise what had happened. The drawers in the hallway were open, half of their contents strewn across the top of the unit and the rest abandoned on the floor; the coat rack was a tangle of jackets and raincoats, as though each had been removed, shaken and haphazardly replaced. I imagined that the search must have taken place recently, and I understood then why they had kept me there for as long as they had. In the confusion of the aftermath, Damien had had no chance to begin to tidy up. And why should he? I thought. Though I had created it unwittingly, this was my mess, not his.

The door to the living room was ajar, and through the gap I could see Damien's legs. I imagined Amelia curled up on the sofa beside him, still in her pyjamas, her legs pulled up beneath her, her head resting on his chest as she sobbed into his T-shirt. She had always been a daddy's girl, something I had mockingly lamented over the years but had secretly been grateful for. My relationship with my own father – with both my parents – had been strained, with physical and emotional closeness an experience to which I had never been exposed, and I was thankful that Amelia and Damien had found the connection I had always craved.

When I heard movement from the kitchen, my first assumption was that it was Lily. Moments later, I realised I was wrong when I was confronted by my mother-in-law, Nancy, who came into the hallway carrying a mug of tea and a hot chocolate topped with a snowy peak of whipped cream and a sprinkling of tiny marshmallows. She looked at me as though I shouldn't be there, as though this wasn't my own home, and I felt my face burn with the shame of what I could only guess she might have heard.

'Jenna. We didn't know when you'd be back.'

Of course not, I felt like saying. Had anyone even bothered to try to find out?

From the corner of my eye I saw Damien move at the sound of his mother's voice; a moment later, he joined us out in the hallway. He looked exhausted, and I was hit by a wave of guilt that left a bitter yet familiar taste in my mouth. He told Amelia to wait where she was for a minute before he pulled the door shut behind him. I shot him a look that said I'd rather he'd closed the door with Nancy on the other side of it. But what had I expected? To be greeted with open arms and a strong shoulder to lean upon, much as I had just two nights earlier? I had kept the truth from him – unnecessarily and inexplicably – and he was obviously still smarting from the fact.

'Why did you lie?'

I felt a knot tighten in my stomach, and that taste, like bile, bitter and acidic, rose again in the back of my throat. For an awful moment I wondered what he was referring to.

'All that talk of running late and getting pizza… Why didn't you say you'd been arrested?'

'I didn't want to worry you.'

He looked at me so coldly that it was as though he was looking through me. I was all too aware of Nancy's presence, so typical of her not to use some tact and leave us to have this conversation alone.

'Didn't want to worry me? I've been trying your phone all night. I've called every hospital in South Wales. If you'd just told me where you were, I wouldn't have been left wondering what the hell was going on.' He lowered his voice to a hiss. 'You could have been dead for all I knew.'

'I'm sorry,' I said, knowing the words would be greeted with resentment. 'I didn't realise they'd keep me there all night.' I looked past him, down the length of hallway and into the glimpse of dining area I could see through the partly opened kitchen door. The table was littered with books, papers and stationery, everything stacked haphazardly and apparently at random. The place had been turned inside out. 'When did they come here?'

'They left just over an hour ago.'

'They had a warrant?'

'They didn't need one, apparently. They'd been granted a "section 18" search, whatever that means.'

I felt sick. My thoughts were snapped back to the previous evening, and to the detective's expression when he had returned to the interview room to take me back to my cell. Had he already known then that they would go to my house, and was that why they had kept me there overnight? When Charlotte had made her accusation against me, had she known that she would bring this to my home? Perhaps her thoughts hadn't stretched as far as the repercussions of her claim; maybe, amid the confusion of her injury, she was unable to see past the association she had made with me.

Whatever her state of mind, it was difficult to regard her words as anything but personal, as though she had done this to ruin me.

Damien turned from me, his eyes following mine.

'Damien called me when the police showed up,' Nancy said, handing him the tea. 'He didn't know what else to do.'

The comment shouldn't have annoyed me as much as it did, but at that moment I think anything Nancy might have said would have caused me frustration. It didn't surprise me in the least that calling her had been his first thought. It was always the case.

'It was the first I knew of where you were,' he said, gesturing with an arm flung in the direction of the chaos. 'I'd been calling round the hospitals – I thought you'd been in an accident. Quite a way to find out your wife has been arrested.'

'It's all a mistake,' I told him, the words pouring from my mouth too quickly. As soon as they'd left me, I heard how they sounded. I was trying to convince myself of my innocence as much as I was trying to convince Damien, as though the hours spent in that station had tainted me with the invisible brand of a criminal.

'Well, I'd assumed so.'

Hostility seeped from him like cheap aftershave, heavy and choking. Had things been right between us, he would have been offering me comfort, reassuring me that he was on my side and that we would work together to prove my innocence. But things hadn't been right for a while now, and it had taken the events of the previous twenty-four hours to highlight a truth I had been trying to ignore. Damien was there, but the husband I knew had left me, and I didn't know where he'd gone or why.

I wondered how much additional poison Nancy had been able to add to a recipe already soured with doubt and mistrust.

'Why didn't you answer?' I asked.

'What?'

'When I called you yesterday. Why didn't you answer? Where were you?'

Damien glanced to his left, and at his side his hand fumbled distractedly with his jeans pocket.

My tone was accusatory, though I tried to speak as casually as possible under the circumstances. I had spent my time in that police cell trying to fight away thoughts of where my husband might have been and who he might have been with, though I knew there was little more than my own overactive brain to justify my paranoia. I didn't want to think it possible that Damien might be having an affair, but his recent uncharacteristic silences and strange behaviour were leading me up paths I'd never thought I'd have to travel, not with him, at least; though I knew from previous experience that nothing could ever be guaranteed, not even the character of someone you thought you knew better than anyone else.

'I'm in for questioning as well now, am I?' he spat. 'I was here, wondering what the hell had happened to you. And looking after our daughter while the police were turning the house upside down.'

I bit my lip, feeling the injustice of his acrimony. 'Is Amelia okay?'

I was still aware of Nancy at my side, lingering there like the ghost of Christmas past.

'No. She's been bloody distraught.'

I looked down at the floor, guilty, but still not able to forget that he had hesitated before he'd answered my question about where he'd been. He could have lied; it would have been easy for him to do so. I hadn't been there to know any different.

'I'll take her the hot chocolate,' Nancy said, finally leaving us alone.

'And Lily?' I asked, when the living room door had closed behind my mother-in-law. 'Is she here?'

Damien shook his head. 'She didn't come home yesterday. She texted to say she was staying at Maisie's.'

My head swam as I realised that wherever she had really spent the previous night, it was all my doing. If I hadn't made her get out of the car the previous morning; if I had dealt with the situation of her mystery man better and earlier; if I hadn't taken that bloody shortcut through the park on Friday night, none of this would have happened. Lily would have been safely home with us, where I could have kept my eye on her.

'I'm glad she wasn't here,' Damien added. He reached into his pocket and pulled something from it before glancing at the living room door as though to check that his mother wasn't listening in on the conversation. 'And I'm glad I went into her room before they turned it upside down. Want to tell me what this is?' He produced a delicate silver bracelet, holding it flat on his outstretched palm. His eyes met mine questioningly, his eyebrows raised as he waited for an explanation.

I recognised the bracelet instantly. A couple of months earlier, when Lily had got her AS results, she had asked us to buy it for her, completely undeterred by the extortionate price tag. She had argued with us when we'd told her that she couldn't have it, and I had reasoned with her that if she wanted it badly enough, she would work hard and save for it. I tried to persuade her of how much better it would feel wearing it with the knowledge that she had earned it rather than just being given it, but my attempts were met with rolled eyes and a comment on how unfair we were.

'It's not like you can't afford it,' she had said, which had made me even more determined that she wouldn't have it, not unless she did as I had suggested, got herself some permanent part-time work and saved so that she could buy it for herself.

I stared at the bracelet in Damien's hand, unable to explain its presence in the house. Though she had earned money on and off with her various part-time jobs, there was no way she could have saved enough to buy it.

'Where did you find that?' I asked.

'In a drawer in her room.'

'What were you doing looking in her drawers?'

'Did you buy it for her?'

'No! We talked about this back in the summer – we agreed it was ridiculous and she shouldn't have it. Why would I go and buy it for her now?'

'Then how has she got it?'

I couldn't answer his question, not because I didn't have an explanation, but precisely because I did. I could only imagine how Damien might react if he knew about Lily's mystery man. There was no other possible explanation for how she had that bracelet, unless she had stolen it. And Lily was many things, but I knew she wasn't a thief.

'Mummy.'

Amelia was standing at the living room door, still crumpled and sleepy in her pyjamas, her penguin clutched in the crook of her arm in a way that made her look so much younger than her eight years. We had given her that penguin when she was two, and for six years she hadn't slept a night without it.

'The police were in my room.'

I'd expected her to be angry with me; instead, she threw herself at me, her arms wrapping around my waist and her face disappearing as she pressed herself against my stomach. As I folded my arms around her little body, I considered how slight she was. She always had been; she had been born five weeks before her due date, weighing just four pounds and fourteen ounces, and she had never quite caught up, always looking younger than the other children her age. I was forever worried that her small stature and childlike temperament would make her an easy target for bullies, but thankfully she had so far gone through her school life a happy, popular little girl.

'I'm sorry, sweetheart. I'm so sorry.'

The sadness I felt for my daughter – for my family – was tainted with anger towards Charlotte Copeland. Though she was a victim, she had made me one too, inflicting upon my children a shame they would be forced to wear like a second skin if this whole sorry mess was allowed to escalate further. I sympathised with her – I pitied her – but I couldn't help the part of me that resented everything she had brought upon me. She could take it all away again with just a few words, but there was no sign of her doing so.

I could feel Damien's eyes on me before his focus left my face and slipped down to the bracelet in his hand. He retracted his arm and returned the piece of jewellery to his pocket, as though realising the silliness of it all. Why were we arguing over a bracelet when there were so much bigger matters at hand?

In my pocket, my mobile started to ring. I pulled it out and glanced at its lit screen. Amy.

'I'm sorry, darling,' I said. 'I've got to take this.' I leaned down to kiss my daughter's head, breathing in the comforting scent of the apple shampoo her hair was always washed with. 'I won't be long, I promise.'

As I stepped past Damien, he ignored me, coaxing Amelia back into the living room with the promise of a Disney film. Then I realised something. When I had asked him what he had been doing looking through the drawers in Lily's room, he had never given me an answer.

SEVEN

I had called Amy after leaving the police station, explaining hurriedly to her answerphone what had happened after I had left the restaurant on Friday night. With hindsight, it had occurred to me that my phone call might have been wasted on Damien even had he answered, and that it would have been better to contact Amy. Her brother was a solicitor, successful and, as such, busy, though by all accounts he wasn't so popular with the police. There had apparently been several cases in which he'd got people everyone had known to be guilty off scot-free. If he could help them, he could help me, couldn't he? *I* hadn't done anything wrong.

'Jenna, thank God… are you all right?' Amy sounded genuinely concerned, and I felt guilty for having dumped my bad news on her in the middle of her relaxing break away.

'No.' I paused. 'No, I'm not okay.'

I did then what I hadn't allowed myself to do since Friday night. My tears were loud and embarrassing, but an accumulation of stress and anxiety meant I had no reserves with which to hold them back. I had never been accused of trying to kill someone before. My freedom had never seemed so fragile.

'Jenna,' Amy said, her voice calm and filled with an attempt at reassurance. 'Where are you?'

'I'm at home. Well… in the garden, actually. Cruella de Vil is here.'

Amy said nothing, more than aware who I was referring to. She was familiar enough with my family details to know that Nancy and I didn't get along.

'I'm sorry,' I said. 'I shouldn't have called you. I shouldn't have left that message.'

'You most definitely should.'

'How was your weekend?'

'Jenna,' she said, ignoring my attempt at normal conversation. 'I'm going to be home by two-ish. I'm coming over, or would you rather meet me somewhere else?'

'I don't want you to cut your weekend short for me.'

'Really, I'm not. I've been with him over twenty-four hours – that's enough for anyone. So, am I coming to yours?'

'Could we meet somewhere else?'

'The Swan?' she suggested.

The thought of going into town filled me with unease. I had no idea how much had already been made public, or what might have been said about me online. I had come from a village where gossip was rife and privacy was hard to come by, and had found that nothing changed with a move to a bigger town.

'Okay,' I said, knowing I couldn't hide forever from what might await me. I still had a business to run, and encountering other people was unavoidable. As well as that, I didn't want to be in the house. The atmosphere was stifling, as though I had already been deemed guilty.

We agreed to meet at four o'clock, and I ended the call. When I went back into the house, Damien was in the kitchen. He had been watching me from the window.

'What was so desperate that she couldn't be kept waiting?'

I glanced into the hallway, not wanting either Nancy or Amelia to hear what I had to tell him. 'They've released me under further investigation.'

'What does that mean?'

'It means they'll be looking for something to try to incriminate me with.'

'But you haven't done anything.'

'I know.'

Damien's face relaxed. It was clear he took this to mean that the whole sorry mess of my arrest was already over; that it was all nothing but a silly mistake and the police would soon come to realise it. In truth, it was far from over. I knew there would be worse to come.

'I'm going to see if her brother will represent me, if needed.'

'Sean Barrett? Are you that desperate? The bloke's a crook himself.'

'That's unfair,' I said, though I understood Damien's concern. Sean's reputation for being able to secure freedom for the bad guy meant choosing him as a solicitor could make me look like one of his usual clients. I didn't know him well enough to trust him, but I trusted Amy and I knew the influence she had over her brother.

'What's the state of Lily's room?' I asked.

'It's a mess.'

'We should tidy it up a bit before she gets back.'

Damien shot me a look I understood – Lily was bound to go nuts when she found out we'd been in her room and had touched her things.

'We'll just deal with the worst of it.'

While he went to the living room and spoke to his mother, I stared out of the kitchen window, my thoughts drifting once again to Charlotte Copeland, wondering what she was thinking about in that moment and whether it included me and what I might be going through as a result of her accusation. Not far from me on the kitchen worktop, its charger plugged into a socket at the wall, Damien's mobile beeped with a text message.

In all our years together, I had never checked my husband's phone, but something made me pick it up. The message appeared in a flash at the top of the screen, accompanied by a number that hadn't been saved to a name.

Hi Damien, are we still on for

I couldn't see the rest of the message – just that, there and gone in the briefest of flashes. To read the message in full I would need to unlock the phone. I knew his passcode – I had never been secretive about mine – yet I had never before used it to access his phone. I had never imagined I would find myself in a situation where I would be tempted to.

'You coming then?'

My hand slid from the phone at the sound of his voice at the kitchen door, and I moved away from it quickly, as though its nearness had burned me, and followed him upstairs to Lily's room. A part of me wanted him to reach out and touch me, to feel his arms embrace me in some sort of act of solidarity and reassurance, yet there was another part that resented his treatment of me since I'd got back from the station. I didn't believe he thought me capable of what I'd been accused of, but it was obvious he didn't trust me, not fully.

Did I trust him? I wanted to believe I did, yet the first few words of an unread message were enough to shake a faith that not so long before had felt indestructible. I was being stupid, I told myself. It was probably a client, someone whose laptop he was servicing; someone confirming an appointment. What had happened to make me so suspicious, or was this simply a resurrection of the old me – a me I had tried and failed to escape?

I stood behind Damien at the door to Lily's room, surveying the mess spread in front of us. Her drawers had been pulled out, clothes flung on to the bed in the police's search for... what, exactly? It hadn't occurred to me until that point, but I realised then what they were looking for, and the thought filled me with anger. I was a wife, a mother. Did they for one minute believe that I would hide a weapon here, in my teenage daughter's bedroom? It made me more determined than ever to prove my innocence, but how I was supposed to go about that, I had no idea.

'I'm meeting Amy later,' I told him as I hooked a denim jacket onto a hanger.

'You've only just got home.'

'I know, but I need to get this sorted out as quickly as possible. I don't want it hanging over us.'

I watched as Damien returned nail varnish bottles and make-up brushes to the drawers of the bedside table and wondered where the man I had fallen in love with had gone. A memory flashed into my mind, so bright it was almost living; a snapshot of a moment years earlier: Damien sitting on this same bedroom carpet with a much younger Lily by his side, his neck adorned with an array of plastic-jewelled Disney princess necklaces, his face a pink flush of lipstick and blusher – the old ones from my make-up bag that I had given Lily for her dressing-up box. I had only just found out that I was pregnant, and the morning sickness had come suddenly and with force, making me shut up the coffee shop early for the day. Nausea had rolled in my stomach as I stood at the top of the stairs and watched my husband and daughter through the partly open door of her bedroom, but I couldn't bring myself to leave the sight, not yet. I'd watched as Lily applied lipstick to Damien's cheeks, smearing it in big pink circles that made him look like a cartoon character, and when she sat back, laughing and holding a mirror in front of him, I'd felt my heart swell with love for them as he proclaimed he had never looked better.

'Is there something you're not telling me?'

I turned to him, affronted by the question. Just moments earlier, it might have been me asking the same. 'What do you mean? Like what?'

'I don't know. Anything. It seems weird that this woman is accusing you like this. Things like this don't just happen, Jenna.'

I can't remember what I was holding – an item of Lily's clothing, an accessory tossed to one side during the house search – but whatever it was, it ended up flung back to the floor. 'What are you suggesting?'

'I'm not suggesting anything. I'm just saying it's strange, that's all.'

We looked at each other for a moment, neither one of us sure what else to say. I could feel myself growing hot with indignation, the thought that he didn't trust me making my heart race and my temperature flare. 'I assumed I'd be able to rely on you for support.'

'And you know you can. You always can.'

It sounded strained somehow, as though even Damien didn't quite believe the words. I wanted to walk from the room, to go back downstairs and leave the house, but I wouldn't go until Lily's room was returned to some sort of state of normality.

We worked separately, continuing the task of tidying up in silence as my mind churned with anxiety about what else could be going on. Why was my husband so suspicious of me? And why was I so suspicious of him?

EIGHT

I waited for Amy in the Swan, a pub just a couple of streets from the restaurant where we had eaten two nights earlier. I found the quietest corner of the bar, feeling that the eyes of every person I passed were upon me, as though somehow the whole town was aware of the accusation made against me. I had managed to avoid the television and the radio, knowing that news of the attack would make the local news.

I took my phone from my pocket and ran an internet search on Charlotte Copeland. Several Facebook accounts registered to that name were thrown up, but as I scrolled the list of faces there was none that matched the woman who had made the accusation against me. I began to trawl through the profiles of other social media sites but found nothing, and my efforts were halted when I looked up to see Amy approaching.

She looked relaxed from her weekend away, chic as ever in a calf-length coat belted around the waist, her hair piled high on her head in a style that on her appeared effortless and on my own head would have looked as though a bird had decided to set up a nest there. The differences in our weekend experiences appeared stark as she slid into the chair opposite me, and I felt guilty once again at having ended her birthday celebrations with my misery.

'God, Jenna, are you okay? You look awful.'

From anyone else, I might have taken offence, but it was honesty such as this that had made Amy one of the few friends I had. I didn't want anything glossed over or avoided for the sake of protecting my sensibilities; I didn't have time for that now. I wanted someone who would be forthright, and Amy could always be relied upon to be that person.

'It's just been mentioned on the local radio news,' she told me. 'Don't worry – your name wasn't brought up. You could bloody sue them if it was.'

In a tactile gesture that was quite unlike Amy, she reached across the table and locked her hand around mine. It felt awkward, but I allowed it to rest there, appreciating her efforts to make me feel less isolated. It didn't matter if the place was suddenly filled with people; I could have been surrounded and still have felt myself solitary, adrift with the unsettling turns my life had taken in such a short space of time.

'Tell me everything.'

Over soft drinks – and in a hushed voice that wouldn't be overheard – I filled her in on what had happened after I'd left her and Laura at the restaurant on Friday night. She remained silent for most of my account, shaking her head at times, her expression changing as I took her through the stages of my weekend.

'Do you think I should go back to the hospital to see her? Perhaps she'll explain why she's done this.'

Amy shook her head slowly, her eyes fixed on mine as though studying them for signs of madness. 'The worst idea you've ever had. Do not, under any circumstances, go back to the hospital – don't go anywhere near that woman at all. It will only make things worse for you. If the police are still considering you a suspect and you try to contact her, they'll see it as a sign of guilt. You could be arrested for intimidation.'

In my lap, I locked the fingers of my right hand into those of my left, squeezing until my knuckles turned white and the veins protruded ice-blue. Near the bar, an eruption of laughter burst through the hum of noise surrounding us, its raucous tone startling me.

'Why is she doing this to me?'

Amy sighed and reached for her drink. 'Perhaps it's not as personal as you think. I mean, it's only natural that you'd take it that way – I think anyone would – but perhaps it's just a case of genuine confusion. Think about it. She was attacked at random. She lost a lot of blood. She might have suffered a head injury when she fell to the ground – we don't know, do we? When she recognised you at the hospital, her brain made an immediate connection to the event, she put two and two together…'

She trailed off with a shrug, her point made. Everything she said made sense, though I couldn't understand why it didn't seem so easily explained to the police. The words 'under further investigation' had lingered with me; I wouldn't be able to tear myself free of them until it was proven that I was innocent.

I fought back tears, determined not to cry in public. 'Do you think Sean would help me?'

'I really don't think it'll come to that, but if it does, of course he will. He never refuses his little sister.' She smiled. I wanted to smile back, to pretend everything was fine, that I wasn't terrified, but my face refused. Instead a silent tear slid down my cheek.

'This isn't just about the arrest, is it? You didn't seem yourself at the restaurant; I knew there was something wrong.'

I wiped a hand across my eye as I thought of the half-read text that had popped up on Damien's phone, chiding myself for this further show of weakness. I had spoken to Amy about the changes in Damien; it had seemed wrong, as though I was being disloyal, and yet talking about it had offered instant relief. By speaking the words aloud, I'd been able to hear them differently.

'It's Damien, isn't it?' she asked, reading my thoughts.

'He's just… I don't know. You know when you just know that there's something not right? He always used to be tactile, but he seems to keep his distance these days. He's started sleeping on the sofa. He says he's having trouble with his leg again, but I know that's just an excuse. And today, when I got home from the police station… It was almost as though he thinks I'm guilty. He just looks at me differently and I don't know what I've done.'

I decided against mentioning the text message. I hadn't really seen it; not all of it, at least. Every logical cell in my brain told me it was something innocent – a sentence that could be finished in a thousand different ways, all harmless – and yet I couldn't help but let myself hold on to the notion that it wasn't.

Amy was listening to me intently, her eyes fixed on my face, her fingers idly twirling a loose strand of hair. 'Maybe what he's saying about his leg is true.'

Amy was right, as she so often seemed to be. She knew all about Damien's accident; though I didn't meet her until after it had happened, she'd seen us at our worst, when we were struggling to navigate our way through the set of cruel circumstances life had unexpectedly thrown at us.

'Maybe,' I admitted.

'Have you spoken to him about it?'

I shook my head. 'There's enough going on already. He still doesn't know about Lily, and I'm worried that if he finds out now, it'll be worse, because he'll wonder why I didn't tell him before.'

'I thought all that was finished with?'

I raised an eyebrow and sighed. 'So did I, but apparently not.' I told her about the bracelet, about how Damien thought I had bought it for her. Like me, Amy couldn't see any explanation for how Lily had come to have it, other than as a gift from the mystery boyfriend.

'We need to find out who this bloke is.'

I smiled at her use of the word 'we'. I should have been approaching this with my husband, and though I appreciated Amy's loyalty and her concern for Lily's welfare, the absence of Damien's help stung. It wasn't his fault, I realised that – I had kept him in the dark about Lily's secret and had made him an outsider.

'I've tried,' I said, though she already knew this. I had scoured through Lily's social media, keeping a check on who she was following and friending, but her accounts had always been kept private and she didn't seem to use them much. I'd always thought it was because she was too sensible to absorb herself in life online as so many young people her age seemed to, but I was quickly learning that perhaps that wasn't the case. Now I feared that her apparent common sense was a ploy to conceal her teenage stupidity.

Amy held her glass to her lips, hesitating before taking a sip. 'You need to follow her.' She set the glass back down, its clink on the table punctuating her statement with the finality of a full stop.

'Follow her? I can't do that.'

'Why not?'

'It's… I don't know. It just doesn't seem right.'

I'd felt uncomfortable enough just checking her phone, imagining how I might have reacted at that age if my parents had done the same. The difference, I knew, was that I hadn't given them reason to suspect me – not at that age, at least – whereas Lily had given me plenty.

Amy pulled a face. 'A grown man getting involved with a teenage girl isn't right either.'

I exhaled loudly and pressed a hand to my forehead. Amy was completely correct. Lily was going to hate me for it, but if it meant keeping her protected, then I was going to have to become exactly the kind of parent I had sworn to myself I would never be.

'I think he's having an affair.'

I watched Amy's face make the leap in conversation from Lily's mystery man back to my husband. 'Damien?' She shook her head. 'You're not serious?'

The words had just escaped me, and I regretted them as soon as they'd been spoken. I knew why to an outsider the possibility seemed implausible. Damien was a family man, always there for his children, consistently supportive of his wife. From the outside, I had it all; now, I sounded nothing but ungrateful for everything I'd been given.

'I've been so wrapped up with whatever's going on with Lily... I think I've just tried to block it out. But something's not right, Amy, I just know it. He's there, but he's absent, you know what I mean? The way he looks at me sometimes... he just isn't him any more.'

I repeated my own words in my head as I watched disbelief play out on Amy's face, and I knew I was being irrational; paranoid even. Perhaps she was right, I thought. Damien was a good man, a man who had picked me up when I'd had nothing and helped me find a life that I could finally be proud of. Perhaps it wasn't Damien who had changed at all. Perhaps I was the one who was different now.

NINE

When I got home from meeting Amy, Lily was upstairs in her bedroom. Though Damien and I had tried to tidy up, we were never going to be able to put everything back in the right place. She was going to know her things had been gone through, and she would be furious. I had hoped to be back before she was, so that I could be the one to tell her about the police, but as always, I was too late, and Damien had done it. I knew my absence would be cause for further argument, and once again, I realised it was justified.

The door to her room had been left ajar, and as I crept up the final steps to the landing, I could hear her crying. Lily never cried. Her emotions tended to make themselves known in exaggerated facial gestures and the slamming of doors, and the sound of tears made her seem more vulnerable than I'd felt her to be in a long time. Though she was seventeen, in so many ways she was still just a child: headstrong, impulsive, impressionable.

'Lily.'

She turned at the sound of her name, quickly wiping the back of her hand across her face, not wanting me to see evidence that she had been crying. In doing so, she smeared a dark trail of mascara across her temple.

'When were you going to tell me about that woman?'

I sighed and closed my eyes for a moment, trying to force back a headache I'd been battling since meeting up with Amy. 'I wanted to tell you yesterday,' I said, going into her room and closing the door behind me. 'But I knew how important that job interview was to you – I didn't want you going there with that hanging over you. And I didn't know she was going to accuse me, obviously.'

'You kicked me out of the car. You were happy enough for me to go with *that* hanging over me.'

I sat at the end of her bed, waiting for her to join me. She didn't.

'You won't say anything to Amelia, will you?'

She rolled her eyes as though I was stupid for feeling the need to suggest she might.

'Have you heard back about the job yet?'

'No. They said I'd hear from them within a few days.'

'I'm so sorry about your things,' I said, taking in the chaos that surrounded us despite our attempts to make things appear as normal as they could be. 'I didn't know they'd do this.'

She looked at me as if I was stupid. 'You've been accused of stabbing someone. What else did you think they'd do?'

I glanced at the bedside table and wondered whether Damien had returned the bracelet to the place he'd found it. No doubt it would have been one of the first things Lily had looked for after discovering the police had been here. She wouldn't want Damien or me to know about it, and I couldn't mention it without her knowing that one of us had also been through her things.

She dropped down beside me suddenly, folding against me like a rag doll, and I put an arm around her, pulling in the warmth of her. The next thing I knew she was sobbing against my chest, clinging to my sleeves as she had done when she was a little girl.

'Why is that woman saying what's she saying, Mum?' she snivelled through her tears. 'You'd never hurt anyone.'

I pulled her closer, breathing in the scent of her shampoo as I'd done with Amelia, wanting to stay like this forever.

'I don't know, sweetheart. I wish I did, I really do – maybe then I'd be able to do something about it.'

'Have you seen what's being said online?'

I swallowed noisily; Lily probably heard it. I had been tempted to look for my name on the internet, wondering how long it would be before news of my arrest circulated among people I knew, but had decided not to expose myself to further unnecessary torment and had successfully resisted.

'I don't want to know. Whatever it is, it's rubbish. I was arrested, but I wasn't charged. I haven't done anything wrong, love – I don't need to tell you that, do I?'

She didn't answer, but her head nuzzling at the crook of my neck confirmed her faith in my innocence. It was comforting just having her there, so much closer to me than she had been in some time. Our falling-out over her boyfriend – or not, as she had so repeatedly and vehemently claimed – had caused ongoing friction that had kept her at arm's length, and it hadn't gone unnoticed by Damien.

'Have I been named?' I asked, curiosity and fear getting the better of me. I wasn't sure whether it was legal for my name to be released when I hadn't been charged with anything, but I knew how cheap talk was and how quickly gossip could be spread.

'No. Not yet.'

'Try to stay off social media for a while,' I advised. 'It'll all blow over soon enough and then they'll find something else to talk about.' I ran a hand over the smooth sheen of her hair. 'No one's said anything to you, have they? Or about you?'

She shook her head against my chest, and a wave of relief surged. I could handle trolls condemning me from behind the safety of their keyboards, but if Lily was dragged into the firing line, that would be a different matter.

'Tell me if anyone says anything to you.'

She nodded again, though I noticed that it was with less conviction.

We were interrupted by Damien, who stepped quietly into the room with a sheepish expression on his face. 'You two okay?'

I nodded, but gave him a look that Lily couldn't see. I hoped he understood what it meant: that we should go easy on her for a while. Regardless of the drama I had unwittingly brought into the house, he was still consumed with thoughts of that bracelet, and the last thing any of us needed was for him to find out that she had been involved with an older man.

'Cup of tea, love?'

The question was directed at Lily, who pulled herself away from me and sat up, shaking her head without acknowledging Damien. His eyes were focused on her, willing her to look at him. Then he glanced at me, and his face changed, aware I had been watching him.

'I'll have one,' I said.

He nodded and turned away. As he reached the door, I noticed the limp that seemed to affect him sporadically.

He closed the door behind him, and I waited to hear him head back downstairs before I looked at Lily questioningly. 'Everything all right between you two?' The exchange – or lack of it – had been odd to say the least, the atmosphere fractious and fragile. Whatever had gone on between them, neither seemed to want to raise the subject in front of me.

'Fine.'

'Has something happened?'

'I said it's fine,' she snapped. She stood and went to the window. The curtains were pulled back and the night sky loomed dark and heavy, not a single star in sight. 'Do you trust him?'

'He's my husband,' I said defensively, at once annoyed and perplexed by the question. 'Why do you ask that?'

'Just wondered,' she said with a shrug, her back still turned to me. 'Perhaps you shouldn't.'

'What do you mean by that?'

She didn't answer me, so I stood from the bed and joined her at the window, feeling my pulse skip a beat. I knew there was something going on with my husband; I had known it for a while. The silences, the absences, the evenings that passed with us barely exchanging a word.

'It doesn't matter.'

'You can't go around making insinuations and then just expect me to ignore them,' I said, folding my arms. 'Come on. What do you know? Why shouldn't I trust him?'

Lily was still looking out of the window, and when my gaze followed hers, it stopped at the park, the events of Friday evening playing out soundlessly in front of me, the memory still sharp.

'Laura was here.'

It was not what I was expecting. We stood in silence for a moment, Lily's attention still averted from me as my thoughts raced along a series of possibilities I hadn't anticipated and was unprepared for.

'What do you mean, here?' I eventually asked.

'Here, in the house, with Damien.' She moved away from the window and picked up a book from the chair in the corner, putting it back on the shelf with the others that were lined up there.

'When?'

'Yesterday, when I got home from the interview.'

'Doing what?' I asked, though I wasn't sure I wanted to hear the answer.

'I don't know. They were in the kitchen together.'

Beneath my clothes, my heart rate slowed a fraction. I had imagined the worst, that Lily was about to tell me she had come upstairs and found them in bed. They could have been doing anything, I rationalised; Laura could have been here for any number of reasons.

'She probably popped in looking for me.' But she hadn't texted me back, I thought. After I'd messaged her outside Sainsbury's, I'd heard nothing from her in return. The thought drew me in a different direction. Had the half-read message I'd seen on Damien's phone been from Laura? The only mobile numbers I knew from memory were Damien's and Lily's – I had a job to remember my own much of the time. Laura's had been entered into my phone years earlier, without me ever having to take in the details of the digits.

Are we still on for

I shook myself for being so foolish and for allowing my mind to take me to such ridiculous, unlikely places. Damien was loyal. Laura was my friend. Friends were something my life had lacked until recently, and I didn't want to lose the few I had because of my suspicion and paranoia. There were reasons why I found it difficult to trust – reasons why I had spent years keeping people at arm's length – but I had made a good life for myself now and I couldn't allow myself to ruin it.

The events of the previous forty-eight hours were making me see things that weren't there and imagine things without justification, and yet a niggling doubt remained. Why had Laura been at the house, and why hadn't she or Damien mentioned it?

'Maybe,' Lily said with a shrug, the word spoken with such cynicism that I knew she didn't believe it.

I had known Laura for almost seven years, having met her at playgroup when Amelia was just a baby. We had clicked in a way I never seemed to with the other mothers, and I'd wondered at the time if my isolation was caused by my lack of enthusiasm for conversations involving sleep schedules and nappy rash. I loved my daughter as much as anyone else loved their children, but it was nice to talk about something that wasn't baby-related, and Laura had been refreshingly happy to oblige.

'Did they see you?' I asked. 'Did you hear what they were talking about?'

Lily shook her head. 'I went upstairs – they didn't see me. But I saw them at the front door. He kissed her.'

I felt my body turn cold. 'What do you mean, he kissed her? Kissed her how?'

Lily shrugged, as though the details weren't important. 'On the cheek. He kissed her and he thanked her, then said something about looking forward to next week.'

He kissed her on the cheek. It was nothing, I rationalised. Just a friendly goodbye. Then I thought of Laura sitting in the restaurant with Amy and me – mentioning circuit training as though it was any other weekend – and I wondered whether she could betray me in this worst of ways. I'd made other acquaintances after opening the coffee shop, but nobody I thought of as a friend. I had just two of those – Amy and Laura – and the thought that one of them might have been betraying me with my own husband made me feel sick to the stomach, as though there was no one in this world I was able to fully trust.

TEN

Lily was three years old when I first met Damien. We were living in a small Welsh village called Llangovney, near the Pembrokeshire coast, in a three-storey terraced house in which the ground floor had been converted into a self-contained flat. The owner – an elderly lady whose decreasing mobility meant she would have benefited from swapping places with us – occupied the rest of the house above. I lived in dread of the day she would tell me she was selling up and moving somewhere smaller and more manageable; my rent was cheap, a reduced price agreed on the basis that I looked after the upkeep of the garden and cleaned for her once a fortnight. I did more than that and was happy to, picking up items from the shop for her and taking her mail to be posted. If anything had happened to her, I didn't know where Lily and I would have gone or how I would have afforded to keep a roof over our heads. The thought often struck me as uncharitably self-obsessed, but at the time I couldn't afford to be anything else.

Six mornings a week, I cleaned rooms at a local B and B. The owners, Brian and Elaine, allowed me to bring Lily with me; she was a well-behaved child, docile and easy-natured, and they would often take her from me for half an hour to walk her around the garden and look for birds, or to play with the collection of toys they kept in a box in the kitchen for her. There was never any mention of children of their own and I never liked to ask whether they had any. They seemed happy to help me, and I was grateful for the employment.

I would spend the afternoons with Lily, playing in the park or out in the garden at the flat, and when it rained, we would often visit the nearest library, a thirty-minute bus trip away. Five evenings a week I worked behind the bar at the local pub, which was just along the street from our flat. One of our neighbours – a woman with three children of her own and a husband who often worked away – looked after Lily during those hours; her fee ate into my earnings but my rent and food bills were still just about manageable. I kept going by telling myself that things wouldn't always be the way they were, that life would get better and easier, but in truth I could never see how that might become a reality. Then I met Damien, and everything changed.

That weekend, an extreme triathlon event was passing through the village. The Ironman took place on the same weekend every year, with two and a half thousand participants undertaking a gruelling challenge of a three-mile swim in the ice-cold sea at Tenby and a one-hundred-and-twelve-mile cycle ride, topped off with a marathon. The local B and Bs were always full, and the pub in which I worked offered a special Ironman menu the day before the event, which consisted of carb-loaded pasta dishes, one of which Damien came to the bar to order.

'Ironman?' I asked, as I had already done with several people that evening.

He nodded and smiled. 'I must be mad, right?'

His accent was different to the Welsh accents in the west; his vowels a little softer, the ends of his words more rounded. It had taken me a while to get used to the local accent, and as a London girl I had stood out like a sore thumb, my voice raising the apparently inevitable question of how I had come to be there.

'You'll be fine. If I can do it, anyone can.'

'You've done it?'

'No,' I said, placing the drink he'd ordered on the bar between us, 'but there was no need to sound so surprised at the possibility.'

We exchanged a smile, and as he placed a twenty-pound note in my hand, I realised I was flirting. This was something that hadn't happened in a long time. There was only one other person who had ever had that effect on me.

'I'll bring your cutlery over,' I said.

'Thanks.'

He had lingered there, still looking at me, before smiling again and going back to his table. When I brought the cutlery, the others with him barely acknowledged me, but I could feel his eyes on me as I moved between them, and I knew I wasn't imagining the attention he was giving me.

'I might see you tomorrow, then.'

I was back behind the bar again at this point, their meals all finished and his friends already headed towards the door. He placed some empty glasses on the bar and met my eye with a smile. My face must have betrayed my confusion.

'The run goes past this way, doesn't it?'

'Oh, right. Yeah, it does. Good luck.'

'I'm going to need it,' he said. 'Wait outside with a pint for me, will you?'

I smiled and he left, but I was still watching him when he turned at the door to look back, and I was surprised by my feeling of disappointment at his departure, and at the thought of never seeing him again.

I looked out for him the next day when I was clearing tables, finding excuses to go near the windows or to pop outside to clear abandoned glasses, on the off chance that he might not yet have finished the triathlon, and I might see him running past. In the stream of colourful T-shirts, tired limbs and reddened faces, none of them belonged to him, and I resigned myself to the fact that that was that, and it had been foolish of me to imagine anything more might have come of our meeting.

The following day, I worked my shift at the B and B. Some of the guests from the Ironman event were still there, and as I watched them head to and from the breakfast room, I kept an eye out in the hope one of them might be him. It wasn't like me to find myself so preoccupied with anyone who wasn't Lily; I had moved to Llangovney to disappear, and as such had managed to keep myself quite anonymous. Yet there had been something about this man – this person whose name I didn't even know – that kept my thoughts returning to him, and I wondered whether, in the past thirty-six hours, his mind had strayed at all towards me.

When I finished work, the weather was terrible, so Lily and I caught the bus into town and went for a swim at the leisure centre before heading home for an afternoon of Disney and popcorn. She curled up against my chest on the sofa, no longer a baby but a little girl, and I remember watching her as she gazed at the television, marvelling at how quickly she was changing and how lucky I was to have her in my life. Later, there were moments when I craved those days, missed it being just the two of us. Despite the loneliness and the solitary nights, it felt as though I had everything I'd ever wanted.

The following evening, I arrived at the pub at just gone six. It was quiet, as it always was on Mondays, and my boss was sitting at the end of the bar eating his dinner.

'All right, Jenna love.' He gestured to the till. 'Someone left that for you.'

I slipped off my jacket as I went behind the bar. There was an envelope at the side of the till, no name written on it, but when I held it up to the landlord, he nodded. I took it with me into the tiny cupboard that passed as a staff room, where I hung my jacket on the back of the door.

I didn't see you waiting with that pint, the note inside read, *but I'll forgive you this time. Maybe we could go for a drink together one day? Damien.*

His phone number was printed at the bottom. I smiled, feeling stupid and juvenile for allowing myself to react to a stranger's attention with teenage butterflies. Since moving to the village, I hadn't really spoken to anyone who existed beyond my day-to-day life: the regulars at the pub, the guests at the B and B; the postman and the couple who owned the convenience shop down the road.

Near the end of my shift, just before last orders, I glanced at my phone.

Lily has been sick. She's OK but crying for you a lot.

I cursed myself for not having checked the phone sooner, and when I told the landlord, he said I could finish early to go and get her.

When I picked her up from the childminder's, she was still awake. She was usually sleeping by that time, and I was able to carry her home in her pyjamas, but that day she was fractious and unsettled. The childminder told me she'd been sick twice in the last hour.

The front door was barely closed behind me when she threw up again, managing to cover us both. I carried her to the bathroom, peeled off her clothes and cleaned her up in a shallow bath before dressing her in clean pyjamas. Then I stripped off my own clothes, throwing on the nearest T-shirt I could find, and cuddled up to her on my bed, smoothing her hair as she fell asleep against my chest. Once she was settled into a deeper sleep, I left her on the bed and went to the kitchen, where I threw her sick-stained clothes and my own into the washing machine, forgetting the note still tucked in my jeans pocket.

ELEVEN

My coffee shop was just off the high street, where the rental costs were a third of those just around the corner. I unlocked the front door and deactivated the alarm before flicking on the lights, knowing I couldn't stay there for too long; if anyone saw the place lit up, they might think it was open earlier than usual. Dealing with customers was something I wasn't ready for; I had gone there purely because I wanted to be away from the house. I needed to be on my own for a while, to give myself a chance to put things straight in my head, and the coffee shop was the only place to which I could escape.

I had been tempted to text or phone Laura, to just come out with it and ask her what she'd been doing with Damien at our house on Saturday. Logic stopped me, along with pride; I knew that if I did, there was a possibility she might mention it to Damien before I had a chance to speak to him about it. The truth was, I didn't want to speak to him about it. My life felt uncertain enough; if the ground was about to give way beneath my marriage, I didn't want to be the one responsible for precipitating the final collapse, not when I was guilty of unwittingly creating the tremor that was already rocking our family. Besides, it seemed too unlikely for it to be a reality, and when the portion of my brain that still retained some sense kicked into gear for a moment, the thought of Damien and Laura together seemed nothing but absurd. Blurting an accusation at either of them would do nothing but make me look stupid.

Yet in the moments when the weaker part of my brain took hold – the part that still saw darkness in everything, believing nothing could ever be truly good – the possibility of an affair between Damien and Laura continued to prey upon me. Laura had been to our house with her kids on plenty of occasions when Damien had been there, but I had never thought of her in any other way than I had come to think of myself – as a mother. Outside of these visits, she and Damien had no connection; we weren't the type to do double dates with our friends and their spouses. Though she wasn't as well dressed or as confident as Amy, perhaps there was something about her I had missed. It would never have occurred to me before to regard her as a threat, and yet a flicker of doubt within me had sparked the fear that perhaps that was what she had always been – a more organised, slimmer, athletic version of me.

I dropped onto one of the sofas near the counter. My legs felt leaden, and I was so tired I could have curled up and gone to sleep there and then had my mind not been so set against finding any sort of respite from the demons plaguing it. The truth, I realised, was that focusing my thoughts on Damien was an attempt to keep my mind from Charlotte Copeland and from the uncertain future in front of me. I wondered how she was, what sort of recovery she was making, though Amy had warned me not to make any contact. Anything I did where that woman was concerned now had the potential to make me look guilty, and I knew that keeping my distance was for the best.

I scanned the books on the shelves near the sofa, realising that Ffion had rearranged them at some point during my absence. The place had been left spotless, as it always was when she was in charge. I was lucky to have found her; a single mother, as I had been, she was hard-working and conscientious, and I could rely on her to run the place without my always having to be there to keep an eye on things.

The coffee shop had been open for nearly ten years, and in that time I had managed to secure a regular and loyal customer base. Thanks to word of mouth and a 4.8 TripAdvisor rating, the business had done better than I could ever have hoped for; so much so that I had come to think of it as my 'forever' job. I hadn't been naive about the chances of success when we'd initially opened, knowing that a majority of businesses failed within the first year, but with hard work, long hours and a gritty determination not to let my family down, the Snug had kept on running while five other coffee shops within a couple of miles' radius had come and gone.

I'd found out I was pregnant just over a year after it had opened. The timing wasn't ideal, and I'd known it would be difficult juggling family life with a newborn while running a business, but Damien could barely contain his excitement at the news, and I was determined to push my anxieties to one side. He was supportive of the shop and did so much to help with Lily, and I spent my pregnancy working hard, doing everything I could to ensure that a solid foundation was in place before the baby arrived. It was during that time that I was lucky enough to meet Ffion, and she quickly became my assistant manager. I saw in her myself as I had once been, and it felt good to be able to offer her a break.

There was a tap on the glass of the shop door. I turned, ready to tell whoever was there that we weren't open. But it wasn't a customer; it was the police. One uniformed officer, with another in plain clothes. The latter held his ID to the glass; it introduced him as DS Maitland. I opened the door cautiously, reluctant to let them in but even less enthusiastic about the thought of leaving them outside the shop for anyone passing to catch sight of.

'We have a warrant to search the premises.'

'What?'

They stepped past me, and I was powerless to stop them. I realised that with a warrant, they had the right to do pretty much whatever they wanted, even though it would be pointless. Another unjustified invasion of my privacy.

'This is starting to feel like a witch hunt,' I told them, my heart throbbing and voice shaking. 'I haven't done anything wrong, I keep telling you.'

I stood back and watched, helpless, as the uniformed officer headed straight to the kitchen, while her colleague went behind the counter and started pulling open drawers and cupboards. I was already mourning the tidiness I had only recently admired, knowing that I would have to get everything back in order by opening time the following morning.

'This is a waste of everyone's time,' I said, trying to keep the anger from my voice.

The plain-clothes officer said nothing, his attention focused on the till. 'Got a key for this?' he asked.

With a sigh, I dug my keys from my jacket pocket and joined him behind the counter. I opened the till and waited as he searched it, wondering exactly what he had been expecting to find there.

I was distracted by the sound of the shop door, my heart skipping at the thought of a customer walking in and seeing the police searching the place. But it was only Ffion. She was in the process of shrugging her jacket from her shoulders; unnerved by the sight of a stranger at the till, she stopped short and looked at me questioningly.

'Everything all right, Jenna?'

'I've had better mornings,' I muttered. I turned back to the officer. 'This is a waste of time,' I said again, as though repetition alone would be enough to hammer the point home. 'What are you looking for anyway?'

'Sarge.'

As if on cue, the uniformed officer appeared at the kitchen door. I turned at the sound of her voice, my heart stuttering to a painful halt when I saw what she held in her gloved hand.

'Hidden behind one of the fridges,' she said.

I looked from one officer to the other, disbelieving. 'That's not…'

My voice trailed into silence, which I realised too late only served to make me appear guiltier. I turned to Ffion. Her eyes had widened, and she looked as though she was contemplating walking back out of the shop and trying again, convincing herself she had walked into some parallel universe.

As the female officer placed the bloodied kitchen knife into a clear plastic bag, her colleague stepped behind me, blocking my path as though fearing I might try to run from the building.

'Jenna Morgan,' he began, 'I'm arresting you for wounding with intent. You do not have to say anything…'

TWELVE

This time, when I was allowed my phone call, there was no hesitation over who to contact. Amy said she would ask her brother to get to the station as soon as possible, advising me not to answer any questions until he did so. I found myself waiting in a cell identical to the one I had been in just the previous morning, only this time the sense of hopelessness that engulfed me couldn't be pushed to one side with logic or reason. Last time, there had been no evidence against me. Now, a bloodied knife had been found on premises I owned, and I had no explanation for how it had come to be there.

Events of the past couple of days played over and over in my head, the sounds getting louder each time, the colours brighter and migraine-inducing. When I tried to view them from different angles, they always looked the same. I cursed myself for having gone out on Friday evening, wished that I had stayed at home with my family, and the thought of how different things might have been had I never taken that short cut home through the park became so overwhelming that it felt as though it would consume me.

I didn't know how long I was waiting before Amy's brother arrived; I had lost all sense of time, and I had no watch or phone with which to track the passing minutes. At the sound of the cell door being unlocked, I stood hurriedly. I must have looked a mess, my hair stuck to the back of my neck with nervous sweat; the leggings and oversized jumper I had thrown on that morning ill-fitting and marked with days-old coffee stains.

In stark contrast, Sean Barrett wore a crisply pressed suit; his dark hair was swept to one side and an expensive watch glinted around his wrist. It had been quite some time since I had seen him, with our last encounter at a family wedding to which I had been invited by Amy as her plus-one. I remembered how, even then, at an occasion that should have been relaxed, I found his presence slightly intimidating, his confidence such that he managed somehow to overshadow other people when making no effort to do so. People wanted to talk to him, to listen to him, and I was happy to do so if it meant staying in the shadows of any unwanted attention.

'Jenna,' he said, once we were alone. 'Nice to see you again.'

I forced a smile, though it felt like the last gesture I was capable of. 'This is all a massive mistake.'

'Amy's told me some of the details,' he said, pulling his trousers up at the thighs as he sat down on the hard blue mattress. 'Here,' he gestured beside him, 'you need to fill in the gaps for me.'

I sat next to him and reeled off for what felt like the hundredth time what I had already told several officers, as well as Amy and Damien, starting with Friday evening and ending at the coffee shop. 'That knife was planted there,' I told him.

'By?'

This was something I hadn't wanted to think about, though I knew I was going to have to. 'I don't know.'

'Was there a break-in?'

I shook my head. In many ways, I wished there had been. Explaining all this would have been easier had there been evidence that someone had forced entry into the building while no one else was there.

'How long can they keep me here?'

'Thirty-six hours.'

'Thirty-six? I thought it was twenty-four, then they have to charge me or let me go.'

He shook his head. 'The severity of the offence here means they've got thirty-six hours. But look, it's very unlikely any fingerprint test results will be back in that time, so the evidence against you is currently circumstantial.'

He sounded confident, but from what I knew of Sean, this was his default setting. I was grateful to have him on my side. If anyone could prove my innocence, I felt sure it would be him.

'I'm sure you were told this last time, but when they interview you today, answer as briefly as possible, okay?'

I nodded. I felt sick. I had been offered a drink and something to eat but hadn't been able to stomach either; now, my head throbbed with dehydration and there was an awful empty burning in the pit of my stomach.

Shortly afterwards, DC Cooper arrived to take us to one of the interview rooms. I was expecting his female colleague, DC Henderson, to be there with him, the same as last time; instead, an older man, maybe mid fifties, was waiting for us, already seated at the table.

'You've met DS Maitland,' DC Cooper said, taking a seat, and belatedly I realised it was the officer who had turned up at the shop. 'He's heading the investigation.'

A look passed between Sean and the detective sergeant, one of familiarity and mutual loathing. There seemed to be a warning delivered by both, that neither was to be pushed or tested. Sean's reputation went before him, but I couldn't have cared less what the police thought of him: if he could get me out of that place, I'd have done anything he told me to.

The DS pressed a button on the recording machine, taking a glance at the clock as he did so. 'Interview commencing at thirteen thirty-five. Present are DS Maitland, DC Cooper and solicitor Sean Barrett.' He stopped and looked at me, holding my gaze for longer than was comfortable. 'Please could you confirm your name for the recording.'

'Jenna Morgan.'

'Mrs Morgan,' DS Maitland said, 'you've already been interviewed regarding an assault against Charlotte Copeland. As you're aware, this morning a bloodied knife was found in the kitchen of the coffee shop you own.' He produced an image of the offending item, though it was something I needed no reminding of. 'Have you seen this knife before?'

I looked at it, bloodstained and incriminating. The thought that it had been in the kitchen while I'd been in the next room, oblivious, made my skin turn cold. I shook my head.

'For the recording, please.'

'No, I've never seen this knife before.'

'Looks like a regular kitchen knife,' DS Maitland said with a shrug. 'How can you be sure it isn't one of yours?'

I looked him in the eye. 'I've never seen it before.'

'Any idea how it might have ended up in your shop?'

'No.'

'How many people have been into the shop since Friday evening, Mrs Morgan?'

I shot him a look that was apparently unappreciated, his top lip curling as though he had caught the stench of something rotten in the air between us. Though I had only met this man hours earlier, I couldn't help but hate him. He wasn't going to listen to me; none of them were going to listen to me.

'I have no idea,' I told him. 'Three staff members, but I couldn't tell you how many customers. I booked this weekend off ages ago.'

'Why was that?'

I knew what the look he was giving me meant. It said that my absence was convenient, as though all this had been planned somehow. And yet none of it made sense to me, so surely he must have seen the flaws in his logic. Why would I have hidden a weapon in my own place of work? Unless I'd wanted to incriminate someone I worked with, someone I knew, the idea of it was illogical.

I found myself missing the presence of DC Henderson. Though she was as stern as her male colleague, I had depended on her gender as a possible source of compassion and understanding of my circumstances, no matter how naive the hope might have been. Perhaps she too was a mother; perhaps she was able to comprehend how frightening all this was for me.

'My daughter had a job interview to attend. I promised her I would take her.'

The detective eyed me coolly. 'And how did that go?'

I looked to Sean, desperate for his input.

'There is no evidence yet,' he said, 'that either Mrs Morgan's fingerprints or the victim's DNA have been identified on that knife. As such, am I right in thinking that the accusation made against my client is based on nothing more than assumption?'

'I'm sure you'll agree, Mr Barrett, that it all looks pretty damning so far. Mrs Morgan has been identified by the victim as her attacker. A bloodstained knife has been found on her work premises. It's enough to bring forward a charge – you know that.'

His words seemed to echo around the tiny room. If I was charged, I knew there was a likelihood I would be refused bail. The thought of being stuck in this place – or worse, inside a prison – for an indefinite amount of time was enough to bring a string of bile to the back of my throat, and I spluttered awkwardly, choking on my fear.

'Would you like a drink of water, Mrs Morgan?' DC Cooper offered.

I nodded. 'Please.'

We sat in silence until the officer returned, and I gulped down the water.

'Are you ready to continue?' asked DS Maitland.

I nodded.

'For the tape, please.'

'Sorry, yes. I'm ready to continue.'

'You say you've never seen this knife before,' DS Maitland said, gesturing again to the photograph, which stared at me accusingly. 'And yet, as we know, it was found in the kitchen of the coffee shop you own and run. Do you have any idea how it might have come to be there?'

'Of course not,' I told him, trying to keep my voice calm. I had already answered the question once, and had no idea what he hoped to achieve by asking it for a second time.

'You're suggesting then that someone else put it there, is that right?'

I glanced at Sean. 'Yes. I mean, I've never seen it, so that's what must have happened.'

'Someone with access to a key then?' DC Cooper suggested. 'Since there was no evidence of a break-in.'

I said nothing. I could see where they were going with this, and I didn't like the direction the conversation was heading in.

'You have three members of staff at the coffee shop, is that correct, Mrs Morgan?' DS Maitland said, looking down at his notes. 'Ffion Weston, who you employ full-time, and two part-time workers, Ellie Jones and Kirsten Howells.'

I nodded, and then, remembering that I would be reminded of the recording, said, 'Yes, that's right.'

'Do all three women have a key to the property?'

I shook my head. 'Only Ffion. On the occasions when neither Ffion nor I can be there for whatever reason, I loan one of the girls my spare key.'

'So they've both had opportunities to get copies cut?' DC Cooper said.

I shook my head again. 'They wouldn't. If you're suggesting that one of them put the knife there, that's just madness. I've known them for years, I trust them. None of this makes sense – why would any of them want to frame me for a crime like this? And it could just have easily been someone without a key, couldn't it? Customers come and go; one of them could have got into the kitchen somehow, when there wasn't anyone there to see—'

Sean coughed, interrupting me from what was about to become an unhelpful display of panic. I reminded myself what he had told me, about sticking to the facts and not becoming overly emotional, but it was difficult to remain calm when it seemed everything and everyone was against me.

DS Maitland cast him a cold glare. 'We've seen the layout of the shop. It seems unlikely a customer would be able to enter the kitchen without a member of staff noticing. The only other keys then would be the ones you keep at home, is that right? The ones you use day to day, and the spare set that you mentioned.'

'Yes, that's right.'

'In which case, what you're suggesting is that the only other people who had an opportunity to hide that knife in the coffee shop are those who live in your home, correct? Your family?'

I looked at Sean again, unsettled by where this was heading. I wasn't going to incriminate one of my own family, and the suggestion that any of them might have been involved was ludicrous.

'My client has already made it clear, twice now, that she isn't aware of how that knife came to be in the coffee shop. Isn't it your job to find out how it ended up there, Detective Sergeant?'

DS Maitland held Sean's eye, and I felt the temperature in the room cool by several degrees. 'Don't worry, Mr Barrett. We intend to do just that.' He shifted his attention back to me. 'You have CCTV at the shop, don't you, Mrs Morgan?'

I nodded. 'At the front and round the back.'

He nodded. 'We've taken the tapes, and officers are checking through them.'

I nodded as he held my gaze. He was waiting for me to say something, as though knowing that I might be caught on camera would force me into an early confession. If the footage did show anything, then good – it would prove who was responsible for planting that knife in my shop. But then another thought struck me. The cameras would only show who had gone in and out of the place; nothing of what had happened inside the building would have been captured.

'They won't prove anything. They only show who comes in and who goes out.' The detective eyed me silently, as though still waiting for me to incriminate myself.

'Why did you come to the shop today?' I asked, another thought occurring to me for the first time. 'You must have had a tip-off.'

DS Maitland studied me in silence. His lack of response told me what I needed to know. Someone had told them to go there, someone who had known what they would find. I just needed to find out who it was and why they were doing this to me.

'Whoever it was, it was probably the same person who put the knife there. What do you think I was doing on Friday night – hiding a knife up my dress while I was giving my statement to that officer? Or perhaps I hid it before you lot turned up?'

I felt Sean's eyes on the side of my face and stopped talking. As difficult as it was, I was going to have to let him do his job, and hope that it would be enough to get me out of the mess I had found myself in.

DC Cooper brought the interview to an end, and within moments Sean and I were left alone in the room.

'I need to see that footage,' I said. 'Can we get it back somehow?'

Sean nodded. 'Do you have other copies?'

'I don't know,' I admitted. Ffion was much better with technology than I was, and I had been grateful when she'd offered to take responsibility for the CCTV. I would need to ask her about it.

'It's not going to prove anything anyway,' I told him. 'I told you, the cameras only pick up who goes in and out. Whoever took that knife in there, it won't show them leaving it, not unless they wandered in waving it around in full view of the street.'

Despite my words, I wanted to see the recordings for myself. Someone was trying to frame me, and if I could see who had been inside the coffee shop then perhaps I might start to understand why all this was happening to me. Perhaps I might see someone I recognised, someone who wouldn't usually have been there.

'I know it isn't easy, but you need to calm down. Outbursts like the one you had back there aren't going to help – they'll use it to make you look unbalanced, as though you're unstable in some way. You see where I'm going with this, don't you?'

It was easy for him to sit there, calm and self-assured, when it wasn't his life about to be blown to pieces. I was convinced by this point that I was going to be charged with attempted murder – at the least, wounding with intent – and I knew there was nothing I could do to stop it happening. The truth, though he didn't want to admit it, was that there was nothing he could do to stop it happening either.

'Have the police spoken to Charlotte Copeland again?' I asked, clinging desperately to the hope that the woman would come to her senses and realise the error she had made in her claim against me. I had reasoned with myself that if she was able to recall the night's events with clearer accuracy, perhaps she might be able to identify her true attacker. If she could do that, maybe I stood a chance of finding out why this currently unknown person was trying to frame me.

'Of course. But they're not going to share the details. All we know is that she hasn't retracted her accusation.'

I couldn't understand it. Surely her memory wasn't so impaired that she still thought I had attacked her? If not, it meant she was lying on purpose... but why?

'I'm not going to get bail, am I? Not if they accuse me of attempted murder.'

'It's obviously trickier,' Sean said, 'but it's not impossible. If the magistrates' court rejects it, which is likely, I'll make an application to the crown court. The quicker I get it done, the better chance we stand. You've got no previous record, so that goes some way towards helping. There's a possibility they'll impose some restrictions – you might have to agree to sign in at the station every couple of days or so. But look... the results of the forensic testing on that knife need to come back first. You haven't been charged yet.'

The word 'yet' bounced around us, echoing from the walls. He may as well have told me that a charge against me was an inevitability, regardless of the results of the forensic testing.

I didn't care about having to sign in at the station; I didn't care that my name would be dragged through the local press until all thoughts of 'innocent until proven guilty' had been abandoned by a community who would come to hate me. All I cared about was getting out of that place so I could prove that I'd done nothing wrong. I needed to find out more about Charlotte and track down the person who had attacked her. Someone was trying to set me up, but I had no idea who or why. No one had broken into the coffee shop, so the knife had been planted there by someone who had access to a key. In many ways, this was the worst thought of all: that whoever was trying to frame me for attempted murder was someone I knew. Someone I trusted.

THIRTEEN

My life in Llangovney had been shaped by the monotony of routine: work, childcare, housework. The noise of the washing machine contributed to the soundtrack of my days, and by the time I remembered that the note with the phone number had been in the pocket of my trousers, it had been going for over half an hour. I switched it off mid cycle and pulled them, soaking, from the tangle of clothes, desperately rummaging for the right pocket. The paper was there, soggy and still folded, but when I opened it out, the words and digits were gone, leaving nothing but smudges of blurred ink.

I sat back on my heels in front of the washing machine and tried not to let disappointment flood me. For the first time in a long time, I had allowed myself to consider the possibility of another person in my life, someone I might be able to talk to beyond the limitations of Peppa Pig and the fairy tales that I read on repeat to Lily before she fell asleep at night. With little else to do, I put what remained of the note in with the rubbish, feeling my heart ache a little as I closed the bin lid. I washed the dishes that had been left from earlier that afternoon, set out clothes for Lily and myself for the following day and then curled up on the bed beside her, holding her warm little body against mine as though we were the only people left in the world.

Over the next few weeks, our lives repeated their pattern, and I decided to feel grateful for their predictability. It was sometimes a tedious, lonely existence, but when I looked at Lily, I was reminded that I had everything I needed. When I considered where my life had gone wrong – when I lingered for too long on the mistakes I had made – I realised that it was wanting something that had always been my downfall, and yet, try as I might, I couldn't help myself from craving more than I had, some little slice of the happiness that had shone so briefly in front of me before its light had been diminished.

And then the light found me again. I was crouched behind the bar at the pub, stocking the fridge with bottles of lager, when I heard his voice. It had been over a month since the Ironman event, and I had done what I needed to put the brief memory of him to the back of my mind, leaving it there with all the other impossible might-have-beens I had managed to collect during my short life.

'You probably see enough drink in this place. Maybe I should have suggested the cinema instead?'

I turned, looked up, and instantly felt my face flush. I can't remember what I said, only that it probably sounded stupid, but whatever it was, he smiled.

'Don't tell me… the dog ate it.'

'I don't have a dog.' I remember saying that much, at least. Then I told him about Lily's sickness bug, the vomit-splattered clothes, the note that went into the washing machine, and all the while I was thinking: there, he knows I have a child now, he won't be interested after this.

He sat at the end of the bar and chatted to me when the pub became quieter, and when my shift ended and it was time for me to collect Lily, he wrote his number on the back of my hand.

'Don't wash,' he told me. 'Not until you've written it somewhere you won't lose it.'

Lily was asleep when I picked her up, and I carried her down the road in her pyjamas, a blanket wrapped around her to keep off the nip of the night air. I tucked her up in bed, then stored Damien's number in my phone before writing it in a notebook that I kept in the top drawer of my bedside table. Then I texted him, thanking him for coming to see me and saying I hoped we would see each other again soon. By the time I had showered and dressed for bed, I had a text back.

Next weekend? X

He was true to his word, and the following Saturday we met at a café in the nearest town. I hadn't wanted him to come to the flat – it seemed too soon, and I had to remind myself that I barely knew him – but there was no chance of my going to see him without Lily. I didn't want to introduce her to someone who might leave her life as soon as he'd arrived, yet it also seemed to make sense that he meet her sooner rather than later. Were he to decide that a woman with a child was someone he wasn't interested in, I wanted to find out before he had a chance to break either of our hearts. And yet something in me already knew that Damien wasn't that type of man, and I allowed myself to believe that for once, things might be different.

Over those next couple of months, we met up once a week. We took Lily to the park, to the library, to the beach; we ate ice creams together though it was November and the temperature was near freezing, and on his sixth visit I invited him to the flat, watching at the kitchen window while I waited for the kettle to boil as he played outside with Lily, jumping in the dry leaves that had fallen from the tree at the end of the garden. I knew so much more about him by then – that he was a firefighter, that he had a close relationship with his mother, that his father had died when he was a teenager – but the more I found out, the closer I felt myself growing to him, and my feelings sometimes scared me with the knowledge that wanting to be with this man would change everything my life had become.

Weeks later, he helped us decorate a Christmas tree in the living room. Lily had turned four at the beginning of December, and I was painfully aware of how underdeveloped her speech still was. Other people had commented on her quietness, asking me why she wasn't yet attending a pre-school, but my answer was always the same – that she didn't legally need to start school until the age of five, and she was doing just fine, thanks for asking.

The truth was, I knew it would be better for her to be mixing with other children her own age, but the longer I'd left it, the harder it had become. When I had moved to Llangovney, I'd had no intention of being there indefinitely, but as time went on, I had come to realise that I had nowhere else to go. Wherever we moved, I would face the same problems of finding somewhere affordable to stay and earning enough money for us to live. The longer we stayed in the village, the more I was forced to accept that this might become home.

After Lily had gone to bed – much later than usual, her excitement at the Christmas tree lights and the snowmen we'd lined up along the front windowsill having a similar effect to feeding her a selection box and a bottle of lemonade – Damien and I sat on the sofa and talked.

'You could do with some better lights,' he said, studying the tree.

'They'll do for now,' I told him. 'It'll only use up more electricity.'

He smiled, though there was sadness rather than humour in the expression.

'What?' I asked.

'Nothing. You just talk like someone much older sometimes.'

I was twenty-four, but I knew what he meant. I realised I wasn't like a lot of people my age, though young people were few and far between in the village. It seemed that as soon as any teenager reached school-leaving age, they were out of there, hurriedly shaking off the sleepy life lived by the locals. There was a time when I might have been desperate to do the same – the old me affronted by the thought of living this kind of life – but for a long while nothing had seemed so appealing as fading into the anonymity of a rural existence. I had taught myself how to disappear.

'That's probably Lily. I've had to grow up quicker.'

'It must be hard, on your own.'

I shrugged. 'We get by.'

Damien had never asked where Lily's father was, though he knew enough to realise that Lily never saw him. He seemed respectful of my privacy in a way I wasn't used to, having grown up with parents whose demands to know my life's every detail had been suffocating. There was something comforting in the space he afforded me, yet part of me wanted to tell him everything, to spill my secrets in the space around us so that nothing could ever emerge to come between us.

Damien was only three years older than I was, yet his life was so different to mine. He shared a rented house with a friend he'd known since college. His leisure time was filled with cycling and running events, which he often did for charity and always for the challenge. I had looked at his social media profiles though I had no accounts of my own, and in every picture, he seemed surrounded by people. No matter where he was training, he tried to make sure he saw his mother once a week. His father had died when Damien was just nineteen, of a brain tumour that killed him within months of diagnosis. Once I knew this, Damien's seemingly relentless training seemed to make more sense. He pushed his body to the limit to prove the life that was in it, testing it, keeping the blood pumping through his veins. I both admired him and felt saddened by it.

'Can I ask you something?' He reached a hand to my forehead, his fingers lightly tracing across my skin, and I knew what he was going to ask me.

'Depends what it is.'

'How did you get this?'

The scar he was referring to was one of many, though it was the only one that anyone ever seemed to notice. I had been lucky; they were fine and silvery, like glittering stretch marks, and they had faded quickly over time; in certain light, even the worst of them was barely visible. Strangely, it was in dimmer lighting that it became more apparent. I had only been asked about it twice since being in Llangovney – once at the pub by a customer I had never seen before and hoped never to have to encounter again, and once by Elaine at the B and B. On both occasions I had lied, but with Damien I allowed the truth to emerge.

'Car accident.'

'Shit. It must have been a bad one?'

I nodded. 'That was when Lily's father died.'

Damien's fingertips had still been on my forehead, still brushing over the route of the scar, but he pulled his hand away then, his eyes fixed on mine.

'God, Jenna, I had no idea. I'm so sorry.'

'I don't really make a point of telling people. The longer I can keep it all from Lily, the better.'

He moved his arm to encircle me, and I turned into him, feeling the heat of him warm me. I felt happier than I had in a long time, the kind of contentment that I'd first known when Lily entered my life, but which before then had been alien to me.

'Thank you for telling me.'

'Oh, you're very welcome,' I said, trying to make light of a moment that could easily alter the mood of the evening. I didn't want to be maudlin or to ruin the time we had together by offloading my life's miseries onto him. There were things I knew I would never tell him; things I had never told anyone.

'I mean it,' he said. 'It means a lot, doesn't it? It means you trust me.'

We sat in silence for a while, his arm folded around me, my head resting on the warmth of his chest.

'Lily's a lovely little girl.'

'She is. I don't know what I'd do without her.'

'Does she look like him, like her dad?'

I wasn't surprised by the question; I had already realised it was one I was going to face on multiple occasions as she grew older. Her hair was thick and dark like his, her eyes the same shade of almost-black. She was already beautiful, and so nothing like me.

'Just like him.'

There was another moment's silence, this one less comfortable than those that had preceded it. Damien kissed the top of my head, then he said something that I had been both longing and dreading to hear; something I knew would change everything.

'It doesn't have to be just the two of you forever, you know.'

His fingers rested on my chin as he tilted my face towards his, and when he kissed me, I allowed myself for the first time in a long time to abandon my thoughts of Lily's father.

FOURTEEN

I was kept in custody for as long as the police were legally able to detain me and greeted on Tuesday evening with the news that I was to be released, once again under investigation. I desperately wanted to see my family, to explain to them that I was being framed. I needed to tell them all how much I loved them, and that anything they might hear about me was a lie. The police weren't going to look for evidence that I was innocent; I already felt certain of that. DS Maitland was intent on bringing forward a charge against me, and I was trapped in a battle of me versus them, not sure who I could trust. The police's focus was to find evidence of my guilt, and while there was someone out there readily assisting them in this goal, I feared I was facing a fight I had already lost.

Sean came to meet me at the station. Amy was waiting in the back seat of his car, and when I climbed in beside her, I allowed her to put her arms around me, not caring by that point what I looked like. I hadn't showered, and had barely eaten, any efforts to function like a normal human blocked by the thought that if I was charged – if this went to trial and I was convicted – I would go to prison. Lily would hate me. Amelia would grow up without a mother. My marriage would be over. This would be my life, indefinitely, alone.

'God, you poor thing,' Amy said, still holding me in a vice-like grip, her words breathed into my greasy hair. 'We're going to sort this out.' She pushed me away, holding me at arm's length and urging me to make eye contact. 'I promise you we're going to find out what the hell is going on.'

She meant well, but my fear was that only the police would be able to uncover the truth. The chances of us being able to prove that someone had framed me for attempted murder, as well as finding out who that person was, seemed remote.

'Surely when the forensic report comes back and there's nothing linking Jenna to that knife, they'll have to stop all this?' Amy met her brother's eyes in the rear-view mirror before he looked away and pulled out from the station's car park. He wouldn't admit it, but we all knew it wouldn't be as straightforward as that. The knife had been found in a property that belonged to me, and that alone was incriminating enough.

'I just want to go home,' I told her, fastening my seat belt. 'I want to see Damien and the kids, I want a shower, I want something to eat. Everything else can wait.'

From the corner of my eye, I saw Amy deliberate over saying something more before deciding to leave me alone. I appreciated everything she and Sean were doing to try to help me, but even being there with them in the state I was in – emotionally and physically – was a humiliation I could have done without. I wondered how many more would follow. Soon I would have to explain all this to Damien, to Lily, to Amelia, though I was sure that Damien at least would already know what had happened.

I realised that while I'd been at the station, my suspicions about Damien and Laura had been put on hold. I couldn't think about them just now, not with everything else that was hanging over me, though I wondered if Amy knew anything. If she did, it would really feel like the final betrayal – the one that might tip me over the edge.

'Did they tell you Damien came?'

'When?'

'Yesterday, but you were being interviewed. Sean told me he'd been.'

I wondered why he hadn't waited, but the thought that he had at least been there was some consolation. The thought that the police were trying to unsettle me – withholding information that might have offered me some form of reassurance – was affirmation of my lack of faith in them. 'He's really worried about you.'

But not worried enough to stay, I thought again, though I had no idea whether he would have been allowed to see me anyway. I bit the inside of my lower lip so hard that I tasted the metallic tang of blood on the tip of my tongue. Damien had been looking after Amelia, but I still felt, fairly or unfairly, that he could have made more of an effort to see me. His absence spoke louder than any angry recrimination. Already, it seemed, he had found me guilty; or had his feelings for me changed so much that he couldn't bring himself to show me the support that would once have come effortlessly?

'What happens next?'

'You wait to hear from them,' Sean said. 'When you do, contact me before you do anything else, okay?'

I should have taken heart from that, but it was impossible for me to envisage a scenario that didn't involve the worst possible outcome. His casual attitude was only adding to my sense of hopelessness. It was easy for him; he was off home now to his beautiful house and his secure family unit, his life as he had woken to it that morning still recognisable and safe. My future was hanging from a thread as fine as a spider's web, my family already fragmenting under the pressure of what had been so unexpectedly dumped upon us. I wanted to scream with the unfairness of it all, to empty my lungs so that everyone would hear the noise of my innocence and would keep hearing it until the world began to believe in its truth. Instead, I turned my head from Amy and stared unseeing through the car window.

We remained in silence for the rest of the journey back to my house, and when Sean stopped the car outside, I thanked them both before climbing out. Amy said she would call me later, but I already knew that if she did, I wouldn't answer. Whatever conversation with

Damien awaited me, it was guaranteed to be long and intense, and we needed to have it alone, free from interruption.

I turned the key in the door and breathed in the familiarity of the house. I was sure that Damien, in my unexpected absence, would have done everything he could to keep our daily routine functioning as normally as possible. He would have put the girls first, as I wanted him to, though I couldn't escape the crush of rejection that weighed on me with the knowledge. I still didn't know why he hadn't waited to see me when he'd gone to the station the previous day, and I could only reassure myself with the thought that the police must have turned him away.

There was the sound of voices from the kitchen, the radio on the windowsill babbling in hushed tones. I took off my shoes and jacket and walked down the hallway, wondering what sort of welcome would greet me.

Damien was sitting at the table, his laptop open in front of him and an array of papers scattered around. He closed the lid when he saw me; the action filled me with anger. I wanted to ask him about Laura, and what was going on between them, but I knew I was in no position to question him.

'Amy told me you came to the station.'

Something flashed behind his eyes – guilt? Sadness? I couldn't read it. I couldn't read *him* any more, not in the way I once thought I could. I waited for him to stand, to come over to me and offer me some sort of physical comfort, but he didn't move. He looked at me as though he wasn't sure of who I was, as though a stranger had just walked into the kitchen and he was uncertain whether to let her stay or ask her to leave.

'Have you been charged?'

I shook my head. The relief that flooded his face was obvious, and yet he still looked away. I watched him bite his bottom lip, his teeth clamping down until the flesh turned white. Whether he was angry at the situation or angry with me, I couldn't tell.

'I am so sorry,' I said, realising as soon as the words escaped me that I sounded as though I was about to make a confession. 'I don't want any of you to be going through this. All I tried to do on Friday was help that woman, and then…' I couldn't find the right words. And then what? And then she decided to make a false claim against me? She decided to try to ruin my life?

But why? None of it made any sense.

'Amy said there's not much evidence,' Damien said, keeping his eyes averted. 'That's got to be a good thing, surely?'

'I hope so.'

I saw him flinch and realised my response was the wrong one. I didn't know what was right; I had no idea what to say to him. 'How was Amelia this morning? I thought she might not have gone to school.'

'She didn't want to go, but I thought it'd be the best place for her. Try to keep some sense of normality.'

'Where is she now?'

I'd assumed she was upstairs in her bedroom or watching television in the living room, but if she was here, she'd have heard my voice and come into the kitchen.

'Mum offered to give her tea.' He glanced at his phone, checking the time. 'I'm due to pick her up soon.'

I tried to push back the flicker of resentment that sparked in my stomach at the mention of Nancy. I wondered what had been said in my absence; whether she'd made attempts to turn Amelia against me.

'And Lily?'

'College. They've got a rehearsal.'

Lily had applied to the Royal Welsh College of Music & Drama for the following academic year, and her drama group was deep in preparation for a production of *Under Milk Wood*. It continued to amaze me that the quiet girl who had barely spoken until the age of five had grown into a confident teenager who seemed to come alive on the stage. I could have tried to take credit for the way in which she had bloomed, but I knew that much of it had been down to Damien's influence.

Damien shifted in his seat. 'So what happens next?'

'I wait.'

I wished that he would get angry, question me about the knife; that he would blame me for bringing the police into our home and inflicting this suffering upon our family, yet he did none of those things. He had always been level-headed, never falling into self-pity when things didn't go his way or getting angry when something affronted him; instead, he dealt with life and all its blows with a calmness and practicality I had sometimes envied, wishing I could be as controlled when faced with something unexpected or unjust. As a firefighter, he had been required to stay calm under pressure, and though the incidents that had challenged him most had happened before we met, I had heard enough to know that he was regarded with respect and admiration by his former colleagues. Even after the accident that had forced him from the fire service, I had rarely seen him angry, though I realised everyone had a breaking point. I was still waiting to see what Damien's would be.

'Why is this happening to us, Jenna?'

The question, though it was one I could find no answer to, filled me with hope that maybe all wasn't lost. He had asked why this was happening to *us*. Surely this meant that he still felt connected, that we were still a team, and that my troubles were his, intertwined, to be solved together.

'I don't know. I wish I did.'

But in my head a voice screamed, *Why didn't you stay at the police station? Where did you go after you left? Who have you been with?*

'You don't believe I did it, do you?' I asked, needing to hear him say it, to be reassured that he was still on my side. He knew me better than anyone else did; if he didn't believe in my innocence, no one would. But he didn't answer my question; instead, he reached for the papers on the table beside him, pushing things aside until he found what he was looking for – an A5-sized plastic wallet. When he opened it and tipped out its contents, it appeared to hold nothing of any interest – just a few envelopes.

He placed each one in front of me. His first name was handwritten on each. I moved towards the table, bending down to read them.

'What are these?' I asked, sliding a small scrap of paper from the first. Damien said nothing as I read it.

How well do you know your wife?

I opened the second.

She's lying to you.

On the last: *Ask her about your daughter.*

FIFTEEN

Damien looked at me expectantly, waiting for a response. His blue eyes, usually alive with warmth and humour, studied me coldly. His jawline was peppered with days-old stubble, and it made him appear older than his forty-one years. He looked exhausted, all of it my fault.

'I tried to write them off as a prank,' he said, 'but then…'

His sentence was cut short, though I knew it wouldn't be long before the truth of his feelings spilled from him. Whatever it was he wanted to say, I was unlikely to come out of it looking innocent.

'But then what?'

He studied my face for a moment, as though expecting to find a silent admission somewhere in my expression. 'But then you haven't really been yourself recently. I've known something's going on, I just haven't known what.'

I could feel my heart rate quickening, sick at the thought of what the notes might refer to. 'When did you get these?' I asked.

'First one came about six weeks ago.'

I nodded, trying to work out just how long Damien's increasingly strange and distant behaviour had started. I couldn't recall exactly, but there seemed more than a chance that it had coincided with the arrival of the first of these notes.

'I was going to tell you.'

'Going to tell me what?' He was waiting for the worst; it was visible in the tension gathered in his shoulders and the rigid straightness of his back. I pushed a hand through my hair, sweeping it back from my face, and sat down at the table opposite him, still aware of the laptop between us, still wondering what secrets it might hide.

'Don't be angry with me, please. I didn't say anything because I thought I could sort it out before it escalated.'

'Sort what out?' His jaw was tensed with suppressed frustration. I didn't blame him for being angry. He had been kept in the dark when I should have told him the truth from the beginning. We were a family. We were supposed to face everything together.

'Lily has been involved with someone.'

It was the only thing the notes could be referring to, or at least the only thing I would allow myself to believe a possibility.

'Someone…'

I sighed, knowing I couldn't avoid the facts, no matter how much I might have liked to. 'An older man.'

I watched Damien's jaw move as he bit down on his tongue.

'How much older?'

'I don't know exactly. Late twenties… maybe early thirties.'

His chair scraped noisily across the tiled floor as he pushed it back and stood. He didn't look at me before going to the kitchen sink, taking a glass from the draining board and filling it with water. His knuckles were white around the glass.

'She's seventeen, for God's sake.'

I said nothing, knowing anything I did say was only likely to make the situation worse.

'How long have you known about this?'

'Not long, I swear.'

He raised his eyebrows, and the look spoke more loudly than any words were capable of. If the first note had come six weeks ago, I had known about it long enough. He didn't think I could be trusted. There was a part of me that was beginning to wonder the same.

'How long?' he asked again.

I paused. 'A couple of months.'

He dropped the glass into the sink. 'A couple of months. Jesus, Jenna, why didn't you say anything?'

'I sorted it out,' I told him, though the words sounded stupid as they were given air to breathe. I hadn't sorted anything out. Lily was still seeing him, still sneaking around behind our backs as though Damien and I were a couple of idiots. 'She promised me she wasn't involved with him any more.'

Damien tutted. 'Oh, right, well that's okay then. And you just believed her? Because teenagers are known for telling their parents the truth, aren't they?' He looked at me as though I was simple.

'Please don't say anything to her. I'll speak to her again, I promise.'

'And that'll achieve what? Do you think she's going to take anything you say seriously after all this?'

He had a point, but its delivery left a sour taste in my mouth. Perhaps I deserved his animosity, though for the most part I was left smarting at the injustice of it all.

'Why don't you want me to talk to her, Jenna? Because I'm not her real father?'

It was a low blow, and I felt it like a punch to the gut. Yes, I had said it before, twice – on both occasions during the worst of our arguments – and as soon as the words were out, I had felt like the worst kind of person for having spoken them. Damien had always treated Lily as though she was his own daughter, and even when Amelia had arrived in our lives, his love for her hadn't diminished. He had given her everything, yet with a few spitefully chosen words, I had the power to snatch it all away from him.

'Don't say things like that. Please.'

He came over to the table and sat back down opposite me. It felt like some small peace offering, a suggestion that perhaps everything was going to be okay and we would find a way to work through all this.

'I just think she's more likely to talk to another female,' I tried to explain.

'What about my mother?'

'God, no.'

Damien immediately responded defensively to my reaction, his shoulders squaring and his jaw tightening. His mother was too often the cause of friction between us, but he could never see any wrongdoing on her part, only on mine.

'Please don't tell her about this. She'll only think the worst, especially of me. Things are bad enough without adding fuel to the fire. I'll sort it, I promise. Don't say anything to Lily – if we come on too strong, it might only push her closer to whoever this man is.'

The truth was, I didn't trust Nancy with Lily. She didn't regard her as family, not proper family in the way she saw Amelia, and I didn't want to offer her further ammunition with which to attack my parenting abilities. In her eyes, Lily's involvement with an older man would mean I'd failed in every way possible.

'Haven't you even seen him then?'

I shook my head.

'Name?'

I raised my hands in an admission of defeat.

'Then how do you know he even exists?'

I hesitated on the answer, fearing it was likely only to make things worse. 'Amy saw them together.'

'Oh, so Amy's known all this time as well? Anyone else you've forgotten to mention?'

An image flashed involuntarily into my brain: Damien and Laura together, their bodies tangled beneath the duvet I shared with him. I pushed the image to one side, chiding myself for lingering over something that should have been of little importance at that moment. Yet the hypocrisy stung. Damien was attacking me for my secrets, but what secrets was he hiding from me? I should have just come out and asked him, but I was too scared of what until then had seemed almost an impossibility.

'She saw them together and she told me about it,' I said, trying not to snap at him. 'I spoke to Lily at the time; she told me they weren't even together, then she promised me there was nothing going on between them. The first I knew of anything different was when you showed me that bracelet.'

Once again I wondered why we were arguing over Lily when there was a potential charge of attempted murder hanging over me. Damien seemed to care more about that bloody bracelet than he did about me, though I tried to convince myself that it might be a distraction technique, a way of keeping his mind focused on things other than an imminent trial. That, or there was something else he wasn't telling me. Lily's words in her bedroom echoed at the back of my brain, refusing to let me forget them. Damien didn't trust me, but I had reason to doubt whether I could trust him.

'"How well do you know your wife?"' he said, and I realised that he was quoting one of the notes. 'Seems a strange thing to say, doesn't it? I mean, "She's lying to you" could refer to Lily, but the other one… Something doesn't seem to add up.'

'Where did you get them?' I asked. As far as I knew, there were only four people who had been aware of the relationship – if that was even what it was: me, Amy, Lily and the mystery man.

'They came through the door. Amelia picked one of them up, asked me what it was.'

I wondered why I had never seen them. I was often up before anyone else in the house, though the post nearly always arrived after I'd left for the coffee shop. These hadn't come in the post, though; they'd been hand-delivered, with only Damien's first name written on the envelopes. It occurred to me that whoever had sent them had done so when they'd known I wasn't home.

'It's not about Amelia?'

'What?'

'The last note,' he said, exasperated. 'It says I should ask you about my daughter. Could it mean Amelia?'

'Why would it mean Amelia?' My tone was starting to echo Damien's.

'I don't know.' He looked at me questioningly as he digested the possibility of some unspoken truth between us.

'Who do you think they're from?' he asked, after a lengthy and uncomfortable silence.

'I don't know. Could be one of Lily's friends playing what they think is a joke, maybe.'

He didn't buy it. He glanced down at the notes again, their implications staring him out as he studied the lettering. 'Lot of trouble to go to.'

Reaching across the table, I placed my hand on his. It was the first physical contact we'd had in days, and I realised how much I'd missed him, how much I needed to have him there beside me even when I knew there was nothing he could do to help. 'You know I'm innocent, don't you?'

'You mean do I think you're capable of stabbing someone? Of course I don't. It's ridiculous.'

He pulled his hand away and moved it over mine, squeezing my fingers tightly. I should have taken solace from his faith in me, yet I noticed how cold his hand felt; how it was there but he was not.

SIXTEEN

After spending what little of that Tuesday evening was left having a shower and picking at a meal that I couldn't face swallowing, I finally climbed into bed. Lily and Amelia were both home and gone to bed, and Damien was already in our room, having gone upstairs before me. The gap between us felt suddenly huge, his back turned to mine as he pretended to be asleep. He had left the notes on the table, and I had cleared them away, hiding them in the washing machine – a place to which neither the girls nor Damien ever ventured – so I could return to them the following morning.

We went through the motions of Wednesday morning on autopilot, avoiding each other as we made cups of tea and breakfast for the girls, exchanging the minimum of conversation. Lily was quieter than usual, but Amelia was her usual exuberant self, chatting animatedly at the table about some science project her class had almost finished. If Nancy had tried to pour poison into her ear, Amelia had apparently shaken it out.

Sitting next to one another in what was a rare moment of sisterly calm, the girls couldn't have appeared more unlike one another. Lily's dark hair hung straight around her face, framing her sad eyes, while Amelia's much lighter curls bounced as she rattled away, rehearsing her lines for the assembly she was due to be part of in a few days' time. Though Amelia was so much younger, it was Lily who worried me. There was a weariness in her expression, something far older than her seventeen years. I blamed myself for it repeatedly, though I wondered sometimes whether her issues were related to something beyond my control.

'Is everything okay?' I asked, clearing her empty plate and mug from the table.

'Just had an email,' she said, shoving her mobile away from her and nearly knocking Amelia's glass of orange juice over in the process. 'Didn't get the job. Not enough experience.'

'I'm sorry, love. Keep trying – something will come up.'

I watched her stand and retrieve her phone before going out into the hallway to get her bag for college, and I wondered whether the email was invented. Lily worked hard for the things she was interested in, but those were few and far between, and again I blamed myself for her attitude. There had been a time when we'd had next to nothing, and when our fortunes had changed, I had sometimes made the mistake of trying to overcompensate, buying her everything she wanted, and allowing myself to get carried away at Christmas and on birthdays. By the time she hit her teenage years, I realised the mistake I had made, but by then the damage was done and she was already far too fond of material things.

As soon as Lily had left to catch the bus to college and Damien had taken Amelia to school, I retrieved the notes from the washing machine and set about studying them obsessively, as though the straight edge of a *d* or the curve of a question mark might offer up some clue about who had written them. As I sat there, I realised there were things I hadn't asked Damien the night before. I hadn't got close to bringing up Lily's accusation against him. It hadn't felt right to question him, not when my own guilt had weighed so heavily in my chest. Had it even been an accusation? I wondered. She had seen him and Laura together; that didn't mean anything. The two of them could have met up for any number of reasons, though it raised the question of why neither had thought to mention it to me.

How well do you know your wife?
She's lying to you.
Ask her about your daughter.

I stared down at the three notes, hating every word of them; hating the fact that I couldn't be sure what they referred to, despite what I'd said. Who would have gone to the trouble of sending them, and what had they hoped to achieve? Whoever was framing me, it seemed likely that the same person was responsible for sending these messages. I couldn't shake the thought that all this was somehow connected to Damien, and to whoever it was he was having an affair with. I didn't want to accept that maybe it was about me, and me alone, so I allowed the fact of an affair to become concrete in my mind, as though all that needed proving was the other woman's identity.

The other woman. Laura. The thought wouldn't go away. She had last been to our home a couple of months earlier, and I fought for the memory of what she had worn that day, convincing myself that she appeared to have made more of an effort than usual, her hair pinned up in an unusually elaborate way and her make-up more appropriate for a night out than a play date with a friend's daughter.

I hadn't heard from her since she had texted me back on Saturday, though there was no reason why I should have. If she had been responsible for the notes, I could see no purpose in them. Perhaps their only object was to create friction between Damien and me, and maybe that was enough.

I remembered that Damien had never explained himself when I'd asked what he'd been doing going through Lily's things on the day he'd found that bracelet. Did he think Lily was involved in the notes somehow? It would have explained the friction I'd noticed between them, yet it still didn't make sense. Causing trouble for

Damien meant causing trouble for me, and I didn't think Lily would be cruel enough to do that.

I put the notes back in the washing machine before leaving the house, concealing them beneath a tea towel. When I got to the coffee shop, I was grateful that it was quiet. There were only three customers: a middle-aged woman who was talking on her mobile; a man staring into an empty mug; and a young mother, her eyes rimmed with a familiar reddened tiredness, her baby asleep, for that moment at least, in its pram. Ffion was there alone; she emerged from the kitchen as I walked into the shop. She offered me a welcoming smile but couldn't hide the furtive glance she gave the customers, as though fearful that everyone already knew what had happened there on Monday morning. I had inadvertently involved her, and if it hadn't happened already, it would only be a matter of time before she came to resent me for it.

'Stupid question, I know,' she said, as I followed her into the kitchen, 'but are you okay?'

'No, not really.'

I sighed and leaned against the worktop, wondering where to start. I had been hoping to keep this from as many people as possible, but Ffion had been here when that knife had been found, and I was going to have to explain the situation somehow. For once, the truth seemed the easiest option, and so I told her everything, starting with what had happened in the park, pausing the story whenever someone came to the counter to be served.

'God,' she said, when I had finished. 'I'm sorry. I mean… How do you think that knife ended up here?'

'I don't know,' I admitted. I didn't add that I was determined to find out.

'What happens now?' she asked. 'With this place, I mean.'

'It's probably best that I take some time out for a while. I don't know how long I'll need, but I'll make sure you get a bonus, okay?' I glanced at the mother in the corner, who was watching her sleeping child as though it would disappear if she dared to look away for the briefest of moments. 'What's she drinking?' I asked.

'Cappuccino.'

'Make her another one. No charge. And look, get the girls in for work as and when you need their help – I'll leave it with you. That sound okay?'

Ffion nodded, but I could tell from the concern etched on her face that everything was far from okay.

'There's one more thing,' I said. 'The CCTV. Have you got copies of the footage the police took?'

There was a time when Ffion had always copied the week's recordings after closing on a Saturday evening. An attempted break-in had made us extra vigilant, and when the police had taken the hard copies to use as evidence, we'd realised it might be handy to keep duplicates. Since then, however, I had let my focus slip and had no idea whether she was still doing so. I felt anticipation rise in my chest, almost thankful now for the tanked-up chancer who had tried to leave with an empty till all those years ago.

She nodded. 'Shall I email them over to you?'

I could have kissed her. Instead, I asked her to do it as soon as she got the chance. I needed to see who had been at the shop; who was so determined to ruin my life.

Her thoughts were transparent, and I couldn't blame her for feeling as she did, not after what she'd seen. Any previous opinions she might have had of me had been shaken by the presence of the police and the sight of that knife, bloodied and incriminating. I could tell she didn't feel safe there any more, and neither did I.

SEVENTEEN

Despite promising myself I wouldn't look, I searched for my name online. I didn't find myself mentioned in anything other than a few articles related to the opening of the coffee shop, which I had tried at the time to keep to a minimum. Reports on the assault referenced the fact that a female had been arrested and released under investigation. I was grateful I hadn't been named, though it was of small comfort. I knew what the phrase meant, and knowing I was a suspect felt as incriminating as having already been charged.

People had already started to speculate in the comments section, and I was aware that a trial by media would follow, regardless of my innocence.

This is sick… my kids play in that park.

Why has this woman been given bail? Probably turned on the waterworks – if she was a man, she'd be locked up till they had proof.

Anyone know how the victim is? The article doesn't say.

Never think things like this will happen on your doorstep.

I scrolled through the comments as they slid from curiosity to vitriol, devouring the words as though feeding on their intensity before stopping at one that read differently to the others.

I know her. This is bullshit. She didn't do it.

I looked for the commenter's name, wondering whether I really did know this person. I must have done; there were only a handful of people who knew that I had been arrested in relation to the incident. I was grateful for his or her defence, though in a sea of blame that rendered me guilty until proven otherwise, it would be washed away by a tide of venom. If it was a member of my family, I didn't want them getting involved. The username MC2020 told me nothing about the person behind the words. Still, it was one voice of support, albeit solitary and silent.

I flipped the lid of the laptop closed when I heard Lily come through the front door. Damien and Amelia were still not home; I had tried his mobile, but there was no answer and I could only assume he had decided to take her over to his mother's for tea again. Anything, it would seem, to delay having to come home and face me again.

Lily slammed the front door shut behind her and headed straight upstairs. I was in our bedroom, sitting on the bed with the laptop on the duvet in front of me, and I listened to her go to the bathroom first before heading to her room. When I got up and went out onto the landing, I could hear her crying. They were angry, raw tears, the kind that can't help but produce noise, and when I pushed the door open she did nothing to try to stop the flow of frustrated sadness that I imagined she had been holding back all afternoon.

I braced myself for a verbal onslaught. It never came. Instead, she kept her head lowered, her face shielded by the hair that fell like a curtain in front of her.

'What's happened, love?'

'Nothing,' she said, too quickly. The opposite was clearly true. It was something to do with *him*, of that I was certain; though she had cried tears over my predicament, these were different somehow, angrier and more personal. I wanted to ask her, but I was fearful of her reaction, knowing that the further I pushed her, the harder it would be to pull her back.

I sat on the bed next to her, careful not to make physical contact. When she wanted me closer, she'd let me know. Slow and steady had always been the best approach in dealing with Lily's moods.

'Why the fuck is this happening to us?' she said, her words an echo of Damien's. I decided to ignore the language. It wasn't really the time or place to reprimand her for coarseness. On more than one occasion I had pictured myself standing at the top of Caerphilly mountain, the town's lights stretched out in front of me like a blanket of glittering diamonds, screaming the same word until my lungs were raw and empty of air and the sky could carry away all the toxic energy that had been poisoning me from the inside out.

'I don't know. I wish I did. I was just in the wrong place at the wrong time.'

Lily couldn't bring herself to look at me, and I feared for a moment it was because she suspected I was guilty. 'Why do they think you're involved?'

For so long she had demanded to be treated like an adult, quick to chide Damien and me when she believed we were talking down to her or not respecting her maturity. So now I gave her everything she had wanted, making sure not to gloss over the details as I might once have done in an attempt to protect her.

The only thing I didn't mention was the knife. I waited for her to bring it up, but when she didn't, I assumed she hadn't heard about it. A part of me had wondered whether Damien might have told her, but since I'd got home the previous evening, he had barely seen her. I hoped that if he had told his mother, she would be sensitive enough to keep the information to herself; Lily didn't need to know, not when it might come to nothing. I would wait for the forensic results to come back before deciding what to do next. Surely there would be nothing on the knife linking me to the crime, and therefore I hoped its existence was one detail Lily could be spared.

'They must know you didn't hurt anyone,' she said. 'It doesn't make sense.'

'I know it doesn't. All I tried to do was help that woman. You believe me, don't you?'

She looked at me then, her eyes wet with tears, and when she nodded, I felt my heart heave with relief at her faith in me.

'The truth will come out,' I told her.

She rested her head on my shoulder, and I was taken back to another time and place, her small, warm body tucked close against mine in the flat we shared, just her and me.

'Lily,' I said, putting my hand over hers. 'We need to talk about this man.'

She pulled her hand away and sat up, removing all contact between us. 'Really? Now, after all this, you think that's the most important thing?' She was glaring at me, her eyes filled with a deep resentment.

'Something's upsetting you,' I said, 'and I know it isn't just about me and the arrest. I'm right, aren't I?'

I watched as a tear slipped from her right eye, but it was one of anger rather than sadness. It was easy to assume the anger was directed at me when I felt so deserving of it.

'What do you care?' she said, stifling a sob. 'You don't give a shit about me – you're too wrapped up in yourself and Damien.'

I didn't know what to say. I had avoided the truth of it, but the fact was, she was right. For weeks I had been worrying about Damien, aware that he was drifting from me; fearing the worst of whatever it was that was going on inside his head. I had become distracted and insecure, but I had never considered myself negligent. Had Lily grown closer to this man through a desire for attention?

She had never told me exactly how long she had known him, and I had no way of knowing just how involved they were. Had I been so consumed with my relationship with my husband that I had taken my eye off the one I shared with my daughter?

'I'm sorry if I've made you feel that way, Lily. I never meant to.'

My relationship with my own parents had come to an end when I was not much older than Lily. They had got what they had wanted, their only daughter accepted on to a medical degree, her whole future mapped out with a plan they had carefully drawn up together, regardless of my wishes. When I had suggested that what I wanted was perhaps different to what they hoped for me, it was regarded as defiance. I was ungrateful and disobedient, too immature to make such important decisions for myself. Neither of my parents was ever violent towards me, but I came to fear their disappointment as I might have any blow, doing everything I could to please them and to keep life as quiet as it could be. Revision became a form of escape, and I used it to run from everything that had happened, hoping that one day they would become more lenient, more understanding, and would start to see things from my point of view.

The day my A-level results came out, my parents insisted on accompanying me to the school to collect them. I remember the embarrassment I felt at having them there, lurking behind me like a double shadow, when the rest of my year group were in their friendship cliques, their parents having done the normal thing of waiting at home for a phone call. I was ashamed to admit it, but I had always been a bit embarrassed by my parents. They were older than everyone else's – in their early forties when a longed-for but unexpected pregnancy made a surprise appearance – and their views were old-fashioned, their ways out of touch.

I opened the envelope with a feeling of dread embedded in the pit of my stomach. I wasn't sure why I was so nervous; I had been predicted strong grades and my coursework marks had all been good, but still I felt the unrelenting pressure of having to prove myself. When I looked at the results, a wave of relief flooded over me. Three As and a B. Enough to secure me a place on the course they had chosen for me.

My mother eyed me expectantly, and I smiled as I handed her the sheet of paper. My father was at her shoulder, but when he glanced down and scanned the short list of grades, his face darkened as though a thunderstorm had just passed above us. I waited for him to say something, and when he didn't speak, I turned my focus on my mother. As though sensing his mood, she too remained silent. My father turned and walked away, my mother offering a small smile of apology, as though she recognised the unfairness of it all but wouldn't bring herself to admit it.

'Jenna.' I heard my biology teacher speak my name and turned to show her my results. She beamed at me, placing a hand on my shoulder as she told me how brilliantly I had done and how proud she was of me. It didn't matter; none of it mattered. All I could think in that moment was how much I hated my parents and how much I wished I had never put myself to such trouble to prove that I was worthy of their approval.

I never wanted my children to feel the way I'd felt that day, least of all to be the one responsible for inflicting such a sense of failure on them. As Lily and I sat together in silence, I worried that the damage was already done. Perhaps I wasn't as far from my own parents as I had hoped and planned to be. I had always based my parenting on being nothing like them. I would never burden my children with impossible expectations; I would never enforce a path purely designed to please myself. I would be understanding, patient, kind, the type of mother with whom a daughter could share her darkest fears and her closest secrets.

'Has he done something to you?' I asked eventually. 'You're still seeing him, aren't you?'

She looked at me, her jaw tensed, her mouth set firm in a defiant grimace. 'No, he hasn't. And no, I'm not.'

She couldn't tell me what was distressing her so much. I'd allowed a gulf to develop between us because of all I'd done, because of my worries about Damien. And as I sat in Lily's bedroom, listening to her lie to me again, I knew that I had failed both of us.

EIGHTEEN

That night, I couldn't sleep. I was too hot, too cold, too uncomfortable; there were too many thoughts intent on keeping me from finding any kind of peace, and it felt wrong to even seek it, as though there was something I should be doing, something that might help me pull myself from the mess I had unwittingly been dragged into. Of course, there was nothing productive I could do at 2 a.m., and so I gave in to the urge to climb into bed beside Amelia, wrapping an arm around her sleeping body and breathing in the soft scent of her hair.

Before long, I was crying, my tears hot against the cool skin of her cheek. Everything seemed worse in the darkness, my blackest fears and biggest secrets gathering at the bedside to loom over me. The police were going to charge me with attempted murder. They would take me away from Amelia. She would grow up with a mother behind bars, the stigma of my conviction attaching itself to her with the permanence of a chain for which the key had been misplaced. She would spend a lifetime dragging my guilt around with her, every opportunity weighted with my crime.

I feared for Lily too. She was on the brink of adulthood; about to move on, to shed her old life and start anew, and I knew from experience that the transition from one life to another was anything but easy. She might well move on, but the past had a way of lingering and was always close at hand, waiting somewhere nearby in the shadows.

In the darkness, I wiped my eyes with the back of my hand and kissed Amelia on the forehead. She stirred slightly, but my presence wasn't enough to wake her. I wished I could explain all this to her while she was safe in slumber; that my words would enter her sleeping ear and stay there until morning, held in her subconscious and carried with her through all of her tomorrows, making every day a little easier, a little more manageable. But of course, I couldn't, not when I was unable to explain it to myself.

Holding that thought with me, I eased myself from beneath the duvet and crept from the room, pulling the door shut quietly behind me. I had left my laptop in our bedroom, so I tiptoed back in to retrieve it. Damien was sleeping on his front, the side of his face crushed into the pillow. I wanted to touch him, to wake him so that we could talk, but instead I watched him for a moment, not wanting to disturb his peace.

Downstairs, I sat at the kitchen table. As I waited for the laptop to load, I went to the sink to get myself a glass of water, mentally prioritising the things I needed to do. The things I needed to know.

I still didn't know the name of the man my daughter had been involved with, but even had I known it, there was another name repeating itself in my head until its presence dominated every other thought. Charlotte Copeland had become an obsession, a woman I thought about while I lay in bed at night; a person whose existence had come to shape my own, every move I made and word I spoke moulded by the effect she had had upon my life.

I had already searched for her online, trawling through the social media accounts of people with the same name, but I had found no profile that matched the woman I'd encountered in the park. It seemed impossible to me that a person of her age – late thirties, early forties at most – could have left no trail on the internet, and yet it appeared that she was invisible, or had at least chosen to keep herself that way.

As I sat down again at the table, I heard a bang. It came from outside, as sharp and sudden as a gunshot, and I jumped up and hurried out into the hallway. Through the frosted glass of the front door, I could see a burst of orange glowing in the darkness of the night. I opened the door and stepped outside, the concrete sending a chill through my bare feet; the heat of the flames rising in clouds from the burning car.

'Jesus, Jenna, get away from there!'

I heard footsteps thudding down the staircase behind me, then Damien's hands were on my shoulders as he pulled me back inside the house. Within moments he had called 999. When I turned, Lily was halfway down the stairs, her hair dishevelled and her eyes bleary with sleep.

'What's going on?'

Her question was cut short by a second explosion, which filled the air outside the opened front door with a blaze of fire and smoke. Lily screamed. Whether it was the explosion or the scream that woke Amelia, I wasn't sure, but soon we were all there, the four of us gathered in the hallway, Amelia crying tiredly in her sister's arms as we waited for the fire service to arrive.

I didn't want to look, but I couldn't tear my eyes from the sight of my Peugeot 5008, its white frame encased in a blaze of orange heat. I had only had it a couple of years – I had bought it second-hand as a gift to myself once I felt certain the café was secure enough to afford such an indulgence – and seeing it burn felt like witnessing the demise of everything I had worked so hard for. I glanced at Damien, who was watching helplessly as the fire engine drew up, blue lights flashing. I knew exactly what he was thinking: that once upon a time, before the accident that had changed everything, he would have been one of those firefighters, actively doing something to stop the blaze from spreading. Now he was dependent on the help of others. His pride was burning with that car, his sense of purpose going up in smoke into the night air. Yet again I wanted to reach out to touch him, but I knew the contact would be interpreted as a gesture of pity and would be rejected.

Unable to watch any longer, I ushered the girls into the kitchen.

'What's happened to the car?' Amelia asked, using the sleeve of her pyjamas to wipe her nose.

'There must have been an electrical fault,' I told her, and glanced at Lily, shooting her a look that pleaded with her not to contradict me. We both knew that the fire was arson, but what Amelia was unaware of wouldn't be capable of scaring her. 'When the fire's out, they'll be able to have a look at it.'

Thankfully, the blaze was extinguished quickly. I put *Mary Poppins* on in the back room and was grateful when Lily didn't make a fuss about sitting with Amelia to watch it. With a hot chocolate each and a packet of biscuits on the sofa between them, I was able to go out to the front of the house and hear what the fire crew had to say about the incident. One of them was speaking to Damien when I got to the front door.

'Arson?' I asked when he turned to greet me.

The fireman looked at me apologetically. 'Know anyone who might be responsible? Could be a random attack, but seems unlikely, to be honest.'

I nodded, reluctant to make the admission. This was no random attack. Somebody was sending a message, and I was hearing it loud and clear. My family had been inside the house, my daughters sleeping in their beds. What next?

'The police are on their way.'

I nodded again, thanked the fireman and turned away from the burned-out wreck that had been my car. Thankfully, there had been nothing inside it of any value or importance, though that seemed to offer little compensation. My life had been sabotaged yet again, and this time the attack had moved uncomfortably close to home.

'Are you okay?' Damien asked once the fireman had left us alone. I shook my head, waiting for the reassuring touch of his hand on mine, or the welcoming gesture of an outstretched arm I could curl my body into. The promise of either disappeared with his next question. 'Do you know more than you're letting on?'

'What?'

'All this,' he said, flinging his hands in the air. 'It's not a coincidence, is it?'

'What do you mean?' I was trying to remain calm, attempting to voice my responses in a way that wouldn't make me sound automatically defensive. It was difficult not to feel affronted, though, not when his tone was so accusatory.

He threw his head back and inhaled a deep lungful of cold night air. When he looked back at me, I wanted to believe he didn't resent everything I had brought upon us, but it was impossible to try to fool myself into thinking that way when I could see the hostility so clearly in his eyes.

'I'm just wondering what's going on here, Jenna. Things like this don't happen out of the blue, do they? Why you?'

I felt tears spark at the back of my eyes, and I hated myself for them. Whatever was going on – whatever the reason behind it – I didn't want to be reduced to tears. I wanted to fight back, to prove my innocence, but the longer I waited for something that might help me do either of those things, the weaker I felt my resilience become.

'I don't know,' I said, feeling a solitary tear fall down my cheek. 'If I did, don't you think I'd be doing something about it?'

'The police are going to ask questions. You need to answer them honestly.'

I turned to look at the open door, mindful that at any moment Lily might make an appearance in the hallway. 'And why wouldn't I?'

Damien looked at me sadly, the tiredness in his eyes fading into something deeper, more ingrained. 'I don't know. I don't know anything any more.'

*

By the time the police and the fire crew left, it was nearly 5 a.m. Amelia had fallen asleep in Lily's arms while watching television, and Damien carried her up to her room and put her back to bed. When he came downstairs again, Lily was in the kitchen, a dressing gown pulled tightly around her and a cup of tea clutched in both hands. Our earlier argument hadn't been mentioned, though she had barely spoken to me, and eye contact had been even more limited.

'Your sister doesn't need to know the police were here,' I said.

Lily rolled her eyes. 'Of course not.'

Amelia had fallen asleep before the police arrived, which I was grateful for. There would have been more questions, more answers I'd have failed to find; it was already hard enough trying to explain things to Lily.

'Well… that was no accident, was it?' Her tone was accusatory.

I could feel Damien eyeing me expectantly. Despite my hopes that some sort of solidarity might be achieved between us, I was encased in a feeling of increasingly familiar isolation.

'You should try to get a couple more hours' sleep. We all should.'

My suggestion was met with pursed lips, but Lily took the hint to leave, and flounced from the room with an overly dramatic swish of her dressing gown. My elder daughter was many things, but she wasn't stupid. She knew as well as Damien and I did that the attack on the car was intentional, aimed at me personally, and that the repercussions would have an inevitable impact on us all.

I set about clearing the mugs she had left on the table, busying myself with the mundane so that I didn't have to concentrate on what I knew was coming.

As though seeing what was going on inside my head, Damien announced, 'We can't keep the girls here. It isn't safe.'

I should have said something, but the words – all of them – were trapped on my tongue. I knew he was right, but I hated what he had said and everything it implied. I hated what this stranger was doing to my family.

My silence seemed to infuriate him, and he passed me with a shake of his head and an audible sigh before heading up the stairs. By the time I reached the bedroom, he had already pulled down the suitcase from the top of the wardrobe and opened it out on the bed. I stood in the doorway and watched as he moved around the room, folding clothes haphazardly before placing them in the suitcase. He looked so different to when we'd first met, and not just because of the inevitable changes of time. He was still only young, just forty-one, yet he was lean in the way of a much older man, the strength that had once defined his muscles having faded since the accident and given way to a visible weakness.

'Please don't do this.'

'I'm not doing it because I want to,' he said without looking at me. 'What choice do I have? It isn't safe here.'

As I watched him, I realised I was witnessing my family fall apart. I didn't want him to take the girls away from me, yet I knew he was right: our home wasn't safe. What if next time a burning rag was pushed through the letter box? The thought made me feel sick.

'Where are you going?' I asked, already knowing the answer.

'My mother's.'

'Lily won't go.' Or Nancy won't have her, I thought, though I kept the words to myself.

'That's up to her. She's got the option.'

'It won't be for long, will it?' I asked, hearing the desperation in my voice. 'Sean is going to sort this out, I know he will.'

Damien scoffed. 'If he's our best chance, then God help us.'

I clung again to the 'our' and the 'us' – maybe all wasn't yet lost.

'I know his reputation, but this is different. I'm innocent. Innocent people don't get sent to prison for things they didn't do.'

I sounded like a naive child. We both knew how untrue that was. I could think of too many well-documented examples of men and women sentenced for crimes they'd later been found innocent of.

When Damien turned to me, I was taken aback by the tears in his eyes. In all the years we had been together, I had only ever seen him cry on two occasions: the tenth anniversary of his father's death, and the day Amelia was born. Even when he was in recovery after his accident – after the multiple operations he'd had to try to repair the damage to his leg – I had never seen him shed a tear, despite the fact that he was going to lose his career and so many of the things that had come to shape his life.

I wanted to say something, but I didn't have the right words. I moved closer to him, tentatively reaching out a hand, convinced it would be pushed away. He didn't reject me. Instead, his body crumpled onto the edge of the bed, and I sat beside him, holding his hand in mine and resting my head on his shoulder as he cried, my own tears following not far behind.

'I love you, Damien, you know that, don't you? I always have. And whatever happens next, none of it changes how I feel about you, I need you to know that.'

Once they were given air, I heard my words as he heard them, almost as an admission. There was more to come, and I already knew it.

NINETEEN

I must have slept for a couple of hours at least, yet it felt as though I had not long ago been downstairs, still poring through the results my searches had thrown up. My mobile phone on the bedside table woke me up; beside me, Damien's side of the bed was empty. Ffion was calling me, and I realised with a panic that it was already nearly 8 a.m.

'Ffion. Everything okay?'

Avoiding work felt like hiding away, but I needed to take some time to figure out how I was going to get my life back in order. I was worried that it made me look guilty, but hoped Ffion knew me well enough to have faith in my innocence. Had she believed me capable of such violence, I doubted she would have continued to work for me. I needed my name to stay out of the press for as long as possible; if people were to learn of my suspected involvement, it would only attract negative attention. We needed the regular income the coffee shop provided, particularly when everything else in our lives seemed so fragile and unsteady.

'Jenna, I'm sorry to call you, but something's happened at the shop.'

I felt my heart plummet at the words, wondering what else could possibly go wrong. I pictured the police there again, the place turned upside down; everything I had worked so hard for brought to ruins in a matter of minutes.

'What is it?'

'Someone's graffitied the front window. I've tried to get it off, but if I keep going, I'm not going to be opened up in time.'

'I'm on my way over,' I said, getting out of bed and reaching for the clothes I'd left strewn around the evening before. 'What does it say?'

There was silence for a moment. 'Don't worry about that, it doesn't matter. Have you got some cleaning stuff there? I don't think what I've got is strong enough.'

I told her I'd stop at a hardware shop on the way over and wouldn't be long. If we were going to try to keep things as normal as possible, I needed to get the window cleaned up before too many customers saw it. I tried to imagine what was sprayed there, but I feared that whatever words or phrases I could conjure up, the truth of it might yet prove to be something I was unprepared for.

Damien was at the kitchen sink, washing up the breakfast dishes.

'Why didn't you wake me?' I asked.

'I thought you could do with a lie-in. You must be shattered after last night.'

Amelia was dressed in her school uniform, playing a game on Damien's mobile phone. She looked surprisingly fresh for a child who'd been disturbed during the night, though in many ways she always seemed far more resilient than the rest of us. I noticed she didn't look up when I entered the room, and I knew it was more than just her being engrossed in what she was doing. I doubted Damien had told her about his plans to take her to stay with Nancy. It would only have caused an argument, and there was no point in upsetting her before she went to school. Though I hated it, I knew he was right. While there was even the smallest possibility that it wasn't safe here, taking Amelia away was the sensible thing to do.

I moved in close beside him and lowered my voice to a whisper. 'Have you asked Lily about going with you to your mother's?'

'She wants to stay here with you.'

I suspected Lily's reluctance to go to Nancy's was more to do with keeping a distance from Damien than it was with staying close to me. Though I was grateful for her loyalty, I wanted her to be protected. I was glad she wanted to be at home – I had so much making up to do, and I needed to try to keep things as normal as possible – yet I was unsure whether it was the best thing for her.

'It's not safe,' I mouthed.

'You'll have to talk to her. She made it clear she didn't want to discuss it with me.'

'What's going on between you two?' I asked the question before my brain had time to talk me out of it. I wondered how he might try to excuse the frostiness between them, or whether he was even aware of it. It occurred to me that he might have been too consumed with other things to have noticed.

'Nothing that I'm aware of.'

I looked across the room at Amelia, making sure she was still lost to our conversation. I had left my laptop on the kitchen table, and I wondered whether Damien had checked my search history. I doubted that it would have been a priority, though it didn't matter if he had; I had nothing to hide. I wanted to know who Charlotte Copeland was and why she was trying to ruin my life; surely he wouldn't find anything incriminating in that? Had he been in my situation, he would have done the same.

'Did you talk to her about it this morning?' I asked in a whisper.

He shook his head. 'Last night. I heard her get up this morning, but she'd left before I had a chance to see her. Have you spoken to her again about this boyfriend?'

When I looked over at Amelia again, she was watching us, the phone still clutched in her hands.

'Can we talk about this later? I've got to go over to the coffee shop… I'll explain later.'

The truth was, I had no intention of mentioning the graffiti. I had already given Damien enough to cope with; I didn't want him to have to worry about the business too.

He opened his mouth to say something, but glancing at Amelia, he changed his mind. 'Whatever,' he mumbled.

I wanted to stay and talk to him, to sort things out, but I knew I had to get over to Ffion. If things became too difficult for her and she decided to look for employment at a place where the boss hadn't been accused of attempted murder, we'd be screwed financially. Damien couldn't help at the coffee shop – the injury to his leg meant that he couldn't spend extended periods of time on his feet – and though he made some money doing laptop repairs, the work was sporadic, meaning the income was too. I needed to provide for my family, but I also needed to ensure Ffion was protected. If she went, everyone would suffer.

I stopped at the kitchen table and crouched beside Amelia, wrapping my arms around her in an embrace from which she was keen to wriggle free. She gave me a questioning look, as though wondering what was going on, and I realised that the more fuss I made, the harder it was going to be for Damien to explain to her that evening that she wouldn't be going home tonight.

'I love you,' I told her, trying to make the words sound as casual as possible. 'Have a good day at school.'

I thought about asking Damien if I could borrow his car – there was no reason why he and Amelia couldn't walk to school – but he had made it obvious that he wanted to get over to his mother's sooner rather than later, and I was too proud to beg him to stay and help me. If he wanted to go, I had to let him. It wouldn't be forever – or so my remaining strands of optimism assured me.

I called a taxi and asked the driver to stop and wait for me at B&Q, where I bought some extra-strength window cleaner, paint remover, a packet of sponges and a wire brush. By the time he dropped me near the coffee shop, town was busy, the main street flooded with teenagers in uniform making their way up to the comprehensive. I wished I had a hood to put up, though the lack of rain would have only made me look more conspicuous.

My resolution to not look at the shopfront until I was right outside fell to pieces as soon as I was close enough to see the window; close enough to see the blood-red paint that dripped down the glass in horror-movie capitals.

PSYCHO

My fragile hope that I might stay anonymous was instantly dashed; people knew who I was, where I worked. And if last night's incident was anything to go by, they knew where I – and my family – lived.

When Ffion greeted me at the door, it was all I could do to stop myself from bursting into tears.

'Where's your car?'

'Wouldn't start,' I lied.

She rolled her eyes. 'Typical, isn't it? I've got everything prepped,' she added, raising a hand as though she was going to reach out to me, but changing her mind mid gesture. 'Come on… let's get this sorted out.'

We worked as quickly as possible to clean the window before too many people saw the evidence of my shame. 'I didn't do it,' I said in hushed, urgent tones as I scrubbed at the paint, my arm working furiously as though it might be able to undo not just this but everything that had led to it.

'Christ, Jenna, you don't need to tell me that.'

Her words were a comfort, and as I scrubbed, I wept. Ffion, tactful enough to know when words weren't needed, allowed me to cry in silence, picking up her pace to match mine.

It was ten minutes past our usual opening time of 9.30 by the time we finished, and thankfully there had only been a small number of passers-by. I was grateful none of them had felt it necessary to comment on the vandalism, though I knew it wouldn't be long before something was said. I had no idea how I would react. If I said nothing, I would look guilty; if I protested my innocence too loudly, I imagined it would achieve much the same effect.

The first customer of the morning arrived while I was still there. He ordered an Americano and I waited in the kitchen while Ffion served him, feeling like a fugitive.

'I think it's probably best I go,' I told her when she came to join me. 'You sure you don't mind?'

'It's probably a good idea,' she agreed, glancing at my hands. They were pink from the paint, raw-looking. 'Go and do what you need to do. If there's anything I can help with, you know you only have to ask.'

'Thanks, Ffion.' Her kindness was appreciated, but I was finding it hard to handle. I couldn't deal with the attention, as though I was undeserving of it.

'Is there anything on that footage I sent you?'

I shook my head. 'Nothing,' I lied. The truth was, I hadn't yet looked at it. I knew I needed to, but I was too scared of what – or who – I might find.

TWENTY

When I got back to the house, it was eerily quiet. Even before I unlocked the front door, things felt changed, as though some irreparable damage had been inflicted upon the place and it would never look the same, smell the same, feel as it once had. It would never truly be home again.

What remained of my car was gone from the driveway. Damien had taken Amelia to school in his own car, which had been safely parked on the other side of the street, and I assumed that he had returned to the house to wait for the Peugeot to be taken away. I needed to arrange a rental car as soon as possible, though there was something far more pressing competing for my attention.

'You okay, love?'

I was snapped from the sight of the blackened concrete on the empty driveway by one of the neighbours, an elderly man who had lived in the street for as long as we had been there and who seemed to follow the same routine every day, walking his dog once during the morning and again in the early evening.

'Thanks,' I said with a nod. 'It's only a car, isn't it?'

'Terrible business.' He shook his head. 'I saw them take it away,' he added. 'Lucky you weren't driving it when it happened.'

I breathed an inward sigh of relief that he didn't appear to realise it was arson. It was only a matter of time before the rumour mill caught hold of what was happening to me and my family, and I knew that when it did, I would be powerless to prevent the inevitable repercussions. All I could hope was that the worst of it would land upon me and not on the girls. Whatever my mistakes or my misfortune, neither Lily nor Amelia deserved to suffer as a result.

'Exactly. Things can be replaced, can't they?' I smiled, faking a cheery optimism, when inside I wanted to cry. The kindness of people I barely knew felt unmerited, as though this man was offering his platitudes to the wrong person. And then a thought hit me, almost knocking me from my feet. The wrong person. What if that was all this was? What if I was being targeted not because someone meant me harm but because they intended it for someone else? Someone they mistakenly believed to be me.

I bid the neighbour goodbye and hurried into the house, making sure to double-check the lock on the door behind me. I opened the laptop at the kitchen table and made a cup of tea as I waited for it to load. When I logged into my email account, the attachment from Ffion was at the top of my unread messages, the link to the CCTV footage there as she had promised.

I was almost afraid to look, as though by doing so I would be exposing myself to something from which there would be no return. I knew there would be no footage from within the coffee shop itself, something I berated myself for before opening the first recording, wishing that the cameras had been better placed. But why would I ever have thought to put one at the kitchen door, where no one other than staff went?

The task was tiresome, and I sped through much of the footage, pausing on the face of each new person as they entered the building, waiting for someone I recognised. Whoever had taken that knife into the coffee shop had done so with the intention of framing me for the attack on Charlotte Copeland, and why would anyone who barely knew me – why would someone who didn't know me at all – want to inflict that kind of suffering upon not just me but my family too? Of course, there were plenty of faces I knew, customers we had welcomed to the coffee shop for years and others newer to us, but there was no one who prompted any suspicion. I started to think I was wasting my time. What exactly was I trying to find anyway?

At just after 2 p.m. I had a text message from Lily telling me she was staying on after college for rehearsals. I believed her on this occasion, knowing that the show was just a couple of weeks away, though I realised that the amount of time the production was taking up had made her lies easier to fabricate, giving her plenty of opportunity to be in places other than where she had claimed to be. I tried to push those thoughts aside, grateful for the extra time to submerge myself in my task, knowing that when Lily arrived home, I would have to pack my laptop away and pretend I had been doing something different.

I picked up my pace and continued to trawl through the footage captured since Friday night. With each man I watched enter the coffee shop, my thoughts returned to that evening, and the darkened figure I had seen running away from Charlotte Copeland. It occurred to me that this unknown person could be anywhere, anyone, and no one was looking for him. I doubted whether the police even believed he existed, considering him nothing more than a figment of my imagination; a character invented as a way of shifting the blame from myself. It was my word against Charlotte's, and as she was the one lying injured in a hospital bed, why should anyone believe a word I said?

I felt my fingers shake on the laptop keys when I saw the figure of my husband appear on the screen. Why had he been at the coffee shop that day? He had known I wasn't there, that I had booked the weekend off, and he had made no mention of dropping in. I rarely saw him when I was at work. There had been times, years earlier, when he would come to see me, always bringing me something savoury – a distraction from the temptation of cakes and brownies on display at the counter – but those days were behind us and we had settled into our separate day-to-day lives, making time for each other when circumstances allowed.

With my attention back on the screen, I ran the tape forward, wondering how long Damien had been at the shop. Perhaps he had only popped in for something, though I couldn't think what that something might have been. I didn't need to wait long; within minutes, a second familiar face arrived at the door.

I paused the footage, tasting the sour sting of bile at the back of my throat, then replayed it, watching again as Laura entered the shop. I wound the recording back, checking the times. She had turned up less than eight minutes after Damien, but they had left together just moments later. I paused on a shot of them stepping through the front door, searching for an incriminating touch of a hand or a momentary look stolen as though unseen, but there was nothing. They were just two people leaving a coffee shop together, with the obvious unanswered question of where they were going and why.

Neither of them looked happy, though at the time the footage had been recorded, Damien wouldn't have known of my arrest. I felt my face flush with anger at the possibility that while I'd been sitting in that police cell, terrified of what might be about to happen to me, he had been elsewhere, with someone I regarded as a friend. Then I remembered that this was the same day that Lily had seen them together in our home. What the hell was going on?

There was a knock at the front door. I closed my eyes, already knowing it could only be bad news, and my heart sank further when I opened the door, the sight of DS Maitland enough to obliterate any scrap of positivity I might have had left.

'Mrs Morgan.'

He didn't need to speak the words that followed; I had heard them too many times already. This time, I knew there would be no release without charge, no 'under further investigation'. My fate lay in the hands of someone else – everyone else – and I was incapable of doing anything to stop what might happen to me.

TWENTY-ONE

On Friday morning, a week after the assault on Charlotte Copeland, I was charged with wounding with intent. Bail was initially refused, which came as no surprise to me, considering the severity of the attack; Sean had already warned me that this was likely to be the case. He was quick to remind me that it could have been worse – the charge might have been attempted murder – as though this might in some way soften the reality of what I was facing.

'The DNA results on the knife retrieved from the coffee shop have confirmed that the victim's blood is present,' he said, studying me as though checking that the information was finally seeping in.

We had been through all this during my interview with detectives prior to the charge being made, yet I wanted – needed – to hear it again, convinced that somewhere a mistake had been made and all it needed was for someone other than me to recognise it for what it was. I felt as though I was watching myself from outside my own body; as though everything was happening to someone else and I was merely a spectator, a viewer shouting with frustration at a scenario I couldn't change.

The news that the blood on the knife was a match with Charlotte Copeland came as no surprise to me. Whoever was trying to ruin my life was unlikely to try to frame me using pig's blood.

'And there are no other DNA results or fingerprints?' I asked.

Hearing it all again felt like confirmation of events, as though through repetition the truth of my situation became less easy to argue against. Sean tapped his pen on the edge of the desk in a way that was both irritating and somehow obnoxious, his silence dragging out my trauma in the way a talent-show presenter lingers on a set of phone-in results, almost enjoying the state of anticipation in which he was keeping me.

'One set of prints lifted. Unidentified.' He raised the pen to his lips and chewed it. 'I'm sorry, Jenna. It doesn't matter how many times we go over it, the facts aren't going to change.'

I lowered my head and squeezed the fingers of my right hand with my left, trying to hold back the anger surging inside me, fighting for release. I knew we were being watched, our conversation listened in on, and the knowledge kept me from screaming with all the fight I had left in me. The most important fact – the only one that should matter to him – was the fact that I was innocent.

'But that's a good thing, isn't it?' I asked between gritted teeth. 'It means there's nothing linking me to the knife. So why have I been charged?'

Yet again I was asking questions that had already been answered, raising arguments already presented during my interview, yet still I refused to accept what was happening to me. It all seemed so unfair.

'They've had the forensic results back a couple of days now,' he reminded me. I saw him raise his eyes to the ceiling, so close to an eye roll that I felt ready to lunge across the table at him. 'They've applied to the CPS, who have obviously decided that the knife being found on your premises is sufficient to bring forward a charge. This isn't what either of us wants, Jenna, but we can't argue with the courts – they get the final say.'

'So what do we do now?'

Sean sighed and sat back, smoothing the front of his freshly ironed shirt. Amy's brother or not – my only lifeline or not – in that moment I hated him.

'Prove your innocence.'

I looked at him with raised eyebrows.

'I'm working on it,' he said, reading the look.

'The knife was planted in the shop by someone else,' I told him, though I'd said it so many times by then that I wondered why I needed to keep repeating it. 'Surely the forensic results prove that, and surely that's enough to prove my innocence?'

'It definitely helps,' Sean admitted, though I could see in his face that he wasn't wholly convinced. 'When this goes to trial, the prosecution is going to need more. They already know that.' He was quiet for a moment, looking at me for the first time not as a client, someone little more than a stranger, but as someone he knew, a woman his sister called a friend and towards whom he had a loyalty, whether he liked it or not. 'Look,' he said, his voice softening as he spotted the tears I was failing to hold back. 'You're intelligent, Jenna, and there's no point in sugar-coating it. There's an overwhelming amount of circumstantial evidence against you.'

I hurriedly ran the back of my hand across my face, desperate to hide the signs of what I knew would be perceived as weakness. 'I thought circumstantial evidence wasn't enough to take a case to trial?'

My thoughts drifted back to my accuser, to that woman who seemed by all accounts untraceable. It seemed impossible that anyone could remain anonymous, not with the amount of daily intrusion all our lives were now subject to. And yet Charlotte Copeland remained invisible, or at least when it suited her to do so. I wondered what the police knew of her, and to what extent they had bothered to look. Her status as victim was keeping her protected, while my assumed guilt had left me almost entirely exposed.

'I'm afraid not. Look, there are things I'm looking into. Leave it with me.' He gave me a knowing look that told me he didn't want to discuss whatever he was working on while the police were listening in on the conversation. I nodded, acknowledging his intention but wondering whether there was really any substance to what he said, or if it was easier to suggest he was doing something practical to keep me quiet for the time being.

'Nothing's been said about what happened to my car. Or the graffiti on the shop. It's like they're just not listening to me – they don't want to have to consider the possibility of someone else being responsible for the assault.'

Sean held my eye, willing me to stop speaking. 'Leave it with me,' he said again.

'What happens with the bail refusal?'

'I'll apply to the crown court. Look, you know I can't make any promises here, but like I said before, there are certain things that will go in your favour. You've got no previous record – that always helps.' He stood and took his jacket from the back of the chair. 'The sooner I get on to it, the better your chances. I'll be in touch, okay? Stay strong.'

His words remained with me, echoing for the remainder of that day and beyond. To stay strong, I needed to have been strong in the first place, but there was little left in me other than despair.

For the first twenty-four hours following the charge, I didn't see anyone other than police officers. On Saturday afternoon, the monotony of my existence in custody was broken by the news that Damien had come to the station to see me. We hadn't seen each other since Thursday morning, when we had tiptoed around the drama of what had happened to the car and everything that had been said the night before.

We were permitted to sit together for a short time in one of the interview rooms. Neither of us seemed to know what to say to break the silence, the unfamiliarity of the setting and the unlikelihood of the situation we had found ourselves in rendering us lost for words. I couldn't stop thinking about what I had seen on that

CCTV footage just moments before the police had arrived at the house. Too many hours spent alone in a cell had done little to help my suspicion and bitterness, and with Damien in front of me, all I could see was him and Laura together.

'Thank you for coming,' I said, trying to focus on him rather than the images in my mind.

Damien glanced at the camera in the corner of the room and I knew what he was thinking: that just being here made you feel guilty even when you'd done nothing wrong, in the same way that too much time spent in a hospital waiting room could make a person with a minor ailment convince themselves they were seriously ill.

'How are you keeping?' He cringed at his own words, hearing the everyday normality of them.

I shrugged. 'The room service is terrible.'

There was no smile; no reaction. His features were taut, as though he was suppressing any emotion that threatened to make itself visible, and I worried for a moment that he might cry again. I didn't want him to do that here, not while we were being watched, and I didn't want to be left alone with the thought of what all this was doing to him.

'I'd better get used to it, I suppose,' I added.

He shook his head. 'You mustn't think like that. Amy reckons the case will collapse unless they can find stronger evidence, so we've got to believe she's right, okay?'

'You've seen her?'

Damien nodded. 'And Sean. I'm never going to like the bloke,' he added, reading the look on my face, 'but I think he's doing his best by you, even if it's thanks to his sister.'

'I don't know how I'm going to pay him,' I said, my voice cracking at the thought of the bill I would be greeted with when all this was over, whether I ended up a free woman or faced with a custodial sentence. If I was sent to prison, it would be Damien who'd be left with the financial mess.

'Don't think about that now. We'll sort it out somehow. You've got to focus on getting through this, okay? The girls need you. I need you.'

'How are they?' A sob caught in the back of my throat at the thought of what all this might be doing to them.

Damien hesitated as though considering a lie that might soften the truth. 'They've taken it really badly.'

'Has Lily been staying with you at your mother's?'

He shook his head. 'She's at Maisie's. I've checked with her mum,' he added, witnessing my reaction.

'We don't know she's there now, though, do we?'

The suggestion sat between us, clear in its meaning. The thought of my daughter being with this mystery man while I was incarcerated here, powerless to do anything to stop what might be happening, made me want to claw at the walls, but I was mindful of what was being seen and heard, aware of the facade of composure I needed to maintain.

Damien was quiet for a moment. 'As you've said before, she's not a kid any more. We've got to trust her to make the right decision.' His jaw had tightened with the statement, forcing back the words he really wanted to say. He knew as well as I did that though Lily was seventeen, she was far from being mature enough to be considered an adult. The events of the past week had been enough to push her closer to this man, whoever he was, and now all I could think was that the charge brought against me might be the tipping point for every wrong decision she might make. Just as my own parents had done, I had pushed her into the arms of someone I already knew in my heart would be nothing but trouble.

'You hate me, don't you?' I asked, letting my resolve slip.

Damien's eyes narrowed. 'Hate you? I hate this, Jenna, but no, I don't hate you.'

'It's just, you've been so… I don't know… so off recently.'

He raised his eyebrows, as though the reason for his aloofness was self-explanatory. 'There's been a lot going on.'

Before all this, I wanted to say. *You were acting differently before all this.* Our relationship had been subtly sliding into half-spoken sentences and strained silences for a while, though I couldn't be sure of when the shift had started. I couldn't be sure of anything anymore. It was the wrong time and the wrong place to be airing problems in our marriage. How could I bring up the subject of my fears about him and Laura when doing so would make me look like a paranoid, jealous wife? I needed to appear to the police to be calm and rational, a hard-working mother who had been dragged into a set of circumstances beyond my control.

We were interrupted by the arrival of a uniformed officer, telling us our time was up. I wanted to reach out to touch Damien, but I knew that any physical contact between us was forbidden.

'Tell the girls I love them,' I said. 'I love you too.'

He gave me a sad smile before following the officer out into the corridor. There was no parting gesture, no words of reassurance; no sign that he loved me back.

TWENTY-TWO

The week after we slept together for the first time, Damien didn't turn up at the flat as arranged. I had swapped a shift with someone at the pub so that we could spend an afternoon and evening together, and in his absence, I played with Lily, trying to avoid the temptation of checking my phone every thirty seconds. I gave her a bath, read her a story and sat beside her bed long after she had fallen asleep, by which time I had finally resigned myself to the fact that he wasn't going to show up. I checked my phone yet again, but he hadn't called or texted. I contemplated texting him but quickly dismissed the idea, worried that it would only make me look desperate. I had chased a man before. I had promised myself that I would never do it again.

I continued to sit with Lily as she slept, watching the rise and fall of her chest beneath her Peppa Pig pyjamas. They were a present from our landlady, and she had refused to be parted from them, throwing an uncharacteristic tantrum when I'd had to peel them from her to get her dressed to go into town. As I listened to the tiny purr of her breathing, I felt reassured by the notion that I had all I needed, and that as long as Lily and I were together, we didn't need anyone else. Nonetheless, the memory of Damien's warm body in my bed filled me with a sense of yearning. I had allowed my mind to run away from me, picturing days that had never been spoken of and a life that had never been promised. My foolish naivety had made me hope there could be more to it than there had been.

I fell asleep on the carpet, and the following morning woke late. I hastily pulled my clothes on before dressing a half-asleep Lily, then hurried over to the B and B, where Elaine was awaiting our arrival with toast for Lily and a cup of tea for me. My phone went off in my pocket as I made a start on the first bedroom, but when I glanced at it, I didn't recognise the number. Ignoring it, I carried on with my work. Lily had joined me by the time I got to the third bedroom, watching cartoons on the TV and entertaining herself with a couple of dolls she'd brought up with her from the box in the kitchen. At eleven o'clock, the same phone number tried me again, this time leaving a voice message.

'Hi, Jenna, my name's Jim, I'm Damien's flatmate. Look, he asked me to contact you, to let you know why he wasn't there yesterday. The thing is, there was an accident. He's okay… well, he'll be okay, but he wanted you to know. Give me a call when you can. Thanks.'

I abandoned the duvet I'd been changing and called the number back.

'Is that Jim?' I said when a male voice answered. 'It's Jenna. You left me a message. I'm sorry I kept missing you – I'm at work.'

'It's okay. Look, Damien—'

'Is he okay?'

I already knew what the answer was; I could tell from the tone of the message that everything wasn't okay. Whatever had happened, Damien was hurt. Able to speak, at least, but injured in some way.

'He was knocked off his bike yesterday morning. He had emergency surgery for a leg injury and is still in hospital. They reckon he could be there a while.'

'Which hospital?' My mouth had gone dry. There I'd been, thinking the worst of him – that he was just another user – and all the time he'd been in recovery. I couldn't bring myself to start thinking about what might have happened to him or in what way

he might have been injured. His job, his running, his cycling…
everything he loved depended on his body's ability to function.

'The University Hospital in Cardiff,' Jim told me.

'Can I visit him?'

'Of course, but I thought you were down west? It's quite a long way.'

'I'm coming. I don't know when I'll get there, but tell him I'll
come as soon as I can.'

We ended the call and I finished the room as quickly as I could.
Then, scooping Lily and her dolls up into my arms, I headed
downstairs to the kitchen, where Elaine was pulling a load of wet
bed linen from the washing machine.

'Elaine,' I said, stooping to put the dolls back into the toy basket,
'I need to ask you a favour.'

'What is it, love?'

'Can I…' I felt embarrassed to ask – I had never relied on charity
and I didn't want to start now. I told myself that it wasn't really
charity: I would earn back what I asked for, so it was little more
than an advance. 'Is there any chance I could have next week's wages
up front? I know it's cheeky to ask, but you know I'll do my hours,
and I'll work my day off for free. I wouldn't ask if it wasn't urgent.'

'What's happened?'

I explained to her that a friend had been in an accident and that
I needed to get to Cardiff to see him.

'You'll be wanting tomorrow off then. You won't get there and
back in a day, not unless you drag Lily home late tonight, and that
won't be fair on her.'

'Would you mind? I know it's asking a lot.'

Elaine smiled. 'You never ask for anything, love. I'll have a chat
with Brian – he'll have to go into town to the bank.'

'Thank you so much.'

She picked the washing basket up. 'A friend, you say?' she said,
a knowing smile creeping across her lips.

I felt the colour rise in my cheeks. 'Thank you, Elaine,' I said again. 'I'll make it up to you, I promise.'

At the end of my shift, Brian handed me that week's money and the following week's pay in advance. I called one of the other part-time staff members from the pub and asked them to cover my evening shift, promising to cover one of their weekends in return, then I took Lily back to the flat and packed an overnight bag for the two of us.

With my heart filled with uneasy anticipation, we caught a bus to the nearest train station, twenty miles away. Whatever I might find waiting for me when I got to Cardiff, I felt certain that Damien and I would face it together. I would help heal him, just as he'd been healing me.

TWENTY-THREE

Sean came to the police station on Tuesday morning to let me know that the crown court had accepted his application, though as he had predicted, there were conditions surrounding my release. I was to go back to the station once a week to sign myself in, had to hand in my passport to the police, and I was under instruction not to attempt to make any contact with Charlotte, though by this point I had no intention of doing so. My time spent in custody had drained what little energy I had, giving me just a taste of what life in prison would be like. I was afraid I hadn't the reserves to survive it.

He drove me back to the house and I thanked him for everything he had done for me so far. He remained quiet, and I was unsure what his silence indicated – whether he was withholding any developments until he had something substantial to work from, or whether in fact there were none, and he didn't want to have to admit it.

The first thing I did when I got into the house was to call Lily. Her phone rang through to voicemail and I hung up, then rang back again and left a message.

'Love, it's Mum. I'm home. Where are you? I was hoping we could meet up – I've missed you all so much. I am so sorry, darling. Call me when you get this.'

I phoned Damien next, but there was no answer from him either. I left a message telling him I was going to shower then go over to his mother's house. I was desperate to see Amelia and wanted to be there when she got back from school. I dreaded the reaction my presence might provoke from Nancy, but thoughts of drawing my family back together were stronger than any concerns about her animosity.

I stayed in the shower far longer than was necessary, allowing the too-hot water to scald away the dirt and shame of the past five days. I washed my hair twice, still feeling even after it was rinsed through that I was carrying the grime of the police station, as though the place's every association had ingrained itself in my scalp and my skin. I was putting on clean clothes, my hair still wet, when I heard the doorbell.

It was Amy. Her car was parked on the drive, in the space where my own had sat the previous week, and she was holding a bunch of flowers and a two-pint bottle of milk. 'I did consider wine,' she said, 'but I thought this might be more practical.'

I ushered her into the house, mindful that the neighbours might be watching. People would surely have noticed that no one had been home since before the weekend, and gossip rarely took long to spread. I had tried not to linger on thoughts of what might have been said about me, but my mind kept returning to the possibilities.

Amy sat at the kitchen table as I made tea. I was grateful for the milk – there was nothing in the fridge other than a lump of cheese that had turned blue at the edges, three cloves of garlic and half a tub of butter, and I wondered whether Lily had been back to the house at all since I'd been gone. She still hadn't returned my call; I had been checking my phone every couple of minutes; had even taken it into the bathroom with me in case she called while I was in the shower.

'Are you okay?' she asked.

'Never been better.'

'We're going to get this sorted, Jenna, I promise you.'

'You shouldn't make promises you might not be able to keep.'

I placed a cup of tea in front of her. I'd made one for myself, though I doubted I would drink it; the thought of food and drink made me feel sick.

'Damien said he'd seen you.'

She nodded and sipped her tea. 'He's really worried about you. Look…' She paused and set her mug down on the table, her eyes meeting mine. 'Remember what you said before, about thinking Damien was having an affair? You don't still think it, do you? I know it's not the biggest thing going on right now… I mean, well of course it's big, but… you know what I mean.'

It wasn't like Amy to get tongue-tied. She was usually so assertive with her opinions, so sure of everything that left her mouth. It was something I admired, this ability to always seem so self-assured, even when there must have been occasions when, inside, the opposite was true.

I thought about telling her what I'd seen on the CCTV footage. The laptop was there on the table beside us, right where I had left it after being arrested. I could have played it to her, but what would I be showing? Laura and Damien leaving a building together. Even in my current state of mind, I could see how ridiculous it would appear. Plus, she was Laura's friend too. I trusted Amy as much as I trusted anyone, but that was the problem: there was no one – not even myself – that I trusted fully.

'I don't know,' I said. 'I can't think about it at the moment.'

'I understand that. Please don't think I'm interfering, and it's probably best you don't tell him I told you this, but Damien was a mess when we saw him on Friday. He's so worried about all this, about you. If he's having an affair, he's putting on one hell of a performance, that's all I'm saying.'

I heard what she was saying, but it couldn't change what was eating me away inside. I knew how Damien had been behaving towards me, long before that night at the park. The distance between us, the silences, the knowing there was something he wanted to say but didn't seem able to put into words; there was something wrong, whether I was mistaken or not about its origins.

Those notes, I thought. I had told him what they referred to, but what if he didn't believe me?

'You haven't come here to talk about my marriage, though, have you?' I said, realising as the question left my lips how abrupt and confrontational it sounded. 'I'm sorry. I didn't mean that how it came out. It's just… I need to focus on clearing my name. Everything else I can deal with later.'

Amy glanced at her mobile phone on the table.

'What is it?' I pressed.

She sighed and closed her eyes, caught in an invisible dilemma she appeared to be battling within her own head. 'Sean will kill me if he knows I've told you.'

'Told me what?'

'I promised him I wouldn't say anything.'

'And if you'd intended to keep that promise, you wouldn't have mentioned anything, so come on, Amy, please – I haven't got time to mess about with this.'

'You can't say anything, okay?'

She was making me feel like a teenager again, as though we were two schoolgirls swapping secrets over a stolen bottle of vodka rather than two adults discussing something that might change the entire course of my future. I widened my eyes, tired of the charade.

'Sean has found out a few things about Charlotte Copeland. I won't go into details, but all you need to know is that they change everything.'

I bit my lip, trying not to lose my patience with her. She was on my side, yet she was doing the same as everyone else, withholding information that I felt I had a right to know.

'This is my life, Amy. My future. My family's future. I think you can go into details.'

'Promise me—'

'Amy, for God's sake, I won't say anything!'

We sat quietly for a moment, both silenced by my outburst. I was capable of much more, but the previous five days had taught me the benefit of adopting the appearance of calm, if nothing else.

'I'm sorry.'

'You have nothing to be sorry for. I think I'd be screaming from the bloody rooftops if I was in your shoes.'

She sat back and drained the last of her tea.

'Charlotte Copeland has previous involvement with the police.'

'Go on,' I encouraged her, sensing her reluctance to tell me everything she knew.

'She made a false rape claim.'

I put a hand to my forehead and pressed my thumb against my left temple, waiting for what was to come next.

'She eventually withdrew the statement she'd made to the police,' Amy continued. 'That's not all, either. She has a history of mental illness – depression, an eating disorder, a diagnosis of schizophrenia. She spent quite a bit of time in rehab.'

I shoved my chair back and the sound of the legs scraping on the tiles pierced the air. 'So she's a fucking liar, basically? Just as I've been trying to tell everyone. Why are the police listening to a word this woman says?'

My resolution to maintain my composure had been quickly shattered by Amy's revelations. I could feel myself shaking, my body trembling as though some unknown force had taken hold of it. The police knew all this – they must have known for some time – yet I had still been charged and kept in that cell for five days. I was still facing a trial and a future someone else would decide upon.

'Why wasn't she sent to prison? I thought making a false rape claim was considered serious enough for a custodial sentence?'

'It is usually. But apparently, after she withdrew her statement, the man she'd accused said he didn't want charges brought against her. Her history of mental illness was taken into consideration and she was admitted to a psychiatric unit instead.'

'But her history will come out during the trial, won't it? I don't just mean the mental illness – I mean the false rape claim as well.'

'Definitely.'

I sat back down, collapsing into the chair beside Amy. The weight I had been carrying with me seemed to slide from my shoulders and land in a heap at my feet. Though I knew my problems were far from over, I was crying with the relief of knowing that finally something had come my way that would help to prove my innocence. Amy put a comforting hand on my arm.

'Where's she from, this woman?' I asked, wiping away the humiliating rush of tears that had flooded my face. 'She's not from around here, I know that much. She didn't have a Welsh accent.'

'I'm not sure.'

'Where was she in rehab? Please, Amy,' I begged, certain that she knew the answer. 'I just want to know where she's from. If I know that, maybe I can work out why she's doing this to me.'

'Let the defence work that out. Your job now is to look after your kids and get your life back to normal.'

I laughed bitterly. 'There is no normal, though, is there? There won't be until the trial is over, and that could be ages. And there'll be no chance of normal ever again if I'm found guilty.'

I met her eyes, pleading with her to see things from my perspective, though I knew that was impossible. Nobody could understand what the past couple of weeks had done to me, or what the thought of an uncertain future continued to do.

'You know, don't you? You know where she was in rehab, but you won't tell me.'

'What will it achieve, Jenna?'

'What I just told you,' I said, trying not to lose my patience. 'If I know where she's from, I might be able to work out who she is. I might stand a chance of figuring out what the hell is going on. Please,' I said again. 'What do you think I'm going to do – turn up at the place? What would that achieve, given that she's not there any more?'

'You'd be stupid to do that anyway. It could jeopardise your entire defence when the case goes to court.'

'Exactly. So please… trust me.'

Amy deliberated, watching the desperation in my eyes as she weighed up her loyalty to her brother against her friendship with me.

'Oakfield Manor Clinic. It's in Peterborough.'

'Peterborough?'

'Exactly. I doubt that makes things any clearer. Have you ever even been to Peterborough?'

'No,' I admitted. 'But at least now I haven't got to wonder.'

I glanced at my phone. Amelia would be finishing school soon.

'Could you do me a favour?' I asked.

'Depends what it is.'

'I need to get a hire car.'

Amy raised an eyebrow and looked at me warningly.

'I've got no way of getting around, remember?' I pointed out. 'I want to be able to take Amelia out, give Lily lifts. I just want to try to find some sort of normality.'

She hesitated, clearly torn about what she should do. Seeing her indecision, I took pity on her.

'Actually,' I said, 'you're right. I don't need one, do I? Most things are within walking distance, and there are always buses if not. The exercise will do me good.'

'I'll take you to get a hire car if that's what you want.'

'No, honestly. No point putting temptation in my way, is there?'

Amy nodded and gave me a sad smile. 'We'll sort this out, I promise.'

I was desperate to believe that she was right, but I just didn't trust anyone else to find out why this was happening to me. If I wanted to get to the truth, I was going to have to do it myself.

TWENTY-FOUR

Amy dropped me off at Nancy's house; I couldn't wait to see my daughters and try to salvage what little respect they might have left for me. Damien wasn't there, but Amelia was already back from school, and I was faced with the heartbreaking task of having to explain my absence from her life for the past five days. Nancy decided not to allow us any privacy, instead lurking at the doorway as she watched me squirm and apologise, no doubt getting some warped satisfaction from witnessing me fail as a mother and a human being. Had we been in our own home I could have asked her to leave, but within her domain, I was bound to accept her stifling presence, as I had been expected to for so many years.

Amelia was doing a jigsaw puzzle on the living room floor.

'Daddy told me where you've been,' she said.

I wondered exactly what Daddy had told her, and how much had been added to the story courtesy of Granny.

'You know I haven't done anything wrong, don't you, sweetheart?'

Amelia nodded, and I was grateful for the lack of hesitancy. If my own children didn't believe in me, I might have given up trying to prove my innocence.

'Adults get things wrong sometimes. Even the police. They think I hurt someone, but they've made a mistake. It wasn't me.'

'Who was it?' She was bending a jigsaw piece, pressing it back until the cardboard threatened to snap. I put a hand on hers to stop her.

'I don't know. And the police don't know yet either, but once they find the person, they'll leave us alone and everything will go back to normal.'

'It isn't fair,' she said quietly, and the words broke my heart into pieces. I wrapped my arms around her and pulled her close to my chest, resting my cheek against her hair as I smoothed her bare arm. 'I know. None of it is fair. But sometimes in life bad things happen, and when they do, you've got to be strong, okay? You've got to keep telling yourself that one day things will be better. And they will, I promise.'

I heard the words I had spoken to Amy, that she shouldn't be making promises she might not be able to keep. I was doing the same, and yet it felt like the kindest thing in the circumstances.

I turned and looked at Nancy, who was still standing in the doorway. 'Shall I ask Granny if she'll make you one of her special hot chocolates?'

Amelia smiled and nodded. Nancy smiled back at her, but the look she gave me couldn't have been in starker contrast, laced with a contempt she was making no attempt to conceal. As much as I wanted to think I was being unreasonable and that all Nancy really wanted was to see me, Damien and the girls reunited as a family, I just couldn't bring myself to believe that was the case. She was enjoying having Damien and Amelia with her, and had no doubt begun to plan a future in which her son and granddaughter – her only grandchild, as she so often managed to say without breathing a word – lived with her on a permanent basis. Amelia's shoes were lined up by the back door; her coat and school bag were hanging from one of the hooks in the hallway. Damien's laptop was sitting on the dining room table, and in the far corner, next to the sofa, his phone charger was plugged into the wall. All these small, inconsequential things added up to a life; a life that had once been mine but now existed in this other woman's home. I didn't want to feel the burning resentment that flamed inside me, but it was spreading with increasing pace, suffocating me with its heat.

I asked Amelia to finish her jigsaw so I could see what it looked like completed, then Nancy and I went into the kitchen. The fact that my daughter hadn't hugged me back when I had held her – had made no physical contact other than that I had forced upon her – smarted like a slap.

'Is she okay?' I asked, my thoughts coming to life. 'She doesn't seem herself at all.'

'You've been in police custody for five nights,' Nancy said snidely, as though I needed reminding of the ordeal I had endured.

'Yes,' I replied through clenched teeth. 'Unjustly. And when the truth comes out, everyone will realise what a massive mistake all this has been.'

She eyed me with a silent scepticism, her look managing to scorch my skin with its searing heat. 'Really? And what truth would that be, Jenna?'

I hated her. In that moment, I felt more venom towards Nancy than I had felt towards anyone, though my life had delivered a conveyor belt of candidates worthy of my contempt. I didn't want to feel the level of animosity that consumed me – I was too tired to be filled with such overwhelming bitterness – yet I needed to feel anger, to feel something, and it was unfortunate that Nancy was the recipient of my hostility. I knew we were not too dissimilar and that she, as I had always done, was just trying to protect her family, to keep the people she loved sheltered from things that might cause them harm, yet still the overriding wave of resentment was enough to smother any rational thought. I wasn't the thing that might cause them harm, and this was my family, not hers.

'I haven't done anything wrong, Nancy.'

'Who are you, Jenna?'

The question threw me, powerful and unexpected enough to nearly knock me from my feet.

'You know who I am. I'm just a mother trying to do her best – you get that, don't you? I haven't asked for any of this. I was in the wrong place at the wrong time and now I'm suffering the consequences.'

She studied me as I spoke, impassive. 'That's all it is? That simple?' She lowered her voice to a whisper. 'I don't think anyone knows who you are, Jenna, not really. Not even Damien.'

TWENTY-FIVE

Despite her vitriol towards me, Nancy was gracious enough to let me read with Amelia upstairs before she went to bed, without lingering at the doorway like some harbinger of doom. Once Amelia was asleep, I left and walked home. On the way, I tried Lily's mobile again, but it went straight to voicemail. Damien hadn't got back to me either. I wondered where he was that evening, who he was with, and tried not to let my jealousy distract me from the things I needed to do.

Back at home, I turned on the laptop and loaded the CCTV footage from the coffee shop. It had been paused in the spot where I had watched it last, and I let it run, keeping an eye on the screen as I tried Lily's phone yet again, exasperated when I was greeted once more by the voice of the answerphone. I hung up without leaving a message and called Maisie's mother, who answered after a few rings.

'Louise,' I said, 'it's Jenna.'

'Oh. Right… okay.'

She had no idea what to say to me, and why should she? What exactly did you say to someone who'd just been released from police custody having been charged with wounding with intent?

'Look,' I said, equally unsure how the conversation should go. 'Thanks for having Lily to stay. I don't know how much you know, but things have been complicated here and… well, thank you. Is she with you now? Her phone's off.'

'She isn't here. She didn't come back after college – Maisie said she waited for her at the bus stop, but she never showed up and her phone went straight to voicemail.'

'And you didn't think to call me?'

'I didn't know you were out,' she retorted, mirroring my tone, and her words filled me with instant shame. 'I tried Damien, but his phone's off as well.'

I bit my bottom lip and swallowed down my frustration with my husband, wondering again where the hell he was.

'I'm sorry. I shouldn't have snapped at you like that. I'm just worried about her. How has she seemed to you?'

'Quiet. She hasn't really said much. She and Maisie have been upstairs most of the time they've been here – I'm just the chef and the maid.'

'I know that feeling.'

'Let me know when you hear from her, okay?'

Louise ended the call and I wondered whether I should phone the police. They were unlikely to do anything; Lily wasn't missing – she had been at college that afternoon – and with everything that was going on in her life, no one would consider it suspicious her disappearing for a few hours to get a bit of time to herself.

I was working my way through the contact numbers I had for her friends' parents when I heard the front door slam. I hurried out into the hallway to find Damien already halfway up the stairs. I followed him up to Amelia's room, where he began opening and closing drawers, looking for something.

'What are you doing?'

'They let you out then?'

'It would appear so. I thought you might have visited again.'

'I've been a bit busy, you know, trying to keep what's left of our family together.'

Except I knew that wasn't what he'd been doing at all. From the slur in his voice, it was obvious how he'd spent most of the past five days, letting his mother care for Amelia while Lily lived with people who were little more than strangers to us.

'What are you looking for?'

'Amelia's medical record book. She needs it for school tomorrow, apparently – they're having a vaccine or something.'

'It's not in here. It's in our room.'

Damien followed me into our bedroom, and I opened the wardrobe, reaching up to the top shelf for one of the shoeboxes lined up there. I opened it, found the book and handed it to him.

'Where have you been this evening?' I asked.

He narrowed his eyes. 'Why?'

He wasn't the same person who had sat in that interview room at the police station with me at the weekend. Something in him had changed, and I knew it wasn't just the effects of the alcohol. For a moment, I saw in him someone else, someone I tried daily to push to the back of my mind.

'I just thought the girls might have been your priority, that's all. Rather than the pub.'

He reached into the back pocket of his jeans, his eyes not leaving mine as he thrust a folded piece of paper in front of me.

'What does it say?' I asked, not wanting to take it from him.

'"Your marriage is a lie."'

He threw it on the bed between us, but I didn't need to see it to feel its repercussions.

'Do you believe that?'

'What?'

'That our marriage is a lie,' I said. 'Is there someone else?'

Once I'd spoken the words, it felt as though a valve had been released, the pressure draining from me, making me instantly lighter. I was fearful of the answer, but I needed to know the truth. I was facing a trial, a possible custodial sentence; I couldn't afford to waste any of my precious freedom on a man who would rather be elsewhere.

'What?'

His face contorted, his expression one I hated. It had made an appearance only a few times, during our worst arguments, and there was something obnoxious about it, something that made me want to walk away from any further discussion.

'You and Laura. Is there something going on between the two of you?'

He sighed and closed his eyes, leaning against the door frame as though propping himself up. When he opened his eyes with a shake of his head, he looked at me as though I was stupid.

'Me and Laura?'

'Ffion told me she saw you together.'

He studied my face. He knew I was lying. He and Laura had been in the coffee shop together for only a minute or two; why would Ffion bother to tell me something so inconsequential? I wasn't even sure that Ffion knew Laura, or was aware that she was my friend. I couldn't tell Damien that I had seen them together without admitting that I had been scouring the CCTV footage from the shop, and doing that meant an indirect confession that I was suspicious of everyone; even, it seemed, my own husband. I didn't know who I could trust, and the feeling was more isolating than being alone.

I replayed the footage like a silent film reel in my head. What had I seen, really? Damien going into the coffee shop. Laura arriving minutes later. The two of them leaving together. That was it. Yet I knew they had been at the house together that same day, unless Lily had been lying to me. I wanted someone else to confirm that I wasn't being paranoid, but the only other person I would have trusted with my neurotic thoughts was Amy, and where this was concerned I didn't want her to know where my mind had taken me. There was nothing going on, I told myself. I was being ridiculous.

Damien hadn't said anything, and I could feel the silence between us starting to feel stagnant.

'You're being serious, aren't you?' he said eventually.

'You haven't answered the question.'

'There's nothing to answer.'

'I know you were at the coffee shop together,' I said, letting my suspicions spill from me. 'And I know you were both here the same day – the day the accusation against me was made. I couldn't get hold of you, could I? Where were you, Damien? Were you with her?'

He held my gaze, defiant. 'Yes, I was with her.'

I tried not to let the reaction that pulsed in my chest show on my face, though I knew it must have been visible. I sat down on the edge of the bed, defeated.

'What's the date, Jenna?'

'What?' I didn't know what the date was; I was only just aware that it was a Tuesday. Being kept at the station for five days had disorientated me; my only concept of time had been waiting for the arrival of a familiar face, someone who might help me out of that place.

'It's the twenty-second. October,' he added, in case I needed a reminder of what month it was.

'And?' I was unable to hold back my frustration. The more he talked, the more slurred his voice became, and his eyes were bleary, ringed with red circles from late nights and insufficient sleep. I knew it was my fault, all of it, but I needed him to handle this better, if only for the sake of the girls.

He shook his head and laughed; a sharp snap of a sound that was gone as soon as it appeared.

'You forgot all about it, didn't you?'

And then realisation crashed down on me, and my body slumped forward, elbows resting on my knees. 'I'm sorry, Damien. I really am. With everything that's been going on…'

The nineteenth of October was our wedding anniversary. We had been married ten years. It occurred to me then that while Damien had been sitting with me in that interview room on Saturday, he had been waiting for me to acknowledge the occasion in some way, if only with the mere mention of it.

'I was organising a surprise party for you, for the weekend. I didn't tell the girls – I thought it'd be a nice surprise for them too. Laura's been helping me. It would have been on Saturday night, but you were otherwise engaged.'

His words cut through me as I realised how much I had let slip from me. I hadn't given our anniversary a single thought, not when there were so many other things keeping my mind occupied. The truth was, I had been so eaten up with concern about Lily's secret relationship and Damien's increasingly distant behaviour that I had forgotten about it even before the night of the attack on Charlotte Copeland.

'I'm sorry,' I said again. 'I suspected there was something going on and I just put two and two together.'

'You really thought I was capable of that? An affair with one of your friends?'

'You have been acting differently, though, Damien. And I don't just mean since the night at the park. I mean before then – things haven't been right between us for ages.'

His jaw had tightened at my attempt to pass the buck. 'Yeah, my mind has been somewhere else for a while,' he said bitterly. 'I kept getting these strange notes, you see, things like "How well do you know your wife?" Yet I'm the one under suspicion.'

I stood up. 'You should have told me about them sooner, then we could have sorted it all out.'

'And you'd have told me about this mystery bloke of Lily's, would you? If that's what these notes are about, you could have just spoken to me when you found out about him and saved us all the secrecy.'

'What do you mean, "if"?'

'You tell me, Jenna.'

Beneath my clothes, I could feel the heat of my skin. My hair was sticking to the back of my neck, slick with a sheen of sweat.

'What were you doing in Lily's room?'

'What?' His single-word response was laced with indignation.

'When you found that bracelet. You said it was in one of her drawers. I asked you at the time what you'd been doing in her room, but you never answered.'

'Because I wasn't ready to mention the notes,' he snapped. The tips of his ears had reddened. Damien rarely got angry, but when he did, this was one of the signs.

'You thought Lily was responsible for sending them?' I asked, hearing my voice waver on the question.

'I didn't know what to think, did I? But she was being secretive about something. I know why now.'

He turned and headed back downstairs, and I hurried after him, panicked that he might see the footage on my laptop. As he put on his shoes by the front door, I made no attempt to stop him from leaving the house. As on so many other occasions, he was right and I was wrong. I didn't blame him for suspecting Lily of some involvement, not when the same idea had flitted through my own brain. When had we both grown so suspicious, and how had I become so consumed with negativity that I had forgotten our wedding anniversary? Despite all the destruction descending upon our lives, I should have clung to the good we still had. Instead, I had begun to believe Damien an unfaithful husband – a good father still, but a man whose loyalties had been swayed by another – when all that time I was the neglectful spouse.

I went to the kitchen, resisting the urge to open one of the bottles of wine that had been stored in the cupboard beneath the stairs since the previous Christmas. I had never been one to turn to drink when times were tough; I preferred to keep a clear head so that I could maintain some control, or the appearance of it at least. The footage was still playing on the laptop on the kitchen table. I had no idea whether anything had been captured in my absence, though I doubted it; when I checked the time on the tape, it was past closing time.

I let it run for a while, distracted by my thoughts of Damien and everything he had been trying to do for me. If he didn't hate me already, he certainly would now. Pulling myself from my self-pity, I pressed a button and watched as the footage sped forward, the empty, lifeless scene in front of me unchanging with the passing of those late-night hours. I was ready to give up when something stopped me dead. My fingers lingered over the keyboard, my body frozen at the sight of what was playing out on the screen in front of me, the images captured in the grainy sepia of the CCTV.

I watched as Lily looked up and down the street before putting the key in the lock of the shop door and disappearing from view, presumably tapping in the code to deactivate the security alarm. I'd had no idea she knew it, though she could easily have watched me when we'd been there together. It didn't seem to matter. By then, I was watching something else, and my thoughts were no longer with Lily but with the figure of the man who followed her into the shop.

TWENTY-SIX

'Move in with me.'

Damien was lying in his hospital bed, propped against the mountain of flimsy pillows that I had arranged behind his head. Lily was sitting in an oversized armchair at my side, her attention captured by the pages of a book we had borrowed from the children's ward; she had collected quite a pile of toys and books during the previous weeks, and I had marvelled at just how calm she had been, taking our new routine of weekly train trips and hospital visits in her stride. She often talked about Damien when he wasn't around, though as she wasn't yet quite able to say his name, for the time being he was 'Damon'. There was no denying the effect he already appeared to have had on her: she was speaking more and interacting with other people with a greater confidence; she seemed happier than she had ever been. It seemed she needed a father, and though we had only known each for four months, I had seen enough to understand that Damien was a good man.

'What?'

'What do you reckon? Jim's hardly ever at the flat – he hasn't said anything yet, but I'm guessing he'll probably move in with his girlfriend soon; he's over at hers all the time anyway, and there's no point in them paying rent on two places. I know it's not the biggest house, but the garden's all right, and there's a school just down the road; we could get Lily's name down, and—'

He stopped abruptly, his face changing as he studied mine. 'I'm sorry. I'm not trying to take over; I would never do that. I got carried away. Sorry. Forget I said it. I don't want to spoil things.'

'What's that? A horse?'

I looked down at Lily, who was pointing at something in the book on her lap. 'It's a zebra. A bit like a horse, but stripy.'

'I'm sorry,' Damien said when I looked back at him.

'You don't need to keep apologising. It's a lovely thought, but...'

'But?'

We were interrupted by one of the nurses, who came over to check the notes at the end of Damien's bed. 'The doctor shouldn't be long,' she told him. 'He's been held up on another ward.'

'No rush. I'm not going to be running off anywhere just yet.'

She smiled at his humour, and I wondered how he could remain so cheerful in the aftermath of what had happened. The Ironman event he had taken part in on the day after we first met would be his last, though at the time he could never have predicted the turn his life would take within a matter of months. His career was likely to be over. I ran my fingers along my temple, tracing the scar there. Our worlds were opposites, mine and Damien's, and yet in some ways they had been brought together by our shared experience of disaster.

Even so, I couldn't share my own experience, not all of it.

He waited until the nurse had left before saying, 'It's a lovely thought, but...?'

'I don't exactly have a lot to offer, do I? I've got no qualifications, no savings. I'd have to find a job, but then there'd be childcare to pay for... I wouldn't make enough to cover everything.'

'You'll get a job easily,' Damien said, with his usual enviable optimism. 'Lily will be in school for part of the day and I can look after her the rest.'

'You need time to recover. You can't commit to looking after a child.'

'Yeah,' he said, with a nod towards Lily. 'Look at her... she's a nightmare, isn't she?'

I smiled. Lily was a good girl, but she was my child and my responsibility. For years I had been her sole provider, and I wasn't ready to relinquish that role. Though I had wanted a third person in our lives, I didn't know how to let him in. A part of me was scared at the thought that everything would change, though I knew that Lily's life – my life – was never going to get any better unless that happened, and I feared losing a chance at happiness that might not offer itself again.

'What if Jim isn't going anywhere?'

'I'll kick him out. You smell a lot nicer – it's a no-brainer. Plus, it turns out I'm not in love with Jim. Who'd have thought it?'

The room fell so silent, I almost wished Lily would burst into an uncharacteristic tantrum just to offer a distraction. No one had told me they loved me for as long as I could remember; no one, at least, who had meant it. And I believed that Damien did. I had heard enough lies and seen enough badness to recognise the truth and know where there was good.

'I love you and I want to look after you – both of you. You've been looking after me, haven't you? Let me do the same. Unless you've decided you love Llangovney and can't be parted from the smell of cow shit, which I'd completely understand.' He slapped a hand over his mouth and glanced at Lily, who was still looking at the book, now engrossed in a page of jungle animals she was naming softly to herself one by one.

'Cow shit,' she said, without looking up, and I poked Damien's arm, trying not to laugh at the innocent repetition.

'Damien said a naughty word,' I told her. 'Don't say it again, okay?'

'Okay.'

'That'll be a great way to start school, won't it? Going in and repeating that on the first day.'

Damien's eyes met mine and the cautious start of a smile played upon his lips. 'Is that a yes, then?'

I nodded, still too unsure of myself to say the word.

'Lily,' he said, and she looked up from the book. 'See that drawer there?' He pointed to the bedside table, nodding encouragingly as she reached for the handle. 'That's the one. Can you pass me that pair of socks?'

She handed him a rolled-up pair of blue cotton socks, which he opened out on the blanket. Shoving his hand into one of them, he produced a ten-pound note and held it up with a flourish. 'Could you take your mum to the shop and get some chocolate and some drinks, please? This deserves a celebration.'

'You keep your money in your socks?'

'Would you have thought to look there?'

Lily's face had lit up as soon as chocolate was mentioned, and she was already at the end of the bed, clutching the note in her fist. I followed her out into the corridor with a smile on my face. I was blissfully happy, yet at the same time filled with trepidation about the new chapter in our lives that was about to begin.

Within a month, the three of us were living in Damien's rented house. Lily had started at the nursery attached to the school just down the road and had settled surprisingly quickly. Everything was going well, though I had been greeted with a frosty reception by Damien's mother.

It was a Sunday and we were at her house for dinner. As the four of us sat at the table together, I'd watched Nancy silently assessing Lily's use of her knife and fork, her lip curling when Lily chewed with her mouth open. The table had been cleared, the dishes washed and put away, and Lily was playing on the rug near the television when I'd gone to use the bathroom.

'She should be seeing someone about that child's speech delay.' Nancy's voice carried up the stairs.

'She's fine, Mum. She's a quiet kid, that's all. Doesn't mean there's anything wrong.'

'Your speech was better at two than hers is at four.'

'Well, wasn't Master Damien a clever little bean.'

I paused halfway up, listening to the conversation behind the closed living room door. I couldn't see Nancy's face, but I could guess her reaction to Damien's sarcasm, and I had to suppress a smile.

'She's been through a lot, Mum. Who knows what's going on in that little head of hers?'

'Through what? She was only a baby when her father died, wasn't she? She won't even remember it.'

I heard Damien sigh. 'I thought you of all people would have been a bit more understanding.'

'You were nineteen when your father died – it's completely different. And anyway, this isn't about me. Just be careful, please, that's all I'm saying.'

'Careful of what?'

'Careful that you're not a rebound. She's lost a partner, she's a single mother… Make sure you're not being used.'

'She's hard-working and she's honest. You're not really giving her a chance here, Mum.'

'You barely know the girl,' Nancy said, her voice lowered to a hiss. 'She's not exactly baggage-free, is she, and now she's living in your home. Don't you think it's all a bit rushed?'

There was silence for a moment, and I wished I could see whatever look was on Damien's face at that moment. Was he hesitant because he was tired of her judgement, or did he fear deep down that she was right?

'You don't know the first thing about her, that's all I'm saying.'

I'd heard enough, so I trod gently up a few steps before hurrying back down, letting my presence on the staircase be known. As expected, the conversation came to an abrupt stop. Lily's attention had been stolen from her toys by the cartoon playing on the television.

'We were just saying how pretty she is, weren't we, Damien?' Nancy gestured to Lily, offering her a moment of attention that had been withheld until then. 'That lovely thick hair. Gorgeous.'

I didn't want to hate her – I didn't know her well enough to harbour feelings of such intensity – but there was one thing I was already certain of. Nancy would be watching me like a hawk, just waiting for me to trip up, and when I did, it was unlikely she would offer me any help in getting back on my feet.

TWENTY-SEVEN

I tried Lily's phone again, and again there was no answer. I had put my coat on and was by the stairs looking for my house keys, ready to go out searching for her, when she burst through the front door. I didn't have time to hide the tears I'd shed so freely ten minutes before; the dark clouds of the last couple of weeks had opened over me, drowning me in their downpour. We were a mirror of each other in that moment, her wet face and reddened eyes a reflection of my own. I thought she might say something, but she didn't; instead, realising the path to her bedroom was blocked, she hurried down the hallway and disappeared into the back room, slamming the door behind her.

The back room was a small corner of the house furnished with a sofa, a television and a disproportionate number of blankets and cushions. The people who had lived in the house before us had used it as an office, but with no real need for one, we had decided to get a second TV in the hope of avoiding the common argument of what to watch. As it happened, it tended to get used most when someone was in a bad mood – when Amelia had taken something from Lily's bedroom without asking first and Lily refused to be in the same room as her for the remainder of the day; or when Damien and I had disagreed over something and had used conflicting viewing preferences as an excuse to keep the argument from the girls. The conversations that took place within the room's four walls tended to consist of reprimands and apologies, and I regretted having a space in the house that had become so associated with tension and discord.

I knocked tentatively on the door and waited for Lily to tell me to go away. When she said nothing, I opened it slightly. She was curled up at the end of the sofa, her long dark hair falling in front of her face, concealing her from sight.

'What's happened, love?'

'Other than the fucking obvious?' She spoke through tears, snotty and snivelling. Anger radiated from her, but then she did something I wasn't expecting.

'I've missed you so much.'

She flung herself against me, her arms wrapping around my waist in the way she had held on to me when she'd been a little girl.

'Oh sweetheart. I am so, so sorry.'

As she sobbed against me, I was taken back to those days in the flat when it was just the two of us, when she would cling to me as though I was the only other person in the world. But then I *had* been the only person in her small and fragile world. No one should have been inflicting this suffering on her now, least of all me.

'Are they going to send you to prison?'

She sounded like a small child, her words so like Amelia's, and it struck me then just how vulnerable she was. Despite the attitude she often tormented me with, she was still just a little girl, and it made that man paused in the image on the laptop screen all the more hateful.

'Honestly? I don't know. There are things that have come up that are going to help me, though – things Amy's brother has found out about this woman.'

Lily looked up and wiped the back of her hand across her eyes. It smeared her make-up, leaving a black smudge at her temple. 'What things?'

'I can't go into it, love, I'm sorry. It's enough to prove she's a liar, though.'

Lily took a deep breath as she tried to calm her breathing. It seemed she had regained some of her lost composure, but a moment later she was crying again, her head slumped against my arm as she sobbed like a little girl. This wasn't just about me, I thought.

'Where have you been this evening?' I asked gently.

Her tears came hard and louder, and I felt her body shudder against my own. Her breath caught in ragged gasps as she tried to form an answer. 'He's not who he said he was, Mum.'

I didn't need to ask her who she meant. I wanted to shake her for lying to me for so long, while at the same time wanting to hold her and tell her that everything was going to be okay, regardless of my uncertainty about such a promise.

'You have to tell me who he is, Lily. Everything you think you know about him – I need to hear it all.'

I couldn't tell her that I'd seen them together on the CCTV from the shop – not yet. If I did, she would hate me for it; she would consider that I had spied on her, and she wouldn't thank me for it regardless of what this man had now done. Any chance of getting her to confide in me would be lost. I thought of him sitting in the coffee shop, sipping at a black coffee as he browsed the titles on the bookcase. I hadn't needed to see his face any more clearly to know that I recognised him. I was sure he had been there more than once, though he was just like any other customer passing through, coming and going. Yet he wasn't, was he? He had been there for a purpose, and I was beginning to think that purpose was me.

'Where did you meet him?

'In the canteen at college. I dropped a folder and he helped pick up the papers that fell out.'

I cringed at the cliché of it, imagining myself as I had been just a couple of years older than Lily was now. Her father had approached me in much the same way, striking up conversation when I had dropped a tray of cutlery in the café where I was working. Listening to Lily's words, it was as though history was repeating itself, and I wanted to scream at the thought of it and at all those things that might follow that I never wanted for her life.

'And then what happened?' I already knew how it went. Girl meets boy and the rest is history, though this was no boy and there was still time to put an end to whatever might come next.

'He asked me my name, said he'd seen me around the campus. He told me his name was Matthew Cartwright, that he was doing an art course. I liked him, Mum. I know it was stupid, that he's too old for me, but he was different to all the other boys.'

I tightened my hold around her and kissed the top of her head. She wasn't the first to be fooled by a handsome face, and she wouldn't be the last. 'You said he's not who he said he was. How did you find out?'

'I just… You know when you get a feeling something's not right? Maisie knows someone on the art course, and this girl had never heard of him. And sometimes he was just so weird, like his phone would go off when we were together, and he'd just become really quiet.'

When we were together. The words made me feel sick, and I wondered exactly what she meant by them.

'Lily, I know I've asked you before and I'm sorry to do it again, but I have to. Have you had sex with him?'

There was another surge of tears as she shook her head against my chest. 'No. I swear to you, Mum, we never did anything.'

She must have felt my body sag against hers as relief surged through me. For the first time, I finally believed her.

'I think he lied about his name. No one seems to know who he is. When we met, he told me he didn't have Facebook or Instagram or anything like that, and I liked that about him, it made him different, you know? He wasn't loud like some of the boys at college – he was thoughtful, more interesting to talk to. And he used to listen, you know, like really listen to me when I was speaking. But now I think it was all just lies.' She sat up and put her head in her hands.

I took a deep breath. 'When you went to the coffee shop with him that night, did you leave him alone at any point?'

I asked the question quietly, bracing myself for the storm I believed would blow up beside me. It didn't. Instead, Lily looked at me through her parted fingers, and when she pulled them away, I could see that her cheeks had already flared pink.

'I'm so sorry, Mum.'

'You don't need to be sorry,' I said, putting a hand on her knee. 'You just need to tell me everything. No more lies, okay? No more secrets.' I felt the irony of the words like a voice whispering in my ear, taunting me with my own hypocrisy.

'How do you know we went there?'

'CCTV. I was looking for something else.'

The realisation of what I hadn't yet suggested seemed to fall upon her with one swift blow, and she started crying again. 'This is all my fault, isn't it?' When she looked at me, my heart cracked for her. She had been naive, too trusting for her own good, but she understood it now, and I could recall only too well the shame and regret that went hand in hand with the feeling. 'Oh my God… That knife the police found at the shop… You think he might have put it there, don't you?'

I cringed beneath the weight of her words and all their implications. She had been exposed to more than I should ever have allowed, and yet how could I possibly have stopped it?

I squeezed her knee. 'Listen to me,' I said, urging her to look me in the face. 'This is not your fault. And I don't think anything yet – I can't think anything until I know the facts.'

They had been at the coffee shop together for twenty-two minutes. I had no way of knowing what might have happened in that time. I had only seen them enter the place and then leave, my imagination left to fill in the details of the time between.

'You took my spare keys, didn't you?'

She nodded. Her eyes were wet with tears and her face was still flushed with embarrassment.

'Why did you go there?'

'I don't know,' she said, still snivelling. 'He suggested it – he said it would give us somewhere quiet to be alone.'

A shiver snaked down my spine. All questions of how and why this man had planted that knife in the coffee shop had vanished, replaced with the sickening thought of what he might have done to my daughter. He had been there with her alone. He had taken a knife with him. I wanted to find him and make sure he never went anywhere near her again. I wanted to fold her into my body and keep her there, a baby bird sheltered from the world in the safety of her mother's wing. I wanted to cry for her, for the possibility of an innocence that might so easily have been stolen from her, though I knew I couldn't keep her protected forever.

'I need to know exactly what happened, Lily. Did you leave him alone at any point?'

She started sobbing again, her guilt making itself apparent in the force of her tears. 'I went to the toilet. I wasn't gone long, not even a couple of minutes. He couldn't have put that knife there, Mum… Why would he do that?'

I didn't know the answer to that question, but I was certain he was the person who had framed me. Yet I had no idea why, and I had no evidence other than the fact that he had been there.

'Tell me what else happened,' I said.

'We sat and chatted for a bit. We both took a drink from the fridge. He asked me a few questions about the shop, you know, just general stuff like how long you'd been running it. He asked if we got on.'

'We? As in you and me?'

She nodded. 'I didn't think anything of it at the time. It just seemed normal, like he was taking an interest in me. Now, though…

I don't know. I liked him, Mum. I thought he liked me. I knew he was too old for me, but he made me feel… important, I guess.'

Inside my chest, my heart sank. Had we really made her feel so insignificant, so neglected, that she had felt the need to seek the attention of this man? I had been so much like her once, young and impressionable, easily swayed by the false promises and lies of a man who turned out not to be what he had claimed, and yet my situation was entirely different to Lily's. My parents hadn't loved me, not in the way I loved her. I had been a trophy daughter, appreciated when doing well and shunned when I failed them. I had done everything I could to give Lily the kind of upbringing I had craved, and yet for all my efforts, it hadn't been enough.

'He kissed me.'

She spoke the words quietly, in little more than a whisper, yet the shame that accompanied them was loud. The worst of thoughts flitted through my head, accompanied by a series of images I didn't want to have to be exposed to.

'Did he force himself on you?'

Though she'd told me they hadn't had sex, and I'd believed her, there were plenty of other things she might have regretted.

She shook her head vehemently. 'No. I…' She ran her hands down her face, drying her tears with her palms. 'I can't talk to you about this, Mum, it's really weird.'

'I know it is, but there've been a lot of weird things going on recently and I wouldn't ask if it wasn't important. Please, Lily. You have to tell me everything.'

She covered her face with her hands again, not wanting me to see her as she spoke. It was the action of a child, a little girl playing hide-and-seek, believing that if she couldn't see me, I couldn't see her. 'I wanted things to go further. I tried to… you know. But he wouldn't. We'd never kissed before and he said he shouldn't have done it – that it was a mistake. He actually apologised. It was really weird. That was when I went to the toilet. I didn't really need to; I just felt so embarrassed, you know. We left not long after that.'

Her hands slid from her face and she exhaled nosily.

'When he turned me down, I thought… I thought he was being respectful, like trying to prove he wasn't just out for one thing. But he wasn't. I saw him with another woman, Mum. And she's older than me – a lot older. Maybe even older than you.' She tried to fight back tears, but the resistance was in vain. 'I thought he liked me.' She sobbed then, and I moved closer to her and put an arm around her again, squeezing her into me as she cried on my shoulder.

'This woman, sweetheart,' I said, my blood running cold at the thought that had taken hold of me and was refusing to let go. 'Did you get a good look at her? What did she look like?'

'Yeah, I got a good look at her. I couldn't stop staring at them. You know when you think something can't be real but it actually is? She was like, I don't know, your height. She was dressed nicely, but a bit gothic – she had this dark dress on that was sort of long, past her knees, and boots that came right up her legs.'

'Her face, Lily,' I prompted. 'Did you see her face?'

'She had pale skin, I remember that. Dark make-up on her eyes. Dark hair too, you know, not quite black, but dark. Long. And she had this weird scarf thing tied around her neck. She was pretty, I suppose, for her age, but I don't get what he sees in her, Mum. Why her and not me?'

I couldn't answer her. A chill had swept over me, racing along my arms and inching its way beneath my skin. Lily had just described Charlotte Copeland.

TWENTY-EIGHT

I persuaded Lily to go back to Maisie's house, making her promise she would text me hourly the following day to let me know everything was okay. I couldn't leave her alone at home – the prospect that the place might face a further attack of some kind was too big a risk to take. I hadn't told her my plans, only confiding in her that I needed to do something that night relating to my arrest. My suspicions had to be confirmed before I shared them with anyone else; Lily would be the last person I'd reveal the full picture to. My job was to protect her, as it had always been.

By the time we had finished talking, it was late, already dark, and we walked to Maisie's house together, where I spoke to her mum, giving a vague explanation about what had happened with the car. I offered her money to cover Lily's food, making her take it when she tried to refuse. I think she felt sorry for Lily, having a mother who'd been arrested. God only knows what she must have thought of me, but by that point I was past caring. So long as the girls and Damien were safe; that was all that mattered.

After leaving Lily, I headed to Nancy's house. It was bathed in darkness, apart from the light that escaped from the edges of the curtains at the front window. Amelia would be in bed, and as I stood outside, I pictured myself sneaking in through the back door and creeping up the stairs so that I could lie beside her beneath the duvet and hold her as she slept. I wondered just how much irreparable damage was being done to our relationship by my absences, and I mourned the life I'd led just weeks earlier; a life I realised I'd taken for granted.

I reached into my coat pocket and took out the spare set of car keys, pressing the lock and watching the lights of Damien's Ford Focus light up on the other side of the road. It was an old car, probably due for an upgrade, but Damien had never been materialistic and regarded it as little more than a means to an end. I doubted, though, that he was going to be happy to wake up the following morning to find it gone.

It took me over four hours to drive to Peterborough, with two stops along the way. During one of them, I ran an internet search for the contact details of Oakfield Manor Clinic before composing and sending an email. I hoped the fact that it would have been received at 1.30 in the morning would testify to my sense of desperation.

When I got to Peterborough, I used the satnav on my phone to find the clinic and its grounds. Unless there were additional buildings that I was unable to see from the road, the place was small, far less grand than the impression offered by its website, though the gardens looked large and well tended. It was almost 3 a.m. by now, but the clinic was well lit, and I was able to recognise some of what was shown online.

I sat at the roadside for a while, scanning through the website. Oakfield Manor offered rehabilitation for a range of addictions and conditions, ranging from eating disorders and depression to drug abuse and alcoholism. The facility looked as though it came with a hefty price tag. I had no clue about this woman's life; her job, if she had one, or whether she was wealthy or poor.

I realised I had got there far too early. I texted Damien so that he would see my message before he noticed the empty parking space outside, then drove to a quiet spot near a darkened industrial estate, where I locked the car doors, set the alarm on my phone to wake me in three hours' time, and put the seat back to try to get some sleep.

I woke before the alarm went off, my neck sore and my throat dry. Despite the two stops along the way, there were no drinks in the car, so to kill an extra hour I found the nearest McDonald's and sat in the car park drinking an ice-cold Coke that woke me up and gave me a much-needed sugar rush.

By 7 a.m., the supermarkets had opened. I bought myself some supplies for the way home, then killed more time until 9 a.m., which seemed a reasonable enough hour to call the clinic.

My proficiency at telling lies is something I'm not proud of, not then and not now. But experience has taught me that lies are often necessary, and as I spoke with the receptionist who took my call, it felt to me as though these particular ones were justified.

Two hours later, I was sitting in the sparse white waiting room, a glass table holding a vase of pink lilies and a small stack of magazines in front of me. I felt sick at the prospect of the trouble just being here could land me in if the police were to find out, but my fears for Lily's safety were far stronger than any concerns I might have had for myself. If Charlotte Copeland knew the man Lily had been seeing, there was no doubt in my mind that my daughter was potentially in danger. I needed to find out why she had been targeted, and I couldn't trust the police, not while they seemed so certain I was guilty. If keeping my daughter protected meant facing jail, it was a risk I was prepared to take.

I had been offered tea or coffee by the receptionist, but I refused, needing to maintain the appearance of someone who was desperate and at their wits' end. I was lucky that the manager was there, and had responded to my email by saying that if I was prepared to wait a while, she would be happy to talk to me. And so I waited, and at just past 11.30, she appeared in reception.

'Philippa?

I don't know where the name had come from, only that when I'd written the email, I hadn't wanted to use my own. I had sent it from an old account – one that had been registered in my maiden name but didn't feature it in the handle. I hoped that if the name

Jenna was noticed, whoever read the email would assume I was using a family member's account.

I stood and smiled tiredly, though this was one act at least that required no pretence. I was physically and mentally exhausted by the drive, the anxiety; the piecing together of things that were starting to take some sort of form, growing more insidious as their shape became clear.

'I'm Annette. Nice to meet you. Come on through.'

She shook my hand and I followed her through a door and into a hallway. We turned right into her office, which smelled of lavender, and she gestured to one of the chairs opposite hers at the desk.

'Thanks for seeing me at such short notice,' I said, putting my bag on the floor at my feet.

'It's no problem. So how can we help you? You said in your email that you're looking for somewhere for your sister?' Annette said.

'That's right,' I said, fighting back a cough. 'Sorry.' I cleared my throat. 'She's struggled for a while now, and to be honest, I don't think her GP has done enough. There's been a lot of talk, but nothing concrete has ever been put in place to help her.'

Annette placed her hands on the desk in front of her. 'What sort of things has she struggled with? You mentioned anxiety in your email.'

I nodded and cleared my throat again. 'She's had problems with her mental health for years, since we were teenagers. But recently, I don't know, things just seem to have got worse for her. She uses cocaine a lot, I know that. We've tried to help her, but nothing's worked so far. I think what you offer could be the best thing for her. She needs to be removed from any temptations.'

Annette was nodding, as though she had heard countless similar speeches recited within these four walls. The place was cold and clinical, and yet its internet reviews were glowing, hailing the staff as miracle workers capable of turning around the lives of people in the most hopeless situations. But some people didn't want to be saved from themselves, and I wondered to what extent Charlotte Copeland was one of those.

I spluttered again, tapping a hand to my chest as I tried to cough up the invented content of my lungs.

'Would you like some water?' Annette asked, looking concerned as she stood from her seat. I had glanced around the room as we entered, wondering if the office might have a water dispenser, but thankfully it didn't.

I nodded. 'If you don't mind. Sorry to be a pain.'

'I won't be a moment.'

As soon as she left the room, I got up from the chair and went behind the desk, where a large filing cabinet stood against the wall. I had no idea how long ago Charlotte Copeland had attended the clinic, or whether everything was already computerised by the time she'd stayed there, but the cabinet held something, and it felt to me as if the truth might be inches from my fingertips, if only I had time to reach it.

'What are you doing?'

I spun at the sound of a female voice, already knowing it wasn't the manager's. A middle-aged woman wearing a tabard and carrying a bucket was standing in the doorway, eyeing me with a mixture of shock and uncertainty, clearly unsure what she should do next.

'How long have you worked here?' I asked, unable to conceal the desperation in my voice.

'Long enough,' she said. She stepped into the office and put the bucket down beside the manager's desk before folding her arms across her chest. 'Now, are you going to tell me what you're looking for?'

'Please,' I said, pushing closed the top drawer of the filing cabinet. 'I'm not here to cause trouble, I promise. I need help. I'm in trouble and I think the woman causing it… well, I know she used to be a patient here. Charlotte Copeland. I just need to find out why she's doing this to me.'

I could hear myself rambling, the words coming quickly and incoherently, but I couldn't help myself. I had limited time before the manager returned to the office, and I'd already seen enough to know that she was a consummate professional; there was no chance of me getting any information about former patients from her. I stepped away from the filing cabinet just in time; as though aware that I was thinking of her, she appeared at the doorway, looking questioningly at first me and then her staff member.

'Everything okay?'

'Fine,' the cleaner replied. 'I'm sorry… the door was open. I didn't realise you were in a meeting.'

The manager gave her a tight smile as she left, and I could see her suspicion when she returned her focus to me. 'Your water,' she said, raising a plastic cup, her eyes still fixed on mine.

'Thank you.' I swallowed the drink down in one long mouthful before sitting back at the desk.

'Does your sister know you're here?'

I shook my head. 'I know she'll agree to it, though. I just need her to see sense. I thought if I saw the place first, I might be able to convince her more easily.'

'Then would you like to?' she asked. 'See the place?'

She reached across the desk and took the cup I had left there, throwing it into the bin by the doorway as we made our way back into the corridor. She proceeded to give me a tour, though it was half-hearted, and I could tell by her tone that she knew she wouldn't be seeing me again, nor the sister she may or may not have guessed I had invented. My anxiety was mounting by the minute. What if this woman was suspicious of me and contacted the police? I feared I had made a massive mistake in going there, acting on an impulse that had seemed like a final chance at finding the truth; risking my bail by exposing myself to something that had led me nowhere.

When the tour was finished, she took me back to reception and I thanked her, telling her I would be in touch once I'd spoken to my sister.

I was outside the building, heading back to the car, when I heard the cleaner's voice again.

'Charlotte Copeland, you said?'

I turned. She was standing close to the wall at the side of the building, her eyes fixed upon me. It took me a minute to realise that she was keeping herself out of view of the security cameras above the main entrance. She wanted to talk to me, but she didn't want to be seen. I fumbled in my bag, feigning a search, then headed back towards the building, keeping my eyes on the ground as though looking for something that had been dropped.

'You know her?' I said, when I was close enough to be heard.

'I can't talk here,' the woman said. 'My shift finishes in half an hour. I'll go to the café at Marks and Spencer's in town – you can meet me there if you want to.'

She turned and headed back through a side door. When I returned to the front of the building, I continued my pretence for the cameras, scouring the concrete slabs near the doorway before returning my attention to my bag and finding whatever it was I had been looking for.

Three quarters of an hour later, I was sitting in the café, waiting for the woman to arrive.

TWENTY-NINE

I had a sinking feeling in my stomach that she might change her mind, yet the fact that she had risked speaking to me outside the clinic suggested that whatever she wanted to tell me was serious enough for her to follow through on her promise. I saw her moments later, entering the café wearing a heavy blue raincoat and carrying a leather handbag. She paused for a moment to scan the room, then spotted me sitting at a table in the corner. I watched her go to the counter and order herself a drink before she came over.

'My name's Cheryl,' she said, putting her coffee on the table before slipping her raincoat from her shoulders. 'Please don't tell anyone I've met you, will you?'

I shook my head. I had no intention of getting her into trouble. I just wanted to learn more about the woman I was dealing with.

'Likewise, though,' I said, stirring sugar I would never usually have taken into my tea, 'you have to promise you won't mention seeing me. This is just between us, okay?'

She nodded and sipped her coffee. 'What's she done now, then?'

The question was enough to confirm my suspicions: whatever else Charlotte was and whatever trauma she had suffered, she was trouble.

'She's accused me of a serious assault against her. I can't be sure yet, but I think she's responsible for framing me.'

I noticed that while I was talking, Cheryl's expression didn't once change. It was as though she was almost expecting what I told her, or at the very least was unsurprised by it.

She put both hands around her coffee cup, warming herself with its heat. I guessed her to be in her early fifties, though she might have been older. She had a kind face, and I could only assume she was there because she wanted to help me. At that moment, I needed all the help I could get, yet I couldn't understand why she would risk her job to help a stranger she had never laid eyes on before.

'How do I know this is real?' she asked, looking at me sceptically. 'You could be someone from management for all I know, checking up on me.'

I took my phone from my pocket, unlocked it and searched online for one of the articles relating to the attack on Charlotte. When I'd last looked, there had been just over twenty comments left in the box below the article; now, I saw that there were almost a hundred.

'Read this.'

I passed Cheryl the phone and waited until she had read to the end. 'That's me,' I said when she looked up. 'I'm the woman who was arrested. I've been charged with wounding with intent. I didn't do it.'

Cheryl shook her head slowly as she handed the phone back. 'I'm not supposed to talk about the patients, but you should know that Charlotte is dangerous. I can't say much more than that, but she was asked to leave after an incident with another patient. The young woman was lucky that staff were nearby at the time, or things could have been much worse.' She looked around her as though checking no one was listening in. 'So she's saying you stabbed her?'

I nodded and returned the phone to my pocket.

Cheryl's eyes widened and she took another sip of coffee. 'I'm sorry. It seems anyone who gets on the wrong side of Charlotte ends up suffering the consequences.'

'But I don't know her. I'd never met her before that night.'

'You were there, then?'

'I tried to help her. I was walking home and I heard her calling for help. I waited until the ambulance and the police came, then the next day she told them that I was the person responsible.'

'Sounds about right. Charlotte always had a way of biting the hand that fed her.'

'This young woman you mentioned… How did she get on the wrong side of her?'

Cheryl shrugged. 'It involved a man, that's all I know. They called themselves friends, the two women, but friendships aren't really encouraged at the clinic. Sometimes they can be more damaging than anything else.'

'How long ago was this?'

Cheryl exhaled. 'Around 2009… 2010, maybe.' She pressed a hand to her face, feeling the flush of pinkened cheeks. 'I shouldn't be here,' she said, reaffirming her discomfort.

'So why are you?'

There was something more, something she wasn't telling me. I got the impression that her connection to Charlotte Copeland was more significant than she was letting on, running deeper than simply having been witness to the after-effects of the woman's seemingly vindictive nature.

'When you mentioned that name, I knew it meant trouble.' She shrugged, as if this explanation was the answer to everything.

'I promise you this won't go any further. You won't see me again after today. I just need to know as much as you're able to tell me – I need to know why she's doing this to me.' I drank some tea, wincing at the sugary sweetness it left on my tongue. 'Why was she admitted to the clinic?'

There was a pause. Around us, the noises of the café – the hum of conversation, the hiss of the coffee machine behind the counter, the crying of a tiny baby on the other side of the room – filled what might otherwise have been an awkward moment of silence between us.

'She'd tried to kill herself. Look, I'm no medical expert – I just clean up other people's messes, so what do I know? But I've seen enough to understand that Charlotte Copeland wasn't like any of the other patients I've come across since I've been working at the clinic, and I've been there nearly twenty-four years. There was something behind her eyes, you know. Something already dead. In my opinion, that makes her the worst kind of dangerous.'

Her words sent a chill through me. Why had Charlotte targeted me? Where would all this stop?

'Do you know what happened to her before she came to the clinic? Before the suicide attempt, I mean… There must have been something that prompted it?'

'I don't remember all the details, I'm sorry. I know bereavement was a big factor, and there was a history of mental illness in the family. I'm sorry, I wish I could help you more. I just think you need to be careful.' She was about to say something else, but instead she stopped herself and sipped her drink.

'Is Copeland her married name?'

Cheryl nodded. 'As far as I know. She was married briefly, I think, before the suicide attempt.'

'Do you know what her maiden name was?'

She shook her head. 'Sorry.' She had clammed up again, holding back something she was reluctant to share.

'Please, Cheryl, I'm desperate here. I don't want to make things difficult for you, but I need help and I'm running out of time. I think she's going to hurt my family. Someone set fire to my car while it was on my drive and my children were asleep in the house. I'm sure it was her. I don't know how much further she's prepared to go.'

Cheryl bit her bottom lip. 'I'm sorry, I really am.' She paused and sipped her drink, and I knew that what I'd told her about my children was making her reconsider. 'There's someone who knows more than I do, but I doubt she'll talk to you.'

'Please… tell me who she is.'

Cheryl took her phone from her bag and I watched as she opened her Facebook app. She typed a name into the search bar and a moment later handed me the phone. 'This is the woman she attacked. Well… she was just a girl then.'

'The one she fell out with over the bloke?'

Cheryl nodded. I looked at the woman in the photograph. She was around my own age – mid, maybe late thirties, a blonde bob and lips that looked as though they had been surgically enhanced. She was pouting at the camera, but there was something distant behind her eyes, something lost and younger than her years. I made a mental note of her name: Zoe Macmillan.

'But if Charlotte attacked her, why wasn't she arrested?'

'The clinic covered it up. They didn't want the negative publicity. Look, I can't be certain, but I think Zoe received a payout to keep her quiet. If the press had got hold of the fact that there'd been a stabbing among the patients, the place might have faced closure.'

'Charlotte stabbed her?'

'In the leg. She wasn't seriously injured, but that wasn't the point. The poor girl was a mess afterwards. She still is.' Cheryl took her phone back and returned it to her bag. 'Look, no one at the clinic knows this, but Zoe used to go out with my son. Years ago, when the pair of them were teenagers. I always had a soft spot for her, even after they'd split up. Bit of a lost soul, Zoe was. Needed a mother figure in her life, but her own was useless. Anyway, I wanted her to get the help, so I paid for her rehab. Nearly cleaned me out, but it seemed worth it at the time. No one knows about that either, so please keep it to yourself. The only reason I'm here is for Zoe. That cow Charlotte has got away with enough over the years. She deserves everything she's got coming to her.'

I reached into my pocket to take out my phone again, knowing that another question – perhaps the biggest of all – remained unanswered. I felt certain that Charlotte was responsible for the notes that had been sent to Damien, though I was pretty sure it would have been impossible for her to deliver all four of them. It meant someone else had been running errands for her, and my heart was sinking under a weight of dread at the thought that I already knew who that person was.

I unlocked my mobile – I had two missed calls from Sean and three from Damien – and went to my photo gallery, searching for the still I had taken from the CCTV footage. Though the image was grainy, I could see what might have drawn Lily to him, imagining myself as I was at her age. He looked younger than I suspected he was – passable as someone in his late twenties – yet there was something about his eyes that spoke of a secret worldliness, one that might only be noticeable to someone else who had plenty of experience of life. The truth would be easily kept hidden from a girl like Lily. She had seen what she had wanted to see, and she had welcomed his attention in the way I felt certain Charlotte had planned it.

Something inconceivable was starting to make itself apparent, and I cursed myself for not having seen it sooner. 'Do you know him?' I asked, holding the phone in front of Cheryl.

She didn't need long to study the photo; a mere glance was enough to confirm that she recognised him. 'Jacob,' she said with a shake of her head. 'He's not still latched on to her, is he?'

THIRTY

As I headed back to the car, I listened to the answerphone message Sean had left.

'Jenna, can you phone me when you get this.'

Then I listened to Damien's.

'Is this some sort of joke? What the hell were you thinking taking the car like that? Call me.'

I called Sean's number, but it rang through to his voicemail, so I tried Amy, hoping that if something had happened, he might have let her know. I was still reeling from what Cheryl had told me. Charlotte wasn't just manipulative; she was dangerous. A new possibility was beginning to take shape inside my brain, something I wanted to find evidence for before I let it take root and grow. Had Charlotte used Matthew to get to me through Lily? If so, why?

'Have you spoken to Sean?' I asked when Amy answered. 'Everything okay?'

'He's been trying to get hold of you. Charlotte Copeland has withdrawn her statement.'

I didn't say anything. I couldn't speak. I didn't know whether to cry with relief or scream with frustration that the woman had put me through hell just to end it all like this, though any potential reaction was then halted by the thought that nobody had yet said it was over.

'I don't understand.'

'Apparently she told Sergeant Maitland that she made a mistake; that she can't remember what happened that evening.'

'Bullshit,' I said bitterly. 'She remembers exactly what happened.'

'I thought you'd be happier.' Amy sounded disappointed.

'Yay,' I said sarcastically. I pressed my fingertips to my eyelids and reminded myself that taking my anger out on Amy wasn't going to get me anywhere. None of this was her fault. 'I'm sorry. I'm tired and I'm just sick of all this. What happens now, do you know?'

I heard Amy sigh. 'The trial will still go ahead.'

I said nothing. It made sense that people who were suspected of crimes as violent as the attack on Charlotte didn't tend to walk free just because the person they had supposedly attacked claimed sudden memory loss. The thought that I should tell Sean what I had learned about Charlotte and her link to the man who had been bothering my daughter for the past couple of months had rooted itself at the forefront of my brain, and yet I couldn't allow myself to divulge the details – not until I knew more and had ascertained the facts for myself. If either Charlotte or Jacob was to find out that I knew about their time at the clinic, I might inadvertently put Lily at greater risk.

'It should help, though, once the police have established there was no coercion involved.'

'Coercion? What… they think I might have intimidated her into withdrawing her statement?'

Just as I had allowed myself to believe that finally something might be going my way, another blow hit me, knocking any sort of hope, no matter how flimsy, from my grasp yet again.

'It's standard procedure, apparently – they do it whenever this happens. Like I said, once they realise you're not involved, it'll work to your advantage.'

'And if Charlotte decides to lie about that as well? What if she tells them I am involved in some way?'

I couldn't tell Amy where I was or what I'd discovered, not when I was this close to uncovering the truth. The best thing I could do to help myself and Lily was to finish what I had started here, then find out what I could about Jacob Perry, the man who had been linked to Charlotte and Zoe while the three of them were patients at Oakfield Manor.

'If she was going to lie about that, she'd have done it by now.'

I put my head back against the head rest, trying not to think about the drive home.

'The man Charlotte accused of raping her. Do you know what his name is?'

'No.'

'Can you find out? Will Sean be able to find out?'

'Jenna,' Amy said, ignoring my questions. 'Where are you?'

'Cardiff,' I said, already prepped with the lie.

'Doing what?'

'I'm in the library. Just researching.'

'Researching what?' Amy sighed. 'What are you hoping to achieve? The fact that she's withdrawn her statement is bound to help your case now. Please just let Sean do his job.'

'What harm am I doing?' I asked, feigning ignorance. 'They can't charge me with reading, can they?'

I paused and exhaled loudly, running a hand through my hair as I checked my dishevelled appearance in the rear-view mirror. 'I'm sorry. I'm tired and I'm worried about my family. You get that, don't you?'

'Of course I do. But I'm worried about you, Jenna. You sound exhausted. Don't try to take this into your own hands, okay? Make sure you're eating properly, spend time with your family, just try to get things back to normal.'

I promised her I would do all those things, knowing that they would have to wait; that there was one other thing I had to do first. I contemplated calling Damien, but the coward in me couldn't face his anger and the lecture that was bound to accompany it, plus he would want to know where I was. Instead, I started the engine and tapped the address that Cheryl had given me into the maps app on my phone.

As I drove, I couldn't stop thinking about Charlotte Copeland and what she had done – what she was doing – to my life. She had withdrawn her statement because she knew the police were delving into her past. She had realised, just as I had, that it was only a matter of time before the truth came out.

Zoe's home was a flat in a tower block, and I realised when I pulled up on the opposite side of the street that I wouldn't get into the place unless she let me in. Dejection pulsed through me in waves as I suspected that what Cheryl had said was likely to prove correct and Zoe wouldn't want to see me.

I locked the car and went to the main doors of the building, finding the intercom button that linked to her flat. The first call went unanswered, but on the second, there was a click as she connected.

'Yeah.'

'Zoe?'

'Yeah. Who is it?'

'You don't know me,' I told her, 'but I was hoping you might be able to help me.'

'Probably not. This isn't a charity.'

'I don't want anything from you. Well… information, that's all. I want to talk to you about Charlotte Copeland.'

There was a second click, and it took me a moment to realise that Zoe had cut me off. I stepped back and looked up at the mass of windows that made up the building's facade, wondering whether she was looking out of one and could see me. Then I tried the intercom again.

I pressed it another three times, but she refused to answer. Did she think I was in some way connected to Charlotte, that the past was catching up with her, ready to repeat itself? Whatever her fears, it was clear she didn't want to return to the subject of what had happened at Oakfield Manor, and I had no choice but to respect her wishes. I had her address; I would write to her. Maybe in words, without my presence, I could make her understand just how much her help was needed.

Or perhaps her help wasn't needed, I thought as I walked back to the car, an air of defeat slowing my step. There was one person I had yet to talk to; one person, it seemed, who might know Charlotte better than anyone else. All I had to do was find him.

THIRTY-ONE

When I got home that evening, music was drifting down the stairs and into the hallway. It was coming from Lily's room. I couldn't believe she was there when she had promised me she would stay with Maisie. My thoughts had taken a nightmarish turn, darkened by the long, tedious drive and the new-found knowledge that had accompanied me on my journey home. As I climbed the staircase, two steps at a time, a series of awful images filtered through my brain, visions that both frightened and disturbed me, and by the time I opened the bedroom door, I was breathless with anxiety.

'Bloody hell, Mum,' Lily said, a hand flying to her chest. 'You nearly gave me a heart attack.'

She was sitting on her bed, her laptop at her side and an array of opened notebooks spread out on the duvet around her. She was wearing pyjamas – soft velour trousers and a T-shirt printed with the words *I woke up like this*, although I hoped for her sake that she hadn't; her eyes were red-rimmed with tears, and there was mascara smudged beneath them.

'What are you doing here?'

'College work,' she said, gesturing at the notebooks as though the answer was obvious.

'No, I mean why aren't you at Maisie's like we agreed?'

'Fuck Maisie,' she muttered beneath her breath.

I sat down on the bed, managing to find a corner that wasn't covered in stationery. 'What's happened?'

'I don't want to talk about it.'

I raised an eyebrow; we were long past the stage of not talking. 'She said a couple of things, that's all.'

'Things about…?'

Lily hesitated. 'About you.'

I nodded. I had known it was going to happen; it had only been a matter of time.

'Don't make me repeat them.'

I shook my head. Though I wanted to know what Maisie had said, a greater part of me knew that ignoring it was the better option, for Lily and for me. We both had enough to deal with.

'Shall I put the kettle on?'

She smiled, and I rubbed her arm, trying to offer a reassurance that I still didn't quite believe in myself.

When I went back downstairs, it struck me how unnaturally quiet the house was without Damien and Amelia there. The pain of missing them was like a piercing through my heart; everywhere I looked there were reminders of the life we had lived and were at risk of losing. Amelia's paint set was still open at the end of the kitchen table, her attempts at abstract art dried on the paper. One of Damien's many pairs of trainers were still at the back door, their soles caked in mud that had flaked onto the tiles.

There were dirty dishes stacked in cold murky water in the sink, and a pile of ironing far taller than the basket it was in waited near the door of the utility room. There were so many things I might have occupied myself with to try to keep my mind from what had happened that day, but I couldn't bring myself to care enough about getting any of them done. All I wanted to do was sleep; sleep, and have my family back, their noise and colours and love surrounding me with the warm reassurance that had been missing from my life for what seemed like an age.

I made tea and took it up to Lily. I put the mug on her bedside table and glanced at her laptop; she closed it hastily but wasn't quick enough for me to miss what she'd been looking at: a news report relating to the attack on Charlotte Copeland.

'Stop torturing yourself,' I told her.

'People shouldn't be allowed to comment.'

I sighed with the realisation of what Lily had been doing. MC2020… Matthew Cartwright? I doubted 'Matthew' himself would have stood up for me, and could therefore only assume that the person behind the words had been Lily.

'Thank you,' I said.

'For what?' she said, looking up from the screen.

'Defending me online. But I don't want you to fight my battles for me, okay?'

I took my own drink to my bedroom, trying not to let my eyes linger on the wardrobe, its half-open door offering a glimpse of the bare space that had once housed Damien's clothes. I put the mug on the bedside table and took my phone from my pocket to check the time, then I drew the curtains and lay on the bed, shutting my eyes and trying to clear my mind of thoughts.

My phone began to ring. Nancy's name flashed up at me from the screen. 'Jenna,' she said, not waiting for me to speak. 'Where are you?'

'At home. What's happened?'

The flurry of her words had sent me into a panic, and thoughts of Amelia crashed into my head. Something had happened: she was unwell; she had been hurt.

'It's Damien,' she said, her voice now lowered to a whisper. 'I don't know what to do, Jenna, this isn't like him at all. He's come home covered in blood.'

I entered Nancy's house through the back door, which I knew she would have left open for me. She was in the kitchen, standing near the kettle, two cups of tea that had been left to brew until the water had turned nearly black left forgotten on the worktop in front of her. Her grey bob was pinned back from her face, and when she turned to me, I noticed the swelling around her knuckles, brought on by the intermittent arthritis that had plagued her for years.

'Amelia in bed?' I asked.

She nodded. 'He's through there,' she said, gesturing to the closed door of the living room. 'He won't speak to me – I thought maybe you could get some sense out of him.'

I didn't know why she thought Damien would want to confide in me, not when he had chosen to move himself and our daughter out of our home, as far away from me as he could reasonably take himself. Whatever had happened, I assumed it was serious; Nancy would never usually ask for my help with anything, and would have struggled in silence rather than admit that I might be able to succeed where she had failed.

'Is he hurt?'

'Doesn't seem to be. Looks as though whoever he fought with came off worse.'

'Shall I take one of those through for him?'

Nancy went to the fridge to get milk. 'Would you like one?'

'No thanks.'

She pulled a tea bag from one of the mugs before adding milk and passing me the drink. I carried it into the living room, bracing myself for whatever might await me there.

Damien was sitting on the sofa with his back to me, his attention focused on the television even though the sound was muted. On the screen, a plastic surgeon was using a black pen to draw lines beneath a woman's eyes.

'Didn't think this would be your cup of tea,' I said, stepping forward and holding out the mug. 'No pun intended.'

The attempt at light-heartedness given everything that had happened was enough to make me cringe as soon as I'd spoken. Beside me, I was sure I saw Damien flinch. As he took the tea from me, I noticed the blood that stained his T-shirt in thick flecks. Nancy had exaggerated on the phone when she had said he'd come home covered, though it was more than enough to justify concern. The side of his face was scratched, as though someone had tried to fight him off in self-defence.

'What have you done?'

'If you'd put an end to it like you said you had, I wouldn't have needed to do it.'

I closed my eyes and tilted my face to the ceiling, feeling a swirl of headache behind my eyes. Lily's boyfriend – or not, as she had so frequently claimed. How the hell had Damien managed to find him?

'It was already over,' I said, trying to calm the anger that was growing inside me. What if Damien was arrested for assault? What would happen to Amelia then, with both parents facing trial for violent offences? I had no control over what was happening to me, but Damien had made a choice. For once, it was the wrong one.

'How did you find him?'

He still hadn't looked up at me, his eyes fixed to the muted television screen. 'I followed Lily. Wasn't that difficult really – I don't know what the hell you and Detective Amy were playing at.'

I could hear the slur in his voice; he had been drinking again. I felt my anger evaporate into something else, something more akin to confusion. Had he followed Lily before or after she had seen 'Matthew' with another woman? Surely she wasn't still chasing him after knowing he'd been lying to her, though nothing seemed impossible any more.

'Who the fuck is Maria?'

My heart stuttered in my chest, my breath failing me for a moment. 'What?'

'Maria. The little prick said he'd never touched Maria, something like that. Then he backtracked, saying Lily, he'd never touched

Lily, like he'd forgotten what her name was. Makes you wonder how many other girls he's been messing about with, the pervert.'

I felt bile rise in the back of my throat, tasting its acidic tang as it spread to my tongue. Trying to distract myself from my thoughts, my eyes found the framed photographs on the mantelpiece, lingering on the large school portrait of Amelia that had been taken at the end of the previous spring term, then on the smaller image of Lily just behind it, partially out of view. Nancy had never made a secret of the fact that she didn't consider Lily family in the way Amelia was, and I had been expected to accept her favouritism, as well as the difficult questions from the girls that inevitably followed her every careless comment and intentional rejection.

'Yes,' I said, trying to swallow back the sick feeling. 'It does, doesn't it.' I glanced around the room, hoping to see Damien's phone lying around somewhere. I was in luck; he had left it on the dining room table, on top of a pile of unopened post.

'I don't think they've slept together,' I told him, and this time I definitely saw him flinch.

'Like you'd know anything,' he replied bitterly. 'If you'd managed to do something before now, it wouldn't have come to this, would it?'

His attention was back on the TV as I moved to the table and slipped his phone into my jacket pocket. He didn't turn as I left the room and went upstairs to the bathroom.

With the door shut firmly behind me, I unlocked the phone. Once in, I went to maps and clicked on the search bar, waiting for a list of previously searched locations. The last was a local postcode, which I copied on to my own phone.

THIRTY-TWO

It took me less than an hour to find Jacob Perry. I had known what to expect of the street when I got there – I'd searched for it online – but what I hadn't been expecting was the calmness that had fallen over me when I eventually found out which number he lived at, any fears for my own safety replaced by a single-minded determination to uncover the truth. The third person I asked was able to tell me where he lived, though she hadn't recognised the name and I'd had to show her a photograph of Jacob before she realised who I was looking for. It seemed he had kept a low profile since moving there, and I knew exactly why that was. Without meaning to, Damien had told me far more than any of my previous attempts at investigation had revealed.

When Jacob opened the door and saw me there, he tried to close it quickly. I shoved a foot in the way and slammed my body against the wood, using everything I had to let him know I wasn't going anywhere. His face was bruised, his right eye blackened with a dark circle that might from a distance have made him look as though he was wearing a patch over it. I had never known Damien to be aggressive towards anyone, and the level of violence he was capable of came as a surprise. He had always treated Lily as though she was his own, but the extent of that love had perhaps sometimes escaped me.

I wondered whether Jacob had already been to the police, and whether he planned to press charges against Damien. While I'd been sitting in the car considering the possibility, another thought had occurred to me. Perhaps he wouldn't. Jacob Perry didn't like to press charges, or he hadn't against Charlotte, at least. Just what hold did this woman have over him?

He was wearing dark tracksuit bottoms and a T-shirt that looked as though it had never encountered an iron. He gave the impression that my knocking at the door had forced him to get out of bed, and as the thought crossed my mind, I felt grateful that I was sure of Lily's whereabouts. He knew who I was as soon as he laid eyes on me, and I recognised him too. I hadn't been mistaken about the fact that I had seen him at the coffee shop before, not just on the night that he had gone there with Lily. I could recall serving him maybe a month or two earlier, making small talk while he waited for his coffee; he had given me a smile as though he was just any other customer passing through the place on his way to somewhere else, and yet the whole time he must have been watching me, and I had been oblivious to it.

'I know you planted that knife in my shop,' I said, fixing my eyes on his face. 'I could have the police here within minutes.'

I was bluffing, of course – the police were as likely to take notice of me at this stage as they had at any other – but the threat seemed to work. He eased his hold on the door and I pulled my foot away. 'Is Charlotte here?'

He shook his head, though I didn't believe him. I knew that by entering that house I could be walking into a trap, but I had no other way of finding out the truth. Above all else, this was the only way of making sure he stayed away from my daughter. I thought about the knife I had slipped into my pocket before I left home, feeling reassured by its presence. If I was forced to, I believed I would use it without a second thought.

The house wasn't what I'd been expecting. It was neat and tidy, well furnished, and I wondered how long he had been staying there. I had no idea where he came from and could only guess that he had followed Charlotte here, blindly accepting her every word as it seemed he might always have done. He was younger than her, my guess was by about five years, and I was beginning to suspect a relationship based on something very different to what usually brought partners together.

My suspicions that he wasn't living there alone were confirmed when I followed him into the living room. There was a pair of glasses on the mantelpiece, red-framed, and by the door to the kitchen a pair of women's shoes. A bag was sitting on the floor near the end of the sofa, and his eyes followed mine as they lingered on it.

'I thought you said she wasn't here?'

'She isn't.'

'She lives here with you, though?'

Jacob said nothing. He shifted from one foot to the other anxiously, his manner twitchy, his eyes darting between me and the floor as though he was waiting for an opportunity to make a bid for escape.

'Does she know you've been messing with a seventeen-year-old girl?' I gestured to the bruising around his right eye. 'I suppose she does now, anyway.'

I was skirting around the truth of what I already knew, wanting him to offer it to me first. Of course Charlotte knew what he'd been doing. She was the one who'd put him up to it.

'It's not like that.'

'What's not like that?'

I sat down on the sofa, feeling an unexpected confidence. Jacob was like a nervous little boy who'd been summoned to the head teacher's office about a playground scrap; any fears I'd had about being under threat in the presence of this man had gone. I wondered just how easy it had been for a woman like Charlotte to manipulate him.

'Charlotte… I mean, Lily… None of it. It's not like that.'

'Not. Like. What?'

He shook his head with frustration, then sat in the chair opposite me. He squeezed his hands together, still twitchy, and I wondered just how deep his problems ran. Was he under the influence of some sort of drug? I couldn't bring myself to care too much; all I wanted was for him and Charlotte to stay as far away from my family as I could get them.

'I never touched her. I told your husband that.'

'And I should just believe you?'

'You can believe what you want. It's the truth.'

'So if it's not "like that", then what were you doing hanging around a teenage girl? You gave her that bracelet, didn't you? What do you expect us to think?'

He was still twisting his hands in his lap, his foot now tapping to the beat of some imaginary sound. What had Lily seen in this man beyond the first glance? I had thought her too smart to fall for a good-looking face, though why I'd assumed that, I didn't know. I reminded myself that I had done just the same once, when I was older than her – old enough perhaps to have known better. I could remember only too well that feeling of wanting to help someone, of thinking that if I could be the one to save him, I would be rewarded with someone who loved me as much as I loved him.

I watched Jacob squirm under my scrutiny, confident that his declaration was likely to be true, though it might be the only thing that was. This wasn't about sex, not when Charlotte had orchestrated the whole thing. She had sent him to get close to Lily in a bid to draw her away from her family. To draw her away from me.

'Charlotte put you up to this, didn't she? I know who she is, Jacob.' I tried to still the shaking in my hands, hoping the lie wouldn't make itself visible.

'You don't know anything,' he said, finally looking up from his hands.

'So tell me.'

I could see him glancing at the door that led through to the kitchen, and I wondered whether he was going to attempt to flee. How things had turned, I thought; this man who had helped terrorise me and my family was now sitting here in front of me, apparently uneasy at the power I might hold over him. What did he think I knew? Whatever he suspected of me, I was mostly in the dark, but he didn't need to know that.

I pulled the knife from my pocket. 'It was a bit like this one, wasn't it? Did you do it – did you stab her? Or did she do it to herself? She's tried to kill herself before, hasn't she?'

Jacob's face paled. I couldn't be sure whether it was at the sight of the knife or because he realised now that I was prepared to force the truth from him if necessary. And that I wasn't going anywhere until I did.

'Did you befriend Lily to get access to the coffee shop?' I asked, knowing what the answer to the question was. Charlotte had planned this, all of it; she didn't care about using Lily or Jacob as collateral, only about getting to me. 'It was you in the park with her that night, wasn't it? I saw you running away.'

The more time I'd had to think, the more complicated things were becoming. Charlotte was mentally unstable, with a history of self-harm. She had a history of hurting others, too. Had she gone to the park that night with the intention of stabbing me, only to change her mind and turn the knife on herself?

'I went there to try to change her mind,' he said, his voice weak. 'I swear… I had no idea she'd do what she did.'

'But you followed her instructions anyway, like a good little pet.'

I made no effort to keep the resentment from my voice. Between them, Charlotte and Jacob had attempted to ruin my life – the lives of my family – and whether he had been coerced by her or not seemed irrelevant.

'Did you set fire to my car?'

He looked up sharply, meeting my eye. 'What? No.'

I already believed him. Something in his face had altered; there was outrage – fear, even – at the suggestion that he might be involved. I wasn't sure he was even aware of the incident.

'Someone came to my house, smashed my car window, poured petrol in and set it on fire,' I told him bluntly, gauging his reaction. He was shaking his head as I spoke, but there was no need for his protest. Charlotte was the dangerous one.

'I had nothing to do with that. I would never—' He cut himself short. 'I just wouldn't,' he added. His expression had changed, morphing from panic to anger.

I stood and stepped closer to him, holding the knife in front of me. I saw his eyes widen with fear, and though to him it must have seemed as though I was capable of anything, I could feel my heart thumping in my chest, my brain questioning what I was doing. I was terrified, but I couldn't allow this man to see it.

'She made a rape accusation against you, didn't she?'

'How do you know about that?'

'Doesn't matter. Why did you let her get away with it?'

Jacob opened his mouth to say something, but stopped himself before he spoke. Watching the fear play out in his eyes, I realised I wasn't scared of this man. I was terrified of what Charlotte was capable of, but Jacob was little more than her puppet. I stepped closer still.

'I've been charged with wounding with intent. My family has moved out of our home because it isn't safe. I'm facing prison for something I didn't do, and it seems to me that Charlotte is responsible for all of it, so you're going to tell me why you're doing what she tells you to, and you're going to do it now.'

I jabbed the knife at him, too close to his face for his liking. He raised his hands in self-defence. 'Okay, okay,' he said desperately, holding his palms outstretched in an act of surrender. 'Don't, okay?'

'Tell me.'

'You don't know anything about Charlotte,' he said, his voice cracking. 'Not like I do. She's…' He stopped, his eyes boring into mine, pleading with me. He was desperate and pathetic.

'Tell me,' I said. 'What hold has she got over you, Jacob? What does she know?'

I stood there as he told me, his eyes resting on the knife in my hand. As his story was laid out before me, his tragic childhood and his disrupted adult life, I wondered if I should be feeling some pity for him, but there was nothing other than the contempt I felt towards Charlotte. She was a parasite, a woman who preyed on the weak and clung to every vulnerability she could find in order to exploit it.

'She's the closest thing to family I've got,' he said, once his admission had reached its conclusion.

My grip around the knife had turned my knuckles white. 'I think you'd be better off alone then, don't you?'

Silence fell over us for a moment before he spoke again, this time in more measured tones, as if unburdening himself of his sad life's story had unshackled him.

'She might have a hold over me, but she's got one over you as well, hasn't she, Jenna? She knows my secret, but she knows yours too.'

THIRTY-THREE

When I got home, Lily was in the kitchen. She was talking on her mobile phone and I stood quietly in the hall for a moment, trying to catch snippets of the conversation. I grasped little, though it was easy enough to hear how upset she was. I was caught by surprise when she opened the kitchen door to find me standing there, and she ended the call quickly, telling whoever she'd been speaking to that she had to go.

Her face was unusually pale, and her dark hair hung limply about her face. She looked ghostly in the half-light of the hallway, something other-worldly about her, and for a moment it felt as though I didn't know her at all. That I had never known her.

'You knew what he'd done, didn't you?'

'Who?'

'Damien!'

I was painfully aware of the knife resting in my pocket, the bulk of my thickest winter coat keeping it concealed while it waited to be returned to the block on the kitchen worktop. I'd had no intention of using it when I'd taken it from the kitchen, though the things I'd heard that afternoon might have been enough to make me resort to behaviour I once thought myself incapable of. I wondered whether Lily knew. Had she spoken to Jacob, or had she seen him? Did she know his real name yet? Did she know that I had been to see him?

'I only knew after it had happened.'

She screamed with frustration, the sound piercing enough to hurt my ears. 'I'm seventeen,' she reminded me, the words spat through gritted teeth. 'I can sort my own problems out, okay?'

'I didn't know he was going there. The first I heard of it was when Nancy called me, telling me he'd come home with blood on him. I'm not responsible for what he does, all right?'

Lily winced at the mention of blood, and I realised that whatever she suspected him of and whatever he had done to her, she still harboured feelings for Jacob. I shouldn't have been surprised by it, not when I remembered my own feelings towards her father. For months I had clung to the hope that he would change, that the version of him that became apparent once we were married wasn't really who he'd always been beneath the charming exterior and the seductive smile. I convinced myself that he needed me, and that I was the only one who could restore him to the man I had fallen in love with. But then I had been forced to admit that that man had never existed.

'Damien loves you,' I said, keeping my voice calm, trying to defuse the situation. 'I'm not justifying what he's done, but he's been worried about you. Whatever's happened, all he wants is to keep you safe.'

'Matthew doesn't want anything to do with me any more,' she said, brushing past me as she headed for the front door, her phone still clutched in her hand. 'So you've both got what you wanted.'

She grabbed her jacket and I followed her outside into the evening air, calling after her as she hurried away from me. Nothing could have been further from the truth. None of this was what I had wanted.

I watched her turn the corner at the end of the street before going back into the house. In the kitchen, I took the knife from my pocket, putting it on the worktop in front of me. I wondered again whether Charlotte had always planned to stab herself. Why hurt me physically, a wound that might heal given time, when she had the potential to cause much greater and longer-term suffering? Jacob had fled knowing he couldn't change her mind, perhaps by then realising that whatever disturbance resided in Charlotte was fixed there with a permanence that neither he nor anyone else could alter.

'What the fuck is this, Jenna?'

I had been so lost in my own thoughts that I hadn't heard the front door, nor had I heard Damien come into the kitchen. My hand flew to the knife still sitting on the worktop in front of me, and I spun around, the tip of its blade hovering just inches from his chest. His eyes widened as he looked down at the glint of steel between us.

'Shit,' I said, lowering my hand and leaning back against the worktop. 'You scared the life out of me.'

Damien's gaze rested on the knife until I had returned it to the block behind me. When I turned back to him, he thrust a photograph into my hand. Tinged brown around the edges, as though it had been damaged by time, it showed a young woman sitting on a sofa holding a baby wrapped in a light blanket, wisps of dark hair escaping from the edges of a knitted hat, its eyes shut in peaceful sleep. The woman was smiling, but there was an emptiness behind her eyes that belied the tilt of her mouth, something more than just the usual exhaustion of those early days of motherhood. I knew her face – I had seen her photograph used in news reports – and I had been expecting to see what I was confronted with then. I should have seen it earlier, but I had been blind to what was right in front of me.

'Turn it over,' he instructed.

On the back were the words *Rebecca and Maria, March 2002.*

'You need to tell me what's going on,' Damien said. 'And don't try and bullshit me any more, Jenna. I'm sick of all these lies.'

I stepped past him and dropped onto one of the chairs at the kitchen table, feeling my life crumble around me, bracing my shoulders as though the ceiling might collapse and leave me crushed beneath it. A part of me wished it would. Anything would have been less painful than what I was about to have to do. I had known this moment was coming, but I had wanted it to come from me, in my own time, in my own way. Not like this. Not forced by her.

I could hear the blood pounding in my ears, as though I was swimming in it. Though I had tried to convince myself that those notes Damien had shown me referred to Lily's mystery boyfriend, there was a part of me – a part I had attempted to suppress for so long – that knew the past was going to catch up with me and that the truth couldn't be kept hidden forever.

'I'll tell you everything,' I said, my voice faltering, 'but you need to hear the whole story. Please promise me you'll hear me out.'

He couldn't promise me anything, not when he had no idea what the story might entail. Perhaps he didn't want to hear the whole of it, and I couldn't blame him.

I took a deep breath, wondering whether he would just walk away, whether these would be the last words he would ever hear from me.

'Maria is Lily. She's not my daughter.'

THIRTY-FOUR

When I was fifteen and midway through my GCSE studies, I got pregnant by the first boy I ever had sex with. I hadn't been particularly attracted to him – I didn't even like him very much – but he had shown me attention and I had clung to it, desperate to feel an affection that had been lacking elsewhere in my life. There wasn't much about sex that I understood at the time, but just knowing that my parents would have been appalled by what I was doing was enough to make me want to do it again and again, which we did every Tuesday and Thursday for the duration of the summer holidays, when my parents thought I was at a science camp.

It took me a long time even after that to learn that sex and love were two very different things, and that the attention I had craved from my parents could never be replaced by a quick fumble that inevitably led to nothing but disappointment and, quite often, an unshakeable sense of shame. In those years that followed, I moved from boy to boy, from man to man, never looking for anything more than a momentary respite from the demons that plagued me and the self-loathing I carried inside me like an extra lung. I didn't care about my reputation; I didn't care too much about myself. I was consumed with thoughts of what had been lost, and the unpredictable void that had become my future; a future that had been designed by my parents but contained nothing I wanted.

We were only a few weeks into the new school year after the summer I lost my virginity when I realised my period was late. They had started eighteen months earlier, and during that time had been so predictable that I was able to forecast the date I would begin my next, never missing an opportunity to use it as an excuse to get out of PE lessons or mixed swimming with the boys. I skipped lunch for a few days until I had saved enough money to buy a cheap kit from a pharmacy in the next town – I couldn't get one closer to home for fear of being seen by someone who knew me, or worse, knew my parents – and the following day I sat on one of the toilets in the science block, knickers around my ankles and head in my hands as I waited for the stick that was resting on top of my rucksack to determine my fate.

My first thought was my parents. Whatever else happened, they were going to kill me, and this thought took hold so firmly that I began to picture my father gripping my throat and squeezing the life out of me until both I and the foetus that was going to demolish my future life's plans were removed from the equation and could no longer cause them the unspeakable shame that would be brought about by a pregnant teenage daughter. I couldn't tell them, and yet there was no one I felt close enough to confide in – no teacher I could speak to or friend I could share my secret with, and the boy who'd got me pregnant had already moved on to someone else. In those weeks that followed, I had never felt more isolated. I went to school, I went home; I stayed upstairs in my room using the excuse of revision for barely showing my face elsewhere in the house. And then came the day when – despite my best efforts to keep it hidden from her – my mother caught me being sick, and everything was thrown out into the open.

She made me promise I wouldn't tell my father, which I'd had no intention of doing anyway. Then she booked an appointment at an abortion clinic. There was no conversation about it – no question of what I wanted to do or consideration of alternatives; with one phone call, my mother made a decision that would come to shape the rest of my life. By the day of the first appointment, something inside me had already died. The pre-tests came and went with little interruption to my life, nothing that might draw attention to me or arouse the suspicion of my father. The procedure was uncomfortable, but there was no pain afterwards, other than that which grew in my head and my chest and came to reside there like dormant tumours.

Years later, and with a teenage daughter of my own, I understood why my mother hadn't wanted me to go through with the pregnancy. I was able to see things from her perspective: I was so young, had barely started my own life, and the prospect of a baby was overwhelming and scary and – yes, for her – shameful. Had Lily come home one day and told me she was pregnant, I might have experienced many of the fears my own mother had had for me, and yet there was one thing I was certain of: I would never have shunned her in the way my mother shunned me. I would never have made her feel the way my mother made me feel.

And yet in some ways, at least, I must have. I had inadvertently pushed her into the arms of Jacob Perry, with Lily clinging to his attention in the same way I had done to that boy at fifteen, and then again almost seven years later to Nikolas Lanza.

I had met Nikolas in January 2003, while working in a café close to the student house in which I lived. I was in the fourth year of a medical degree, and my parents hadn't wanted me to work, adamant that it would only prove an unwelcome distraction from my studies. Money had never been an issue for them – my mother was a consultant anaesthetist and my father was a GP – but although both were successful professionals, it always seemed that neither was fully satisfied; that their perceived failings were something that my own career should go on to correct. They made it clear they would continue to support me financially as long as I followed their wishes, but I worked regardless, needing the break from studies and an outlet through which I could engage with people other than those I lived with.

I was taken in by Nikolas the moment I met him, by the beautiful face and the beautiful accent, but even during that very first encounter it was Lily – Maria – that I was most enchanted by. Her dark curls strayed from the top of the bobble hat she was wearing, and when I passed her the beaker she had dropped from her pram, her chubby little hands reached out to me as though it was me she wanted. To Nikolas, it must have seemed obvious early on that I would be easy prey. I hated the course I was on, I disliked the people I lived with and the house we shared; I wore my misery like an accessory, and it made luring me into his web of lies all the easier. The truth was, I wanted to be taken away from my life. For years, I had craved the possibility of a future that had been stolen from me by my parents, and Nikolas offered me the very thing that had been lost. I would have done it all again without changing a thing if it had meant keeping Lily.

THIRTY-FIVE

The silence that lay between us was deafening, and in the noise of it I could hear the life we had built together crumbling to ruin. There was blood rushing in my ears, the sound of my own pulse thudding like a drumbeat at my temples, and I felt sick at the thought of everything that was about to disintegrate in front of me.

At first, Damien's reaction was to absent himself, as though he hadn't heard what I'd said. He didn't move; his expression showed no sign of changing.

'Say something. Please.'

He sat down at the table opposite me. 'I'm just waiting for the punchline.'

I wished there was one; that all this was just one big, inappropriately timed and ill-judged joke. Yet it was the truth. I had been running from it for most of my adult life, managing to convince even myself at times. Wasn't I the one who had cared for her, who was there for her no matter what? Wasn't I the one she came to first for everything she needed?

'It's a long story,' I said, as though that offered me a get-out clause.

The look on Damien's face still hadn't changed, and it scared me. Since the incident with Jacob, I had been aware of my husband's potential for violence, something I had never seen from him before and had never imagined. Yet I knew that everyone had a breaking point, and he had met his.

What would happen after this?

When he still said nothing, I took my cue to continue. I drew a deep breath, trying to clear my head of all the debris.

'Everything I told you about Nikolas is true,' I said, hating the sound and the taste of his name on my tongue. 'He did die in a car accident. I was there with him, you know that. I hadn't known him long. Lily – Maria – was thirteen months old when I met him. Her mother, Rebecca, had killed herself.' I paused, cleared my throat. There were things I couldn't tell him; things I could never admit to anyone. 'It was a whirlwind relationship, but after we got married, I realised he wasn't who he'd said he was. There were a few other things I realised too. I loved Lily, but I didn't love Nikolas. He didn't love me either, I knew that. I think he'd been looking for someone to take Lily off his hands, and marrying me got him what he wanted – his pass into the UK. He started drinking, neglecting Lily while I was at work. That night… well, you know what happened. He'd been drinking, but he insisted on going to pick her up, and I knew I couldn't leave her alone with him. We never made it to the babysitter's house.'

Damien's eyes had darkened as he stared down at the table, not once looking at me as I spoke. I wished he would do something – scream at me, throw something; anything that would break the awful silence and show me he cared enough to react. I wanted to reach out to touch him. Like me, he was holding everything back to stop himself from breaking.

'I don't get it,' he said eventually. 'Why didn't you just tell me? It wouldn't have changed anything.'

'I did what I thought was best for Lily. I've been the only mother she's ever known. What was I supposed to do – tell her both her parents were dead? What would have happened then?'

'So you just lied? It seems to be a habit, Jenna.'

I sighed, realising too late that the sound was petulant, like something Lily would offer up mid argument. Damien was never going to understand this, any of it. Though his life had been afflicted by its own set of tragedies, our backgrounds and experiences differed entirely. He was a literal thinker, believing things should be one way or another, this or that. He had never been able to see the shadows that appeared to me in every corner.

'You were her stepmother, then?' he asked, his eyes restless as his brain tried to make sense of my admission. 'I'm sorry… I still don't get it. You didn't need to lie, did you?'

'It wasn't that straightforward,' I said, but when I offered nothing more in the way of an explanation, my silence was incriminating.

'How did you think you could keep it a secret?' he challenged. 'What if she'd got ill? What if she'd needed her birth certificate for something?'

This was one of the things I'd had to keep pushing to the back of my mind, knowing that at some point the issue would arise. I'd just hoped it would be way into the future, when Lily was an adult, and perhaps old enough to understand why I'd done what I had. But deep down, I'd known that when the secret came out, its consequences could be disastrous. Lily wouldn't see my commitment to her; she would only see the lie. I knew I was lucky to have made it this far, though it felt wrong to have the truth forced from me by the vindictive actions of a stranger.

'Oh,' Damien said flatly, his face changing in an instant, and I could only imagine what had occurred to him. He shook his head, and a smile crossed his face, weak and fleeting; there was no kindness or humour in the expression, and it was quickly replaced by a coldness that made him look nothing like his usual self. 'This is why you went to so many of Amelia's antenatal appointments alone, isn't it?'

He stared at me, waiting for a response, an admission, yet I couldn't even bring myself to look him in the eye. I knew how much my behaviour back then had frustrated him. He had wanted to be there with me at every step of the pregnancy, displaying a commitment that would have been welcomed by most women, but at the forefront of my mind was the thought that at any scan, any appointment, the truth might make itself known: that I hadn't already given birth, that I hadn't been there and done all that before. I made excuses. It was such a long time ago, I would tell him, when questions about my previous pregnancy arose. I couldn't remember.

'All that time,' he said, when I failed to offer even an attempt at a justification. 'You were lying all that time. You've been lying to me for all these years. Is Amelia even mine?'

The question stung more than any other. 'How can you ask me that? Of course she's yours. Lily's past doesn't change anything between us.'

'Ask her about your daughter,' he said, repeating the words of the third note. 'I didn't want to think it, but now I don't know what to believe.'

'You know she's yours. And we're still a family, all of us.'

But I was wrong. In his face, in the way he looked at me, everything was changed.

'Something's not adding up,' he said, eyeing me with a suspicion that was entirely deserved. 'You haven't kept this a secret all these years just so that Lily doesn't find out.'

'You're wrong. Plenty of adopted children don't discover until they're adults that their parents aren't their birth parents.'

'So is that what Lily is? Adopted?'

I hesitated. 'No, I never legally adopted her. I could never have known what would happen to Nikolas, could I?' I could see that Damien was rapidly forming the pieces in his brain into some sort of shape. 'I didn't lie to hurt you,' I tried desperately to explain. 'I had no choice.'

He shook his head. 'You had a choice. You always have a choice.' He sat back and tilted his head to the ceiling. 'Those notes.' He laughed, but the sound was without humour. 'You know, I could have said something weeks ago, but I didn't. I thought it was a prank, just someone messing around. I know my wife better than anyone, don't I? You'd tell me the truth.' He stood, his chair scraping across the tiled floor, and moved to the back door, looking out at the garden. 'This photograph,' he said with his back to me. 'It's linked to everything else, isn't it? The arrests... the car. Who's responsible?'

'I don't know.'

'Another lie,' he said, his voice rising. 'Where do they all end, Jenna?'

'I didn't hurt that woman,' I told him, desperate to convince him that that at least was the truth. 'You have to believe me.'

'I want to, but how can I?' he said, turning to me. 'How can I believe anything you say any more?'

I rose hurriedly and moved around the table, putting a hand out to him but quickly pulling it away when I gauged his reaction. 'We need to talk about this properly. I can explain everything if you'll let me; just don't walk out on me, not now.'

'It's all a lie.'

'I love you. That's not a lie.'

'You sure? Or was I just a means to an end?'

I felt my jaw tightening at the question. It was true I'd had nothing when we met – no money, no home, no job prospects – but the suggestion that I had pursued our relationship for anything other than to be with him was unfair.

'If you want to believe that.'

'You would have been nothing without me, Jenna, just remember that. If I hadn't come along, you'd still be a single mother scraping together a living.'

Bitterness radiated from him, and I could taste a million angry words on my own tongue. I held them back, knowing retaliation would only make things worse. 'I appreciate how much you helped me, but I paid you back, every penny plus more. What about everything I did for you?'

After the accident, I had moved to Cardiff and nursed Damien back to health. Though it hadn't been much of a life I'd been living, I had given up everything to be with him when he'd needed me, and had asked for nothing in return. The risk was great – there was far more chance of me being exposed in Cardiff than there had been in Llangovney – but it was one I was prepared to face. I loved Damien. I wanted us to be a family. I managed to convince myself that if Lily and I were discovered, the law would be on my side. Legally, I was her stepmother. I was the only mother she had ever known, and who was going to deprive her of the one relationship she had left?

'And what exactly did you do for me?' he said defiantly.

'I looked after you,' I reminded him. 'I took on two jobs while you couldn't work. I never asked you for anything.'

Damien had faced his injuries with stoicism, though I could see how much he had been changed by the accident. Everything in his life – his job, his hobbies, his social circle – involved his athleticism and his physical ability, and when the doctors told him that the damage to his leg was irreversible and irreparable, it was as though a part of him died. For a while, the colour was drained from him, his eyes a blank grey and his smile forced. In truth, there was only one person who managed to raise a genuine smile, and that was Lily.

He was advised to seek compensation for his loss of earnings and for the impact his injuries would have on his future lifestyle. He was reluctant at first, critical of what he referred to as 'claim culture', but in the end, unable to return to his job as a firefighter, he sought legal representation and a case was put together. Nobody was expecting the hefty five-figure sum he was eventually awarded, though no number would have been big enough to replace what he had lost.

'I'm grateful for what you've given me, you know that,' I continued when he offered no response. 'But everything I've done has been for this family. I know I should have told you, but I couldn't. I never wanted Lily to find out.'

'For fear that she'd hate you?'

His words were like a punch to the gut. I had always imagined that if Lily was to ever discover the truth, she would be confused, shocked; devastated. I had never considered the possibility that she might come to hate me for it.

'You know, people warned me that I was jumping in too quickly when I met you; that I didn't know enough about you.'

I rolled my eyes; a juvenile gesture, but it escaped me involuntarily. 'People? Your mother, you mean.'

For whatever reason, Nancy had never liked me. Yes, she was there for us when we needed her, and she had always helped out with Amelia, but the affection she showed her granddaughter often appeared in stark contrast to the aloof restraint that was reserved for any exchange with me. Of course, Damien never saw it, or at the very least refused to acknowledge it, accusing me of being paranoid or overly sensitive, each criticism of my character punctuated with a reminder of all the school pickups Nancy had done and the dinners she'd put in front of us when my time had been consumed by setting up the business.

I'd seen her watching me with caution from the day I arrived, resentful that her son had chosen me to care for him; jealous of the fact that there was a woman in his life threatening to take him away from her, though that was never my intention. A close family unit was all I had ever wanted, and had Nancy welcomed me more warmly, our relationship might have been very different. As it was, she regarded me with a contempt that was almost tangible, making me feel like an outsider at every opportunity.

'You can't resist, can you? This isn't about my mother, Jenna. Take some responsibility.'

His words grated inside my brain, sending tiny tremors of fury racing through me. Taking responsibility was all I had ever tried to do, and was the very reason I had kept the secret for all those years. I had been taking responsibility for Lily's happiness, trying my best to ensure that her childhood wasn't blighted by the sad truth of her past. Was a lie always so bad? I asked myself. Was it always wrong if the reason for it was to protect someone you loved?

'I love Lily,' I told him, as though this would explain away everything. 'Whatever I've done has been about protecting her.'

Damien stared at me then, hard, for longer than was comfortable. 'Are you sure?' he asked, the words cold; his voice not like his at all. 'Or have you been protecting yourself?'

He brushed past me and went out into the hallway, taking his jacket from where he had left it at the bottom of the stairs, searching the pockets for his keys.

'I don't know who you are any more,' he said without looking at me, and a moment later he was gone, leaving me with the silence of the house and the deafening screams of my thoughts.

THIRTY-SIX

That evening, Lily didn't come home. I tried her mobile repeatedly, but it rang through to voicemail. I called Maisie and her mother, but she was with neither. Damien had taken the car when he'd left, so I had no way of driving around to see if I could find her. Thoughts of where she might be plagued me, and I wondered if she would be foolish enough to meet up with Jacob again. Where was Charlotte? I wondered. The darkest thoughts filled my brain, taunting me with possibilities.

I thought about calling the police, but I knew it would be regarded as an overreaction.

I had reason to believe my daughter might be in danger, but how could I admit that without incriminating myself? I had abducted Lily. Not in the traditional sense of the word – not in a way that would be considered abduction by any rational mind – but in the eyes of the law, I had taken a child who wasn't mine, and I would be regarded no differently than an abductor.

I sat on the bottom step of the staircase and stared at the front door as if the power of thought alone could make Lily appear. I only had a few of Lily's friends' numbers stored in my phone. I tried the ones I had, but no one had seen her.

Had I always known that this day would arrive, the truth finding its way into the open through one means or another? I supposed I must have, though I had managed to push the fear to the back of my mind, maintaining a pretence of normality. There had been so many times I had wanted to confide in Damien, to tell him the truth, but I had known how he would react, and the fear of losing him had kept me silent.

We had been safe in Llangovney. Our lives might never have come to much, and we would have found our existence shaped by our daily routine, our isolation making us dependent on one another, but we would have been free to be together without the past hanging over me, an unseen threat. I wondered whether the events of the last two weeks would have occurred if I had never met Damien, though without him there would have been no Amelia, and it was impossible for me to regret any circumstance that had led to her existence.

I found my coat and my house keys and walked briskly to Nancy's house. Neither the car nor Damien was there. I knocked at the back door, and a moment later Nancy opened it. On the way over, I had braced myself for the welcome I might receive, wondering whether Damien had already spoken to his mother and told her what he had found out about Lily. When she ushered me in and told me Amelia was at the dining table doing her homework, I was able to breathe a sigh of relief. So far, she knew nothing more than she had that morning.

'Have you seen Lily?' I asked her.

She shook her head. 'Everything okay?'

'Fine,' I lied. 'She's probably at rehearsals. This show seems to be taking up her life.'

I moved to the living room door and watched Amelia. Her sketchbook was open on the table in front of her, an array of coloured pencils neatly lined up beside it. As soon as she turned and saw me there, she got down from her chair and ran to me, and when she threw her arms around me, I could have cried. I held her tight and said nothing, squeezing her until she wriggled free.

'Want to see my project?' she asked, before leading me by the hand to the table.

Nancy made me a cup of tea, and I sat with Amelia for the next hour, until it was time for her to have a bath and get ready for bed.

'I love you,' I told her before I left. 'You know that, don't you?' She nodded. 'Love you too.'

'I'll come back to see you tomorrow, after school.'

When I left, I tried Lily's mobile for the umpteenth time, but it went straight to voicemail again. I had been checking my phone every five minutes while at Nancy's house, willing the sound of the ringtone or a message notification to put my increasingly anxious heart at ease. Not knowing what else to do, I went back to the house, with the intention of waiting a few more hours before making a call to the police.

In the living room, I searched the sofa for the television remote control. The screen lit with life and I went straight to the planner, scrolling the list of recordings. I knew that what I was looking for was there somewhere, though it took a while to find it.

I pressed play.

'Teenagers across Wales are celebrating today as a record number of students achieve A*–C grades in their GCSE exams,' the flame-haired reporter said, grinning a toothy smile at the camera before turning to a man standing next to her. 'I'm joined this morning by head teacher Daniel Pearson, and two of his Year 11 students, Josh and Lily.'

The camera panned to Lily, and I pressed pause. She had changed so much in the fourteen months since the clip had been recorded, and yet I had barely noticed. As I stared at her image on the screen, one thing couldn't be avoided. She looked so much like her mother: the same dark hair, the same eyes, the same lines around her mouth that framed her smile. If it was obvious to me – to someone who had never met Rebecca Lanza – then it must have been instantly apparent to anyone who had known her.

I had been so proud of Lily's results, but I hadn't shown it. Instead, when she'd got home later that day, I'd asked her what she thought she was playing at getting her face on TV, to which she and Damien had looked at me as though I had lost my mind. Lily's eyes had filled with tears and she had stormed from the room, dropping her results envelope on the floor as she left, and I was taken back to all those years earlier, to my own exam results day, and the disappointment I had felt at my parents' dismissive attitude towards everything I had tried to do, most of it for them.

'What the hell was that about?' Damien had asked me, but of course I couldn't tell him, so I had just made some excuse.

I was still staring at Lily's face when I heard the front door. I turned the TV off and hurried out into the hallway. Lily was bending over, removing her shoes, her mobile clutched in her left hand.

'You've got the bloody thing with you then, I see.'

She narrowed her eyes and followed my gaze to her phone. 'Battery died,' she said, looking at me as though I'd grown a second head. 'What's happened now?'

I stepped forward and put my arms around her, holding her close, tightening my hold as though I could keep her there forever.

'Mum,' she said, trying to free herself from my grip. 'What's going on?'

'Where have you been?'

'Just for a walk. I wanted to be on my own, that's all.' She sighed and I felt her head relax against my shoulder, a gesture that told me she didn't hate me. 'I'm sorry about earlier. I know Damien was just trying to protect me. I just don't think it was the best way.'

Neither did I, though I wasn't going to tell Lily that. I wanted her to love Damien as she always had, without Charlotte Copeland ruining the relationship that had formed between them over the years. He had acted stupidly, impulsively, but we had all been pushed into behaving in ways we never would under normal circumstances.

'What's wrong?' she asked.

'Nothing,' I said, holding her at arm's length so I could look at her beautiful face, her dark eyes with their long lashes. 'I love you, that's all. You know that, don't you?'

'You're acting weird.'

I smiled, faking cheeriness through the gloom hanging over me. 'So what's new? Tell me you know.'

'Know what?'

'That I love you. That no matter what happens, I've always loved you.'

She pulled a face, disconcerted by my behaviour. 'Yeah, I know,' she said, though I was sure the words were uttered just to get away from me and the awkwardness of the exchange. 'I love you too.'

I closed my eyes at the sound of those words, letting them smother me with something other than the sense of despair that had become my default emotion. We were still a family, fragmented but not broken. Whatever Charlotte Copeland's plans, she hadn't succeeded yet. As I looked at my beautiful daughter, I vowed to do whatever it took to keep her safe.

I closed my eyes, the smile that Lily had flashed for the television camera lighting up the darkness behind my lids. The image of her face was as clear as though a younger Lily stood before me now, yet within moments it had faded, blurring into something else. Someone else. Rebecca Lanza stared back at me, her face unsmiling and lifeless; so like Lily's and yet so different.

I saw for the first time then something I should have seen before; something I maybe had seen but had refused to allow myself to acknowledge. In the hard edges of Rebecca's face there was another woman, a woman so similar it could only be her sister. Lily's aunt had tried to ruin my life. I couldn't let her ruin Lily's.

THIRTY-SEVEN

I waited all the following day for Charlotte to find me. I was sure she would come to the house – that she had been watching me and knew I was there – but she never arrived, and her absence did little to reassure me. I had prepared myself for meeting her face to face, this time knowing who she was; understanding the intended purpose of our being there. I might have forced myself into a false sense of security, convincing myself everything was over, that she had done what she had set out to do by intimidating me and ruining my marriage, but I knew that that was far from true. She wouldn't stop until she'd finished what she'd started. She might have withdrawn the statement she'd made to the police, but only to protect herself. What I'd learned of her was enough to confirm my suspicions that once she had decided upon something, nothing would stop her from achieving it. Perhaps she had reverted to her original plan of trying to kill me.

I waited until Amelia would be back from school before heading over to Nancy's. Expecting Damien to be there, I had prepared myself for whatever atmosphere might await me, wondering whether Nancy knew my secret yet. She lived in an end-of-terrace house with a narrow garden – little more than a yard – that was accessible from the side street on which Damien's car was parked. When I got there, Amelia was outside, crouched near the fence.

'What are you doing?' I asked.

She stood and held out a handful of leaves that had blown from the trees that edged the field behind the back lane. 'I need these for my autumn project,' she explained. She pointed to the pencils resting on top of her sketchbook on the low wall that lined Nancy's narrow flower bed. There was a collection of oranges, browns and reds. 'I could do with something really red,' she mused as she studied the colours.

'We could go to the park tomorrow after school,' I suggested. 'It's a bit late now – it'll be dark before long.'

Amelia sighed and muttered a reluctant 'okay', disappointed at being restricted by the small garden and the October nights that were drawing in increasingly early.

'Do you fancy a pizza?' I asked brightly, offering something I knew would distract her from thoughts of the park. 'I could order one in for us, what do you reckon? Thursday evening treat?'

Her face lit up.

'I'll go and tell Granny before she puts something on for you.'

I went into the kitchen, where Nancy was standing at the sink, her back to me. 'I told Amelia I'd get us all a pizza,' I said, removing my coat and hanging it from one of the hooks by the back door. 'I hope you don't mind.'

Nancy said nothing, and it was a moment before she turned to acknowledge me. When she did, she couldn't hide the fact that she had been crying.

'What's wrong?' I asked. 'Has something happened?'

She pressed her fingertips to her eyes as though trying to push the tears back. It was uncomfortable for us both; I couldn't remember ever having seen her cry before, and it was something she didn't appreciate being reduced to in front of me.

'It's Damien,' she said at last. 'I've never seen him like this. Out drinking all the time, coming back in such a state he can't get up the stairs by himself. I'm just grateful Amelia was in bed by the time he got home last night.'

The word 'home' stung, though I realised how petty it was of me to focus on it. This wasn't his home – it wasn't Amelia's home

– though Nancy already seemed to have accepted their residence here as permanent.

'Where is he now?'

'Still in bed. He's been up there all day.'

'I'm sorry, Nancy. It shouldn't be you looking after Amelia. I'll take her out after school tomorrow; it'll give you a break.'

'I don't need a break. I just hate seeing him like this. He loves you and he loves the girls, but these past couple of weeks seem to have broken him. What's going on, Jenna? I don't understand why the charge hasn't been dropped. I know that woman has withdrawn her statement, so why are you still being persecuted?'

For the first time in as long as I could recall, it felt as though Nancy was on my side. She almost sounded sympathetic. She deserved the truth, but it was something I just couldn't give her.

'I don't know.'

We stood in silence, both trapped by our own thoughts. Though I couldn't blame Damien, I wanted to shake him for being so irresponsible. It wasn't like him to react to problems in this way, even in a situation that was far from normal.

'Mum! Mummy! No!'

My blood turned cold at the sound of Amelia's piercing screams. I shot through the back door; the side gate opposite it was open and my daughter was being carried across the road, her arms and legs flailing wildly as the woman holding her struggled to keep her grip.

'Call the police,' I screamed at Nancy, who had followed me out.

I ran across the road, reaching for Charlotte's hair and yanking her head back as she pushed Amelia into the back seat of a car. She cried out in pain, yet she managed to twist free and her closed fist caught me in the side of the head. I heard Amelia crying and calling for me as Charlotte kicked me in the shin, taking my legs from beneath me. I staggered back and fell to the tarmac.

She got into the driver's seat and started the engine as I pulled myself up, tasting blood in my mouth. I yanked open the car door, where Amelia was cowering on the back seat, her face red and stained with terrified tears.

'Mum,' she said, her voice pitiful, but as I reached in to grab her, I felt the car move. 'Mum!'

She clung on to my arms as my body fell forward with the movement of the car. Charlotte accelerated, the back door still open, my legs hanging out. I managed to pull myself inside, and fell on top of Amelia, grasping her tightly for a moment before reaching back to close the door.

'Everything's going to be okay,' I said, desperately trying to reassure her.

Charlotte pressed the door lock, and I tried the handle to find the car was fitted with child-safety locks, keeping us trapped inside. Amelia was still sobbing, her eyes searching mine pleadingly, wondering why I was doing nothing to stop what was happening. The truth was that for a moment I was paralysed. I had been here before, at another time, in another life – a little girl entirely dependent on me, and on what I did next.

I looked through the back window to see Nancy standing in the street, her phone in her hand, watching helplessly as the car disappeared with a screech of tyres around the corner.

I looked at Amelia. 'Put your seat belt on,' I told her, trying to keep my voice as calm as possible. Then, to Charlotte, 'I know who you are, Charlotte. I know why you're doing this.'

THIRTY-EIGHT

I didn't have my mobile phone with me; it was in the pocket of my coat, which I had taken off in Nancy's kitchen. I had never felt so helpless, and I was acutely, painfully aware of Amelia at my side, sobbing quietly.

'You don't need to do this,' I said, desperately clinging to the possibility that Charlotte might be reasoned with. 'None of this has anything to do with Amelia – none of it is her fault. It's me you're angry with, not her. Please... let her go. You can do what you want to me, but she's just a little girl. Please.'

I could see her faltering, and wondered for a moment whether, despite everything she was guilty of, Charlotte was capable of empathy. I knew nothing about her – I hadn't even known her name. I tried to remember whether Nikolas had ever mentioned it, but I was sure that if he had, I would have remembered. Surely there had to be some glimmer of compassion amid the revenge she was intent upon. Amelia was no relation to her, but the two of them were linked by Lily, and I hoped this would be enough to persuade Charlotte not to hurt her.

Her hands were shaking on the steering wheel, her resolve clearly weakened by my plea. 'You knew what he'd done, didn't you?' she said, the words escaping through clenched teeth. 'You knew what he'd done to her and you said nothing. You did nothing. You're no better than he was.'

I glanced at Amelia, who was huddled against me, her little body curled in on itself, her pale face streaked with tears that shone in the darkness. I offered her a look that I hoped might calm her fear, but as she gazed back at me, I saw that nothing I could fake would reassure her. She was only eight, but she was old enough to recognise the threat that sat in the car with us, knowing as well as I did just how dangerous this woman might be.

'I will tell you everything, I swear to you, but not in front of Amelia, please. Let me call her father and get him to take her away from this. Just you and me. What do you think?'

'Shut up!'

The car veered into the middle of the road as Charlotte leaned across the passenger seat and fumbled for something in the glove box. We were already leaving Caerphilly, heading in the direction of the A470, which would take us either south to Cardiff or north towards Merthyr Tydfil and Brecon.

In the darkness, the glint of the knife flashed like torchlight. Charlotte held it clutched in her left hand, raised for me to see, her eyes meeting mine in the rear-view mirror. 'You know I'll use it, don't you? So just stop talking.'

Seeing the knife, Amelia broke out into another fit of sobs. 'It's okay,' I whispered, my face pressed to her head, my words breathed into her hair. 'Everything is going to be okay. No one's going to hurt you.'

My thoughts had been so focused on my elder daughter that I had neglected to worry about the younger. I had assumed that Amelia was safe – none of this was anything to do with her – yet it made some sick kind of sense that Charlotte should exact her revenge in this way.

The car veered off the bypass and stopped at the side of the road. 'Get out.'

I thought she was talking to me, but when she leaned between the seats and pushed the knife towards my face, I realised she was giving Amelia an opportunity to leave. We were near Treforest, just a short walk from the university. Amelia was staring at me, wide-eyed, too terrified by the sight of the knife to do anything but sit there, frozen with fear.

'You can't make her get out here,' I said, trying to keep my voice calm. The blade was inches from my mouth, and I had no doubt that Charlotte would use it.

'She gets out here or she comes with us. Your choice.'

'Amelia,' I said, keeping my eyes fixed on the knife. 'See over there?' I raised my arm and pointed in the direction of the bridge. 'There's a shop just there. I need you to go in and give them your dad's number. You remember it, don't you?'

From a young age, Damien and I had made sure Amelia knew our full names, so that if she was ever separated from us, she would be able to get help. When she was a little older, we repeated our mobile numbers like a mantra, never believing she would ever have to use them.

'Amelia,' I urged when she didn't respond.

'I don't want to leave you,' she sobbed.

I could see Charlotte's impatience growing, her grip around the knife tightening.

'You need to do this for me, sweetheart, please. Your dad will come and get you, okay?'

The thought of her going out alone into the night made me sick with dread, but I knew that if she was to stay in the car, whatever Charlotte had planned for me might prove much worse. Amelia was a smart girl, but she was just a child, and I could only pray that the next adult she encountered would be someone who would take care of her and make sure she got home safely. At that moment, she was better off with a stranger than she was with me.

Charlotte unlocked the doors and I nodded to Amelia. 'I'll be fine,' I reassured her, lying yet again.

Her sobs as she stepped out of the car broke my heart, but her feet were barely on the concrete before Charlotte turned back to the wheel and accelerated onto the roundabout.

'You bitch,' I said, a blast of cold night air rushing at me through the still open door. 'She's just a little girl.'

Through the back window, I could see Amelia's rapidly shrinking figure. She hadn't moved. Why wasn't she doing what I had told her? She was alone on a busy road. Anything might happen.

'Close the door.'

I thought about throwing myself out of the car, but it had gained speed quickly, and if I didn't end up killing myself in my attempt to flee, I knew Charlotte would return to do the job for me.

'Maria was just a little girl,' she said, meeting my eye again in the mirror. 'That didn't stop you from stealing her, did it?'

'I didn't steal her. I was the only family she had.'

'*I* was her family!'

'She didn't know you,' I argued. 'I was the only mother she'd ever known. Hadn't her life been ripped apart enough already?'

'You knew I had more rights to her than you ever did – that's why you ran. You kidnapped her.'

She was wrong, but I couldn't tell her so, not without revealing a truth I had never told anyone. There were other reasons why I had chosen to hide, all of them to keep Lily safe.

'I did what was best for Lily,' I said quietly.

'You did what was best for yourself,' Charlotte accused. 'Were you in on it?'

'In on what?' My words were strangled by the insinuation.

'Did you help him kill her?' she screamed.

I shook my head, feeling tears wet my cheeks. 'I didn't even know him then, you know I didn't. I am so sorry about what happened to Rebecca, I swear to you I am. I know the police didn't believe you, but I do. I know what Nikolas was.'

Charlotte was silent for a moment. 'She didn't fall from that balcony.'

I closed my eyes and tried to suppress everything I had managed to push to the back of my mind. I kept a locked box there, filled with the things I knew would drive me to some sort of breakdown if I allowed them loose to sabotage the attempts I had made at a normal life.

How did you meet Rebecca?

I had asked Nikolas the question early on; he'd never kept her death a secret from me.

She was on holiday with her sister, he told me. *The summer of 2000. They came into the bar where I was working, we got chatting, they came back every evening after that.*

I knew what Rebecca had fallen for when she had met Nikolas, for I had been drawn to those same things. It had taken hindsight to realise the mistake I had made in trusting him. It was then that I began to question his version of the events that had led to Rebecca's death.

She was beautiful, he told me. *But she had this dark side. It was as though a cloud rested over her, and it darkened everything. When Maria was born, things quickly got worse. She was diagnosed with post-natal depression. Her mother had suffered with it too. She killed herself when Rebecca was thirteen.*

Rebecca's struggles had been documented in the media reports of her death, which made no secret of her mother's suicide, nor of Rebecca's own battle with post-natal depression. Doctors' reports showed that she had attended the surgery seeking help with her sleeplessness and anxiety, and the more I heard of her tragic story, the greater my sympathy for Nikolas became.

I already knew how she had died. I had read a news report about her suicide, which had detailed how she had jumped from the balcony of the fifth-floor apartment she shared with her husband Nikolas in Larnaca, having moved her life there to be with him.

Charlotte's right hand was clasped around the steering wheel, her left still holding the knife. She kept meeting my eye in the mirror, waiting for me to speak.

'I know,' I said quietly, giving her what she wanted to hear. 'And yes, I knew what he'd done. But only when it was too late.'

THIRTY-NINE

On the night he died, Nikolas had been out drinking. He was supposed to be looking after Maria while I worked; as with so many other things, I found out too late that his word meant nothing, and that more often than not he left her with a friend, one of the many women it seemed he was able to manipulate to his advantage. I was working as a waitress in a Bristol restaurant three nights a week, with a second job at weekends, trying to earn enough money to cover the rent on the damp-riddled bedsit we reluctantly referred to as home, but we were never going to do any better while Nikolas was busy drinking away the little that was left over. He had persisted in nagging me to contact my parents to ask for money, but my relationship with them had died the day I had married him – in what I realised later was an impulsive act of defiance and rebellion – and I would rather have worked myself into the ground than crawled back to them begging them to rescue me from the mess I had got myself into.

When I returned to the bedsit after work, Nikolas was shoving clothes into an opened suitcase that lay on the bed. The place was a mess, toys and dirty washing strewn over any available surface, and the cold air carried the stale smell of whisky I had come to loathe.

'What are you doing?'

'We're leaving.'

This wasn't the first time it had happened. We had already fled from two other addresses, and I was starting to wonder if this would be my life now.

'Why?'

He didn't answer me.

'It feels as though we're on the run all the time.'

'There's nothing here for us. All you've done since we got here is complain, and now you're making a fuss about moving somewhere new. There's no pleasing you, is there?'

'I just don't understand why we have to go now, right this minute. What's the hurry?'

He grabbed me by my top, yanking me towards him. His face was just inches from mine, and it was then that I smelled alcohol on his breath, sharp and sour. 'Just for once, do as you're fucking told, okay?'

I was scared, and he knew it. There was something sinister in the way he looked at me then, some smug satisfaction that seemed to come with the knowledge that I would do anything he told me to because I was too fearful of the consequences if I didn't. Standing in the bedsit that evening, watching Nikolas prepare to upend our lives yet again, I realised how isolated from everyone else I was, and that it was entirely my own doing. I had cut myself off from my parents, severing our relationship in a bid to escape the authority they had exerted over me, and yet I had fallen into the control of someone else, moving from a stifling situation to one that was potentially dangerous. I had been so desperate to prove my independence, to assert myself as a grown-up who could make her own decisions, yet I had fallen into a trap from which I couldn't see a way out.

Nikolas never admitted why he was so desperate to leave that night, just as he had always avoided addressing the reasons for our previous moves. I could only assume later that he had heard from Charlotte and that she had found out where we were. I knew that Maria's mother had a sister; Nikolas had told me that she and her father lived in France, where he had moved with his job after the girls' mother had committed suicide. It was where Rebecca had been living when she had gone on holiday with her sister to Cyprus – the holiday that would change the course of her life – and as such, I believed it was where her remaining family had stayed.

Charlotte was never going to stop looking for Maria, but running from her wasn't about protecting his child; it was about protecting himself, something else I didn't learn until it was too late. She knew what he was and what he had done; she just needed an opportunity to prove it.

I snapped myself from memories of the past and focused on the darkened blurs that passed outside the window of Charlotte's car, trying to work out where we were and where she might be taking me. I had the same feeling then as I'd had all those years ago with Nikolas behind the wheel, and though I tried to remain in the present, I was flung back to that night once again.

'Slow down, Nikolas, please.'

'Are you scared?' His voice was soft and taunting, his face lit with his pleasure at finding amusement in my fear.

'I just want us to get to Maria safely.'

'One dead mother, two dead mothers… what's the difference?'

I remember the feeling that engulfed me then. When I looked at Nikolas, I saw nothing of the man I had met in that café almost two years earlier. The truth was, the memory of that person had already faded, replaced by the man he had become following our wedding day – a controlling, coercive husband who had tried to convince me that I couldn't survive without him. I imagined he had done the same to Rebecca.

'Don't say stupid things like that.'

His hand flew to my neck and the car swerved towards the pavement. I had lost all sense of where we were; I barely knew Bristol, and I had no idea where Maria had been taken.

'That bitch had it coming, the same as you.'

I don't remember what I felt in those moments that followed. I might describe numbness, or a taste of bile or sickness rising in a swell from my stomach, but the truth is my mind went blank, as though every thought and every feeling was momentarily erased, and I was capable of nothing. I had married a murderer. Rebecca hadn't jumped from that balcony. Nikolas had pushed her.

My thoughts collided, everything I had thought I'd known changing shape and texture in front of my eyes, which were swimming with the darkness of the night and the shadows that raced past the car as Nikolas's driving became faster and more erratic. I was living the wrong life. I should never have been there. There was a little girl who needed me; her mother dead, her father the killer.

He had confessed his crime to me, which I realised meant only one thing: he wanted the same for me. When I grabbed that wheel, I did so knowing it was me or him.

FORTY

'He told me that she had killed herself.'

Charlotte shook her head. 'That's what he told everyone.'

'And everyone else believed it too.' I had run internet searches on Rebecca, as anyone else in my position might have done, and hadn't thought to question what I read there, not until the night I saw him for what he really was. I had swallowed his lies without question, never wanting to see anything but a good man caring alone for a vulnerable child whose life had faced the most tragic of beginnings – an unlikely duo who needed me as much as I needed them. I fell in love with Maria, with the softness of her skin and the smell of her fine dark hair; she was everything my own child might have been had I been given the chance to meet her.

Within weeks of our wedding day, however, it started to become apparent that Nikolas didn't love his daughter as much as I did, nor as much as he had seemed to when we had first met. He barely spent any time with her, and I quickly came to realise that I was little more than a glorified babysitter, and that he had chosen me with this very role in mind. I didn't care; in fact, it seemed that the more he pushed Maria away, the closer she grew to me, and I soon loved her far more than I had ever loved anyone.

'Please, Charlotte, you must believe me. It's the truth. He told me that your sister had suffered from depression, and that after Lily arrived, she couldn't cope. I pitied him. He was charming and convincing, and all the other things Rebecca must have fallen for too. He preyed on both of us.'

'Her name is not Lily,' Charlotte said through gritted teeth. Her hands tightened around the wheel, and when I glanced at the speedometer, I saw that it was pushing eighty. We were nearing Brecon now, the road narrowing and growing darker as the trees on either side became taller. 'Her name is Maria. She was named after our mother. And don't even try to suggest that you are anything like my sister. She would never have stolen another woman's child.'

I felt sick at the sound of her words, and at their echo in my brain. Try as I might, I could not avoid the truth. I had stolen a child. Everything I had tried to run from over the past fifteen years was there with me in that car, my guilt surrounding me, inescapable.

'I didn't steal her,' I said, though even to my own ears the words sounded pathetic. 'Nikolas and I were married – we'd done everything legally. Both Lily's parents… both Maria's parents were dead. I was the only mother she'd known, and I did what I could to protect her. I've only ever tried to give her as normal a life as possible. I know what Nikolas did to your sister, Charlotte – I saw what he was really like, once it was too late to do anything about it. She was a victim, but so was I; you've got to see that.'

I feared that no matter how I worded it – no matter how many different ways I tried to make her see the similarities between Rebecca and me – I would remain nothing but the evil stepmother, the woman who had torn her niece from her remaining biological family.

'You are nothing. Rebecca should be here now. You should be dead.'

'I love Lily,' I said, desperately trying to find some common ground with which I might be able to reason with her. I knew in my heart that I was fighting a lost cause – that Charlotte was too intent on revenge to even consider my circumstances – but somehow I had to try to save myself from whatever she had planned for me. 'Maria,' I corrected myself again, not wanting to anger her further.

'I have always loved her like my own; I've only ever tried to do what was best for her.'

'But you knew I existed, didn't you? You knew she had family, yet you chose to take her away from me.'

'Do you think you could have done any better? I know about you, Charlotte. I know about the Oakfield Manor Clinic.'

The car swerved towards a tree as her head turned sharply, her eyes blazing like wildfire. She had already decided that tonight was the night all this would come to an end. There was no explaining why I'd done what I'd done; no convincing her that I had tried to do what was best for Lily.

'That's where you met Jacob, isn't it?'

'Shut up.'

'You used him, didn't you? You both knew what it was like to lose a sister – you used his grief to form a bond with him. I know about the fire that killed his sister. I know he started it.' Charlotte's head whipped towards me again. No one else had ever been trusted with Jacob's darkest secret; no one other than Charlotte. She had never believed he would tell another person, least of all me.

I remembered him sitting in that chair at their house, his admission falling from his lips as though finally being able to confess to another human being had come as a relief to him. He had been six years old, his sister just three. He had been playing with a lighter his uncle had left lying around, trying to set fire to the stubbed-out cigarette ends in the glass ashtray by the side of the bed in his parents' spare bedroom. His sister had been taking a nap in the bedroom next door, and when the blaze spread, no one had been able to reach her.

'You've exploited him, haven't you? What did you do – tell him he needed to follow your every instruction or you'd go to the police? Is that why you accused him of rape, just to prove the power you had over him?'

'Shut up!'

'You want the truth?' I goaded. 'Yes, I knew you existed, and yes, I knew you were looking for Lily. But I knew she was better off with me – she was safer with me than she ever would be with you. And I was right, wasn't I? You're unwell, Charlotte. You need help. Who would stab themselves like you did – do you think that's a normal thing to do?'

She had started to shake now, her anger rising to her cheeks in a burst of colour. I edged forward on the back seat. Up ahead, the trees that lined the roadside were thinning out, making a clearing before the reservoir that lay ahead.

'You were going to stab me, weren't you? What made you change your mind?'

'I thought death was too good for you,' she spat. 'I wanted to make you suffer, really suffer, like Rebecca had. But I was wrong. You deserve to die.'

Just as I had done once before, I grabbed for the steering wheel. That time, I had reacted in fear, some survival-mode instinct telling me that I wasn't going to die in that car. I killed Nikolas, but I did it to save Lily from him, and to protect myself. If I hadn't, I had no doubt he would have killed me.

Now, the same impulse took hold. If I was going to die, it would be by my own hand, not this woman's. I felt pain sear through my arm as Charlotte lashed out with the knife, but it was in the wrong hand – she was right-handed rather than left – and her wrist flailed at an awkward angle as she tried to find me in the darkness while attempting to keep the car on the road.

I leaned forward and drew my right arm to my face before jabbing my elbow at the side of her head. Her neck snapped to the right and the car veered left as I reached again for the wheel. As it left the road and plunged into the reservoir, I was thrown forward into the front seat. The knife had dropped somewhere between us, but Charlotte was distracted now with grappling for the door handle as the car filled with water. The rush of cold stole my breath, and I pushed myself away from her, trying the passenger door, desperately yanking at the handle. I heard a click as it opened.

Charlotte grabbed at the back of my neck as I tried to get out of the car, and when I swung to fight her off me, I realised she was trapped, her belt locked tightly around her, pinning her to the seat. The water was up to her chest now, rising faster with every passing minute. She released her grip on me and plunged her left hand into the freezing water, grappling with the belt lock, looking up at me desperately.

'Help me.'

Her voice was pinched with shock. I hesitated, faced with a decision that would ruin either her life or mine. She had called for my help once before, and I had gone running to her. It had broken my family and it had broken me. Our eyes met, and she knew what I was thinking. The water was nearing her face now, lapping against her chin, and I reached down below the surface to find the seat belt. I yanked at it, trying to loosen it, but it held fast. There was a muted gurgle as the lower half of Charlotte's face disappeared, and I plunged my head underwater, my eyes burning as they fought to focus. I pushed the red button that held the seat belt locked, and on the second attempt, it released. I resurfaced, and she pushed herself up, gasping for air, but the car was nearly submerged, and we needed to get out.

I flailed for the open door, gripping its metal frame as I pushed myself out of the car. My clothes were weighing me down, and I fought to untangle myself from them as I turned in the water.

Charlotte wasn't there. I twisted from side to side, but I still couldn't see her, and the breath I had been holding was running out fast. I rose to the surface and gulped a lungful of cold air before submerging myself again. The car was completely under now, and when I grabbed for the door to drag myself down, I saw Charlotte's hand pushed flat on the passenger seat. As I lowered my head to see into the car, she turned to look at me, her eyes too wide and too bright, glimmering in the murky darkness of the water. Her right hand was gripping the steering wheel, keeping herself anchored inside the car.

I stretched an arm out, urging her to take hold of my hand. Her face was expressionless and unresponsive. I imagined later that her eyes tried to communicate something to me, some parting message that she was unable to verbalise and might not have been able to bring herself to speak even had she been capable. Whatever it was, she had obviously made the decision to stay, and with an instinct to survive that seemed to take hold of my entire body, I heaved myself away from the door and rose to the surface.

FORTY-ONE

'Tell us what happened.'

I sit up against the flat hospital pillow and try not to focus on the throbbing inside my head. I should feel worse than I do, but I can't allow myself to be injured. I am needed too much.

Two pairs of eyes watch me expectantly, waiting for me to fill in the missing details of last night's events. I have been here before, years ago. It should all feel easier now, but it doesn't.

'Where's…' I begin, but the question is strangled on my tongue as it was all that time ago, lost to a solitary tear that slips from my left eye and slides onto my cold cheek. I picture Amelia fading into the darkness, disappearing as the car speeds away from her, and I want to reach for her as though she is here in front of me.

'She's fine,' the female police officer reassures me. 'She's safe.'

I breathe a sigh of relief, and when I close my eyes I see Charlotte's face in front of me, vivid at first then distorted as she sinks deeper into the water that surrounds us. She fades then disappears, and I am taken back to another time, another accident. I see the tree the car collided with; I hear the screech of the brakes and the crunch of metal as the bonnet crumples against the trunk of the oak, folding in on itself like an accordion. A rush of darkness floods me, greens and browns muted by the night, and I remember the last thought that crept from my mind as my eyes fell shut and consciousness escaped me, that just a split second could change everything, and that nothing was ever going to be the same again.

I open my eyes, put my fingers to my arm and trace the stab wound there.

'Tell us what happened,' the man says again.

'She tried to kill me. Everything happened so quickly.' I wince and bring my hand to my head, finding a bandage covering an injury I wasn't even aware of.

The man nods and glances at his partner, who stands from her seat. 'We'll try again later. Your husband's in the corridor. Shall we send him in?'

I nod. A moment after the police leave, Damien enters the room. He sits on the chair at the side of the bed, watching me in silence.

'Is Amelia okay?'

'Just about.'

'I had to leave her,' I say, desperate for him to understand the choice I was faced with. 'I knew Charlotte would try to kill me – I had to protect Amelia.'

Damien's eyes meet mine. 'You sure? Or were you still protecting yourself?'

I feel a tear slip from my eye and I raise a hand to swipe it away, not wanting to rely on sympathy to make him understand. 'No,' I say. 'I was protecting Amelia. I was protecting Lily. We're a family. We always will be.'

Damien's jaw tightens. 'How will I ever be able to trust you again?'

'Let me tell you everything. Promise you'll hear me out this time.'

I wait for the reasons why he can't or won't listen, but they never come.

'What happened in that car last night, Jenna? How did you get here but Charlotte didn't?'

This time, I don't need to lie.

'She tried to pull me back at first. The car was filling with water so quickly – it all just feels like a blur now. She couldn't get her seat belt undone, but when I managed to do it, she froze. She wouldn't come up to the surface with me; she just stayed there, like she wanted to end it all.'

He studies my face as I speak, only half believing the words I say, but I see the hesitation in his doubt and I know he doesn't want to let go, not yet. Despite everything we have been through, Damien and I are meant to be together. Only he knows my secret – and Jacob, who trusted me with his – but I believe now, as I have always believed, that not all secrets are destructive and that some are for the best, designed to protect rather than destroy. We were happy once. We can be happy again; this time with the truth out in the open. I will have to tell Lily and can only hope that the bond we have – the years I have given her – is strong enough for her to understand why I did what I did.

I wait, hopeful and undeserving, then his hand slides onto the bed and his fingers lock with mine.

A LETTER FROM VICTORIA

Dear Reader,

I want to say a huge thank you for choosing to read *The Accusation*. If you enjoyed it and would like to keep up to date with my latest releases, just sign up to the following link. Your email address will never be shared, and you can unsubscribe at any time.

www.bookouture.com/victoria-jenkins

Like my two previous thrillers, *The Accusation* started with a 'what if' idea – what if someone took a shortcut home, and that shortcut changed the course of their life? The idea of being falsely accused of a crime is something that has always fascinated me, and there are many famous cases of people having served sentences for crimes of which they were later acquitted. I have often wondered when reading about such cases – or watching dramas or documentaries – how such a person manages to move on with their life afterwards, and to what extent the stigma remains even after their innocence has been proven. In the case of *The Accusation*, the 'what if' ran to a further idea of 'what if the person was innocent of the accusation made, but was guilty of something else?'

The Accusation is a little different for me, as it's the first book I have written in first-person. I have enjoyed the experience of being well and truly inside a character's head – if I was Jenna, how would I react to the accusation? What would I tell my family? Would I confront my accuser? Jenna is not without her flaws, but I hoped to create a protagonist readers would be able to empathise with and root for. As in every book I have written, relationships are at the heart of the story, and Jenna's love for her family is the motivation for every decision she makes. Despite her 'crime', I believe she deserves a happy ending, and I hope this is where I have left her.

I hope you enjoyed *The Accusation*; if you did, I would be very grateful if you could write a review. I would love to hear what you think, and it really does make a difference helping new readers discover one of my books for the first time.

I love hearing from my readers – you can get in touch on my Facebook page, Twitter, Goodreads or my website.

Thanks,
Victoria Jenkins

     victoriajenkinswriter

     @vicwritescrime

     victoriajenkins

ACKNOWLEDGEMENTS

As always, a huge thank you to everyone at Bookouture. I am very lucky to work with such a brilliant team and am still pinching myself that I was given this opportunity (and am still here!) In particular, thanks to Noelle and a huge thank you to my new editor Lucy – it has been a pleasure working with you, and long may it continue. Thanks also to my agent, Anne, whose enthusiasm for my writing gives me much-needed confidence and encouragement.

Thank you to Stuart Gibbon for answering my questions relating to police procedure.

To my family, as always, thank you for the babysitting and the pep talks, for the food (I have been mainly powered by sugar while writing this book) and for all your support – I couldn't write anything without you.

My last thank you is to Jenny, who in 2017 offered me my first contract with Bookouture. The last three years have been life-changing – both professionally and personally – and your ongoing support has been invaluable. I realised when midway through writing *The Accusation* that the name Jenna couldn't be any closer to Jenny, but this was purely coincidental, and the character is in no way based upon you! Best of luck in your new position at Bookouture – I hope the future brings you all the success you deserve. This one is for you.

Lightning Source UK Ltd.
Milton Keynes UK
UKHW010828170520
363373UK00001B/42

9 781838 887599